RACHEL'S BUTTERFLIES

Vicki Childs

Copyright © 2021 by Vicki Childs

First paperback edition July 2021

Cover design by *InspiredCoverDesigns.com*

ISBN 978-1-7373077-0-9 (paperback)
ISBN 978-1-7373077-1-6 (ebook)

www.vickichilds.com

To my best friends Pippa and Joe who were the
inspiration for this book.
You truly are my butterflies.

1

Rachel
Monday, January 28th - London

Rachel looked up at the moon, her green eyes, usually so heavy with sorrow, were now composed.

She turned, and her shimmering backless gown flowed and rippled around her. Her long dark hair was swept back into an elegant high bun, and along its crest, tiny diamond studs glimmered in the light, like the first stars in a night sky. The hairstyle accentuated her long neck and delicate features, her only other adornment was a fragile diamond bracelet which matched the diamonds in her hair.

An icy breeze blew through the open balcony doors, running its fingers over the papers on her desk. She no longer felt the cold, she felt nothing but a sense of calm. The car would be here soon to collect her.

Tonight was the industry's most prestigious event, and she was to be honored for her work. Her journey as a photographer would be distilled and narrated, her most iconic photographs projected on a huge screen for all to see. Her life's work, her legacy.

When her name was read out she would stand, smiling at the others around the table, and make her way to the stage as the room erupted with applause. She would take the award and turn to the sea of adoring eyes. She would thank her family, her mentors, and the industry for all their support. Later there would be press interviews, maybe even television appearances. This moment would elevate her to true stardom, securing her a place in history amongst the giants of the field.

She was ready.

Turning, she walked across the hardwood floor to the staircase which lead up to mezzanine level above the living room. She gathered the folds of her dress in one hand and placed the other on the railing. As she ascended the stairs, she stroked her fingertips along the ornate wood. With each step the years slipped away, like heavy winter coats shed in the first warmth of Spring. The weight she had been carrying for so long lifted from her, leaving her light and fragmentary, ready to soar to the stars above.

At the top of the staircase she paused, looking down on her living room, her quiet sanctuary for so many years. The bookshelves, crammed with well-worn books, doorways to the worlds she had loved. Several comfy chairs facing the large fireplace, mismatched and threadbare, but welcoming. She had spent many a night in their warm embrace, her feet tucked up beneath her, reading and sipping a mug of hot chocolate.

She would miss this room.

The rope, secured to the railing, felt rough as she picked it up. The coarse, twisted fibers accosting her freezing fingers.

As she slipped it over her neck, it became a necklace of sparkling diamonds, the reflection of a thousand chandeliers. She was transformed, as if in a fairytale, with no midnight hour to break the spell. No more forced smiles. No more pretense. No more eyes watching her, expecting her to be something that she could no longer be. Now she would dance and spin and be free forever.

She inhaled, filling her lungs with the cold crisp air as she climbed over the railings to the other side.

Looking down to the room below, she thought of her parents, and a deep sadness enveloped her. There were no more tears to shed though, and she stepped forward.

One sharp snap, and then nothingness.

The next morning there were concerned knocks, and then urgent bangs. The front door was unlocked, and the stillness and peace of the living room was shattered by a scream. The screaming faded and was replaced by men and women in white suits.

Then the car arrived to take Rachel away.

*****

Could she have known, in those final moments, the impact she would have on our lives? Could she have known that when our worlds collapsed around us, she would be the thread that would hold us together?

She gave us the strength and courage we needed to get through what was to come, and to come out stronger on the other side, and for that we are eternally grateful.

2

Liz
Friday, March 29th - London

"Hi babe. You home?" Liz shouted as she pushed through the front door of the London penthouse apartment. It was late, but the apartment was still in darkness and there was no sign of Liz's errant boyfriend. No change there then. She threw her keys onto the side table, and her laptop bag, handbag and gym bag onto the sleek oak floor, kicking off her elegant work shoes as she went. She would tidy them away later, but first she was in dire need of a vodka and a cigarette.

After a quick stop in the kitchen to fix herself a drink, she cracked open the sliding doors that ran the length of the living room.

Standing on the threshold of the balcony she breathed in the cold night air while admiring the views of the London skyline. Half in and half out, with the warmth of the apartment at her back, she wasn't willing to commit herself entirely to the frigid evening. The balcony was elegant and minimalist with wrap-around views of the city, but in late March it was still too cold to sit outside comfortably without firing up the heaters.

She took a deep draw on her Marlboro Light, holding the inhale for a moment, before blowing the smoke out into the darkness. She sipped her drink and listened to the clinking of the ice against the sides of the mason jar.

Jesus, that felt better.

Her shoulders dropped, releasing the tension she'd been holding in them all day.

She settled into the silence, letting the calm of the evening envelop her. This view always made her feel at peace. It was the reason she'd fallen in love with the apartment after all. The gentle glimmer of the city lights reflecting on the river. The rumble of humanity from nearby buildings and streets.

London had an energizing effect on Liz, and she couldn't imagine being anywhere else. Yes, it was grimy and noisy and often unforgiving, but it pulsed with the energy of people pushing and thrusting and achieving. It was unlimited, and there for the taking. If you were strong enough, you would survive and thrive, and she was, most definitely, strong enough.

Her gaze followed the river to the shining beacon of the Shard and, smiling to herself, she slid the door shut. She drained her glass and headed to the kitchen for a refill. Drink in hand, she strolled into the large, chic living room, and stretched out on one of the chocolate brown leather couches, its cool texture delicious against her skin. She placed her drink onto the glass coffee table next to her. With her fingers on the rim, she turned the jar this way and that, watching a ring of condensation form on the table. An almost imperceptible smile appeared on her lips as she thought how infuriated her mother would be at the sight of this ring, and it gave her a warm, self-satisfied glow. "*Small pleasures, eh?*" She thought, chuckling to herself.

She shut her eyes for a few moments, enjoying the silence,

before hauling herself to her feet and padding back to the entrance hallway to grab her phone. Back on the couch, she scrolled through the day's personal emails, deleting the usual barrage of junk; unmissable deals and 'one-day-only' promotions. Then her eyes caught an unusual subject line.

'Memorial Invitation.'

She opened the email and read the text that followed.

"Hi Liz, I'm sorry to email you out of the blue like this. Please let us know if you will be available to attend the Memorial Celebration. Regards, Isabelle."

She opened the attachment to find a formal invitation with the following text:

Celebrating the Life of Rachel Sullivan
7th October 1979 to 28th January 2019
Rachel is survived by her mother Isabelle, her father Anthony, and her cats, Miles and Amelia.
Rachel loved photography, poetry and traveling.
Her warm smile and contagious laughter will be greatly missed.
Memorial to be held Saturday 20th April at 2pm
Tortworth Court
Wotton-under-Edge, Gloucestershire

Liz sat for a minute with a furrowed brow. Who the hell was Rachel Sullivan?

Then a distant memory came into focus with a force that hit her like an electric shock. "Oh fuck! That's Rachel from school!" she said out loud.

Really? They had been close friends at school, but they hadn't spoken for decades. Liz knew that Rachel had become a successful photographer, but other than that, she knew nothing about her.

She Googled *'Rachel Sullivan, photographer UK'* and scanned through the results. There was a headline from the Daily Telegraph dated a couple of months back; it read 'Renowned Portrait Photographer Rachel Sullivan Found Dead In Her Home'.

Liz clicked the link and sat back into the sofa in disbelief as she read the article.

'Celebrated British photographer Rachel Sullivan was found dead in her home early on the morning of Tuesday, January 29th. It is believed that she took her own life sometime the previous evening. Her body was discovered by a close family member. Sources say the photographer, who gained an international reputation for her poignant and melancholic photographs, had been suffering from a spiraling depression for several weeks before the incident. A representative from the Royal Photographic Society was quoted saying, "We are heartbroken to hear of the untimely passing of Ms. Sullivan. The world has lost an incredible artist and a precious soul.'

Liz sat in silence for a moment.

Holy shit. Rachel was dead. She killed herself. She couldn't quite believe it.

She wasn't sure how to feel about this. After all, she had no actual connection to her anymore, but here was an invitation to her memorial service somewhere in Gloucestershire. Would she go? It was in three weeks, and she didn't have any other plans for that weekend.

She jumped as the front door opened, and Xander shouted, "Hi babe, it's me."

"Hi. You OK?" she replied, pulling herself back to the present.

"Yeah, long day, but all good. Glad to be home."

Xander strode through the living room, giving Liz a quick kiss on the forehead on his way to the kitchen to grab a beer. Bottle cap flicked and beer in hand, he jumped onto the couch in his casual schoolboy way, and gave Liz a playful punch on the arm.

"So what's up, gorgeous?" he said, giving her one of his million dollar trademark smiles.

Liz answered in a faraway tone.

"I just found out that one of my friends from school died. Actually, she killed herself."

"Oh, Liz. Are you OK? Were you guys close?"

"We used to be, but I haven't spoken to her for decades." She paused. "Her parents sent me an invitation to her Memorial Service. It's in three weeks' time, in Gloucester."

"What? Well, that's shitty. Why in God's name would they have it out in the middle of nowhere? Are you going to go?"

"I don't know. I need to think about it some more."

Xander snorted. "Well, pack your rain boots, and good luck finding any Wi-Fi out there. Hey babe, pass the remote, will you?" he asked as he settled himself back into the couch.

3

Emily
Friday, March 29th - Surrey

"Philip darling, don't forget to bring your football kit, and can all of you please take off your muddy shoes the minute we get inside."

"Mummy, Mummy, look at the picture I painted today. Miss Guthridge said it's very beautiful and colorful!"

"Hang on Harry, let's just get into the house and then I promise I'll look at it."

Emily unlocked the side door, and everyone tumbled into the boot room in various states of disarray.

"Sophie, please say 'excuse me', don't just push past everyone. Right, shoes off everyone and then go and wash your hands. Sophie, did you hear me? Wash your hands, please."

After shaking off her damp wax jacket and storing her boots on the rack, Emily headed to the kitchen to put the kettle on and make herself a much-needed cup of tea. Chilled through from standing around at football practice, she could do with some time to relax and reset before launching into making dinner.

She filled the kettle and set it on the stove, holding down the ignition switch to light both the ring and the Aga. Shivering, she rubbed her hands together as she waited for the heat of the Aga to permeate the cozy kitchen.

"Mummy, please look at my picture now?" Harry looked up at her with wide, pleading eyes.

Emily knelt down beside her youngest, one arm around his shoulders, feeling the warmth of his body next to her. "Wow, it's beautiful. Is this a flower?"

"Yes! And that's a swing, and that's an elephant, and that's me!" Harry pointed at the various objects with a proud, chubby finger.

"I love it, Harry. You really are an amazing artist. Shall we put it on the fridge?"

"Yes, yes!" said Harry, his eyes gleaming. A sweet pain touched Emily's heart as she looked into his little freckled face, so filled with pride. She adored him, her little angel, and she ruffled his red hair and hugged him.

Digging around in the knick knack drawer, she found the sticky tape and taped the picture to the fridge door. Not so long ago this door had been covered with pictures, little artistic offerings from her children, but Harry was the only one who still offered up his efforts for praise and recognition.

Time was passing so fast, and her babies were growing up before her very eyes. Philip, so tiny when he was first born, was now eleven, and almost as tall as her. He was still a sweet, caring boy who found wonder and excitement in the world around him, but now he was self-conscious and had the awkward gait of a boy fast becoming a man and not quite able to keep up with it.

Unlike her enthusiastic, gamboling eldest boy, Sophie, her brooding eight-year-old, already seemed to be entering her teenage years like a storm cloud. She was darker than the boys in every way, with a ruddy complexion and dark auburn hair, whereas the boys' hair was bright, unapologetic red. Sophie's eyes were dark hazel with flashes of green that glinted like shards of emerald when she cried.

Sophie and Emily had never seen eye to eye, but over the last couple of years Emily worried they had drifted even further apart. Now they seemed like strangers who merely existed in the same orbit.

Then came Harry, her youngest. At five years old he radiated light and positivity, despite everything he had been through. Her heart hurt when she thought of his courage and enthusiasm, and she wanted to hold him tight, to stop him growing up and becoming less reliant on her.

Emily loved her babies with a passion, and she wanted to hold them close forever.

Soon the Aga radiated a welcoming heat and Emily, holding her tea in both hands to warm herself, sat at the heavy wooden table and breathed a sigh of relief. *"Another week over, and everyone is still alive,"* she thought to herself with a grin. This country cottage kitchen was her happy place, and she felt the busyness of the day fall away as she relaxed into the comfort of home.

Reaching in to her handbag, she pulled out her mobile phone. She scrolled through emails about upcoming school events. There were the usual requests for the provision of snacks for the children, and an ongoing discussion about the budget for the annual theater production this year.

She stopped when she saw the subject line 'Memorial Invitation'. A stab of alarm ran through her as she opened it and read the contents.

She clicked open the attachment and read through the invitation.

Emily was surprised by the emotions that arose in her. Confusion, followed by guilt, and a whisper of anger.

She put her phone face down onto the table and picked up her mug. The warmth spread through her fingers and up her arms as she stared ahead, trying to process what she had just read.

She and Rachel had been close friends at school, inseparable from the age of twelve, but they had lost touch when they went to university. The four friends had sworn they would never be parted, and yet Emily hadn't spoken to any of them in years. And now Rachel was gone.

Memories formed in Emily's mind. Rachel's striking beauty, offset by her gentle smile and the melancholy in those green eyes. She looked like a woodland nymph, with rich brunette hair the color of bark and almond-shaped eyes the color of moss. She always seemed so sad, though. The warmth and sorrow that emanated from her was so tangible that it made you want to catch your breath and come up for air whenever you spent too much time with her. She was ethereal, a spirit not meant to live in this world. Reality was too harsh for her. It was almost inevitable that Rachel would die young, although Emily had never realized it before now.

"I wonder how she died?" she thought to herself.

Googling her name, Emily realized with horror that Rachel had taken her own life. How awful to be so lonely and desperate that you would resort to something so destructive and final. Her poor parents, they must be distraught.

And yet behind the sadness Emily recognized a rising sense of guilt, as though this was somehow her fault. That she had dropped the ball in some way. Forgotten something that she should have had in hand. There was a quickening in her chest and a tightening in her jaw. How on earth was she supposed to have prevented this? Rachel had never reached out to her to renew their friendship, so why was it on Emily to have done so?

She checked herself, flushing as she thought how

inappropriate it was for her to feel aggrieved when her friend had just passed away so unexpectedly.

She stood and washed up her cup in the ceramic butler sink, setting it carefully on the draining board.

Well, there was nothing for it. She would have to go to the Memorial and honor Rachel, even if it meant going to Gloucestershire. She would speak to Ed about it tonight when he got home. He wouldn't mind looking after the kids for the weekend, he'd always been such a wonderful Dad.

"God, what am I going to wear though?" she thought to herself, sighing with exasperation before rolling up her sleeves and diving into the dinner preparations.

4

Chrissy
Friday, March 29th - Pasadena

Chrissy relaxed into her wicker chair, sipping her cappuccino and breathing in the warm, fragrant air of a typical Los Angeles summer morning. The dappled light streamed through the wisteria above her head, casting soft, beautiful shadows on the stone floor below.

Various chairs and tables occupied the elegant patio area. Although designed to appear casual and weathered, Chrissy could tell that this charming decor was the work of an experienced designer. The pieces had, no doubt, been purchased at great expense from various high-end establishments on the West Side.

She grinned as she saw Livi's head pop up from behind the coffee bar. Her head swiveled like a meerkat to check that the coast was clear, and with no management in sight, Livi headed over to Chrissy carrying a plate with a muffin on it.

"Hey girl!" Livi said with a wide smile, her purple tipped hair catching the light. "Where have you been? I've missed you!" She slid the muffin across the table and sat down opposite Chrissy. "You gotta try this new muffin, it's orange blossom, and it's yummy AF!" Chrissy looked quizzical, and Livi raised her eyes to heaven. "That means it's good. Just try it, woman," she said, in playful exasperation.

Livi watched with glorious anticipation as Chrissy took a bite.

"Oh, wow, this is delicious Livi. You've outdone yourself, you're such a talented baker."

Livi's eyes glistened with joy, and she slapped the table. "Yes! See! I knew it! I've been trying to tell Marcus that we should sell them, but he's all like 'whatever'. I just can't even with that guy," she said, rolling her eyes. "Anyway, what are you working on? Can I read it?"

Chrissy smiled and wrinkled her nose. "I'm not writing articles any more. I don't have the time since I got my realtor license."

"Well, that sucks. You're such a good writer, and I loved reading your articles."

Chrissy snorted with laughter. "It wasn't exactly the New Yorker or the Huffington Post. Not much cutting-edge journalism required when you're writing for a parenting magazine."

"Yeah, but you made it so interesting, plus you enjoyed it, I could tell." said Livi "And don't tell me you didn't make the world a better place with gems like '7 Magical Places To Take Your Kids for Spring Break' and 'The 10 Best L.A. Spas For a Mother-Daughter Treat', you should have gotten an award for those two, I reckon," she grinned from ear to ear.

"Yeah, yeah, just call me Hemingway," said Chrissy with a smirk.

"Who? Oh crap, here comes Marcus. I gotta bounce," Livi said, disappearing through the back door.

Chrissy laughed to herself as she sipped her coffee and finished the muffin.

Her regular table was positioned in the corner of the patio, private enough to enable her to focus on her work, but close enough to people-watch and overhear the fascinating snippets of their various conversations.

The ever-present Lululemon crowd occupied the large metal table in the opposite corner nearest the coffee bar; moms and housewives who had rediscovered themselves through the power of hot yoga and spin class.

Chrissy's husband Scott had always been so scathing about these women, his old-fashioned ideals jarred by the idea of someone being so self-absorbed. Once or twice Chrissy had fancied herself as a Lululemon 'yummy mummy', but she didn't have the time or the dedication to go to the gym every day, as these hard-core exercisers did.

She was no slouch though. She made it to barre class at least two or three times a week, and she owned a wide range of coordinated and flattering workout clothes in order to blend in with the natives. Maybe if she set herself a goal to work towards, then she would go to the gym more often? Like a 10k race or something? She would need to think about it some more.

A group of four women sat at a wooden table in the center of the patio. They screamed PTA as they talked with fervor about an upcoming fundraising event for their school. They weren't from Chrissy's own PTA group though, and she wondered which school their children went to.

Maybe Westridge Girls School? That was the closest high school to this coffee shop, nestled amongst the million dollar homes of leafy Pasadena.

Chrissy smiled at the all too familiar mix of PTA moms. A few had walked the line between working woman and involved mother, but most had morphed into nothing more than an extension of their children, a life support system recognizable only as 'mother of insert-name-of-child-here'.

When Chrissy fell pregnant with their first child, she had sworn this would never happen to her. She would maintain her own identity while still being a devoted mother to her child. That was why she had insisted on working as a freelance writer, even when the children were younger. Scott had said many times that she didn't need to work, and that she could give it up anytime she wanted. True, her freelance writing would never pay the bills, but she enjoyed it, and it made her feel a little more independent.

In fact, it was while she was hunting for a quiet spot to write her articles she had found this very coffee shop, and had taken up residence at this table.

Now of course, she had packed away her writing career, such as it was, for a more challenging role as a realtor. But she still found herself back at this little table, watching the various patrons and basking in the sun dappled tranquility while breathing in the aroma of coffee and jasmine.

"Oh, yikes. I should really look through these MLS listings," she thought to herself.

She scrolled through properties new onto the market. Beautiful airy homes with manicured gardens and sparkling swimming pools. She imagined wandering through these grand houses and she smiled to herself, thinking of her own beloved Craftsman style home.

She tried to stay focused, but before long she was scrolling through Instagram and Facebook.

She flicked over to her personal email and mass deleted the usual junk that piled up in her inbox every day. As she deleted each unwanted email, she considered unsubscribing, but it always seemed like so much hassle.

She stopped when she saw the email entitled *'Memorial Invitation'*.

She read through the contents, and then sat back in her chair, feeling a little light-headed. Reaching for her sunglasses, she inhaled deeply and stared up into the azure blue sky. Everything seemed to go quiet. The humming of the surrounding conversations faded away, and she heard the song of a bird she hadn't noticed before.

She watched it flit through the boughs above her head, before darting over the wall towards the mountains in the distance.

Although she was heartbroken, Chrissy found she wasn't shocked. Rachel had always been an unusual person, drifting through life with the insight and melancholy of an old soul. At school she had been the Cassandra of their tight-knit group, the seer of portentous omens, brushed away so flippantly by the other girls who, at eighteen, thought they knew everything there was to know about life. And now she was gone.

'The Four Musketeers' as they had called themselves, were now just three. Chrissy's mind drifted back to those school days, so fraught with drama. Drama that now seemed so insignificant in the broader context of life.

During the last couple of years of school, the four of them had become inseparable. Each of them so different, and yet all needing each other, like the four elements of nature, each drawing power from their undeniable connection.

Emily, the 'Mother Earth' of the group, was always somewhat nervous and overly prepared for every eventuality. She had her feet firmly planted in reality, and she became the sensible conscience that grounded the other girls. Plump, red headed and ruddy, she provided a safe port in the wild, turbulent storms of adolescence.

Liz was their warrior, tall, blonde and elegant, but also foul mouthed and fiery. She was a handful and not to be trifled with. When trouble was brewing, you could be sure that Liz was at the eye of the storm. Her passions were many, including smoking, drinking, winning at all costs, and infuriating her mother as much as humanly possible.

Then came the dark, soulful Rachel. Oh Rachel, what a wonderful, complicated creature she had been. A 'Will-o'-the-Wisp', never comfortable in her own body, and only ever at peace when she was observing others through the lens of a camera. When a friend had told Chrissy that Rachel had become a photographer Chrissy had laughed and said "when was she ever anything else?"

And now to the last of the mischievous quartet, Chrissy herself. Chrissy's stomach tightened, and she shifted in her seat. What of her? School had been an uncomfortable time for Chrissy, like trying to squeeze into hand-me-down jeans. What role had she filled? Was she the sporty one? The adventurer? She wasn't quite sure. She had never been able to define who she was, and she was always looking to the horizon and beyond in search of the answer.

But now she knew. She knew who she was and what she wanted.

Didn't she?

"Oh crap! Look at the time!" she said to herself, hurrying to pack away her laptop and notepad.

As she waited for the valet to pull her car around, Chrissy's thoughts returned to Rachel's Memorial. Should she go? Were Rachel's parents even aware that she lived in California now? It was a big ask to invite her to a memorial 5,000 miles away for someone she hadn't spoken to in years. Still, it would be nice to see the others again.

Chrissy slid into her black Porsche Cayenne, threw her laptop bag onto the passenger seat, cranked up the A/C and pulled out of the parking lot.

A little further down the street she pulled over, grabbed her cell phone and opened the Facebook app.

"Let's just see what the remaining Musketeers have been up to, shall we?" she said to herself, and started a search.

5

Barracuda
Thursday, April 4th - London

"Listen to me you little shit, if you *ever* try pulling a stunt like that again, I will rip off your tiny balls and shove them down your throat, you hear me?" Liz's manicured finger hovered so close to Charlie's nose that he bent backwards, limbo-style, over his desk, his eyes darting from side to side, searching for an escape route.

James raised his eyes to heaven and said, "Hey BC, can we *please* take this into a meeting room for Christ's sake, other people are on the phone with clients and they can hear every word you're saying."

Liz stormed into the meeting room, followed by her boss James and the terrified Charlie. Her face was flushed and her eyes flashing. She was a formidable sight when she was angry.

Now she turned her wrath on James. "This fucking newbie tried to cold call one of my biggest clients, *again*. I'm not putting up with this shit, James. You need to control your puppies before I neuter them, OK? I'm not having my reputation damaged just because this little dickhead thinks he can play with the big boys, and don't you *dare* try telling me it was a mistake."

James flashed Liz a stunning white smile and said in his usual calm, dulcet tone, "I hear you, and I promise it won't happen again, right Charlie?"

"Absolutely. Sorry, Liz" said Charlie, looking cowed.

"Well fuck you, *Charles*. Other people may be impressed that your family owns half of Suffolk, but I really don't give a shit. Cross me again and you'll wish you'd never been born, you hear me?"

Liz strode out of the meeting room and across the sleek, open plan office. She slammed her notepad down on her desk and tried to control her breathing.

Charles had screwed her over for the last fucking time. From now on, she would make it her sole purpose in life to get that little prick fired.

"You OK?" whispered Vanessa, the beautiful but ineffectual admin who sat at the end of the bank of desks. Her wide, smoky eyes looked terrified. But then she often looked that way.

"No, I'm not fucking OK. Do I look like I'm fucking OK? I'm going outside for a cigarette. You guys are the reason I smoke, you know!" Liz shouted over her shoulder, her middle finger raised high for all to see.

"Ooh, BC is rattled. Hold on to your dicks before she cuts them off," jeered one of the junior associates.

"Now lads, come on, leave her be," said James as he grinned and adjusted the cuffs of his Saville Row suit.

James loved to see Liz angry. He had a great deal of respect for her, after all she was one of the top billing head-hunters in an almost exclusively male dominated industry, but he couldn't resist seeing her eyes flash and her shoulders pull back in that glorious battle stance. She had that look in two situations, when she was on the warpath, or when she was reeling in a deal with a big fat five-figure commission check attached to it.

James had often wondered if she was as resplendent when she climaxed, too. He'd pictured her on top of him, riding him, her long blonde hair trailing on his chest, her slim, elegant body glistening with sweat. Over the years he had tried to make this fantasy a reality, but for all her faults Liz was loyal to that asshole boyfriend of hers. She could smell bullshit from a mile away, but she had a complete blind spot when it came to Xander.

BC was Liz's nickname, given to her when she first started at the headhunting firm as a fresh-faced, single-minded graduate. It was short for Barracuda. It had started as a pet name, used in a somewhat patronizing way by the old guard of the firm to refer to this twenty-something female upstart who had appeared in their midst. But Liz had earned the title, as she eviscerated the competition and took her place as one of the top billers in the organization. Occasionally upper management would ask her if she would consider training some junior Sourcers to help generate leads. Her response was always the same;

"Just because I have a uterus, it does not mean I want to babysit your snot-nosed spawn. If you want a nanny then ask Nigel, he's a bigger pussy than I am any day!"

*****

Liz stood outside the shiny office building, tapping her stilettoed heel on the ground and dragging hard on her second cigarette. God, she was fuming, but she wouldn't let that little fucker wipe out the rest of her day. It was only 11am, and she had some money to make. She'd been on a roll with a pipeline she'd spent the last 6 months building. The chickens were coming home to roost, and Charles could eat her shit in the next bonus round.

She stared ahead, watching the passing crowds in their corporate uniforms; a sea of suits and ties and smug expressions. It was lunchtime, and the pavement was filled with sharp-suited, up-and-coming types. They hurried along, clutching their 'Pret A Manger' sandwiches in one hand, and their mobile phones in the other, eyes glued to the screens. She wondered how they didn't crash into one other, as none of them ever seemed to glance up. They just slid past each other using some kind of built-in anti-impact system.

It dawned on Liz as she watched, that she used to be that self assured, that arrogant, but all she had felt recently was a creeping exhaustion. She pushed the thought away. After all, that kind of thinking could be deadly in this game.

Liz's firm was based in a prime location, just a stone's throw away from the financial giants of London. Merrill Lynch was walking distance from her office, and Goldman Sachs and Deloitte just down the road. It provided a fine hunting ground for a firm that specialized in executive level positions in the financial markets sector.

Liz's eyes wandered across the street to the Viaduct Tavern, where she had spent many a night drinking gin and tonic and retelling old war stories with her colleagues. Her mouth watered as she thought of the pub's amazing array of gins. She wouldn't say no to a drink right now.

"Alright, you lush, back to work," she chided herself, grinning as she ground the cigarette into the pavement and turned to head back inside.

By the time she stepped into the foyer, she had regained most of her glacial composure. She headed for the ladies' bathroom and examined herself in the enormous mirror that hung the length of the marbled sinks.

Her makeup was still perfect. Liz tended toward

minimalism when it came to makeup, applying a light, clear foundation that allowed her skin to glow, a brush of mascara to darken her otherwise blonde lashes, some bronzer to emphasize her high cheekbones and some clear gloss to plump her rather thin lips. "Less is more after all," she could hear her mother whispering in her ear, and she grimaced.

Over the last couple of years Liz had found it disturbing to see with increasing regularity, her mothers' reflection staring back at her from the mirror. Her only solace was that she had inherited her father's middle class nose, much to the horror of her aristocratic mother. There was no love lost between Liz and her father. In fact, she considered him to be next to worthless. He had, however, given her the long-lasting gift of his genetics, a satisfying barb in her mother's side, a constant reminder that even she had made some errors in judgement in her time.

As she looked closer, Liz could make out the telltale lines of age developing around her eyes. Carefully concealed, but still present, like the faintest drumbeat of inevitability. Headhunting was a young person's game, and at forty Liz would already be considered a veteran.

"Well, I'm not done yet. Let's go bust some balls, shall we?" she asked herself as a rallying cry, and headed back into the bullpen.

She was on fire. She had pulled together three candidate shortlists, booked four meetings and finished the drafts for two pitches all before 3pm. The other consultants knew well enough to give her a wide berth. Even Vanessa didn't ask her if she wanted a cup of tea, she merely slid the steaming brew slowing and across the desk until it was within Liz's reach. After four hours of furious activity, Liz took a deep breath, pushed her chair back from her desk, and stretched her arms above her head. She felt satisfied with a job well done, and the sting of the earlier betrayal was well behind her. She felt so content that she thanked Vanessa for the earlier cup of tea.

Vanessa's jaw dropped, and she stuttered, "You're, you're very welcome".

After a trip to the ladies' room to stretch her legs, Liz opened her LinkedIn Recruiter account. Once a day she would skim through new connection requests, messages, and saved search results, to check she wasn't missing any suitable candidates fresh on to the market.

One connection request stopped her in her tracks. Eyebrows raised and lips pursed, she read through the contents.

'Hi Liz, this is Chrissy - we used to go to school together. I'm sorry to contact you like this, but I've received an invitation to Rachel Sullivan's memorial service (I'm assuming you did too) and I was wondering if you were planning to go? If you are, then maybe we could all meet up? Let me know what you think. Thanks. Chrissy.'

"Hmm. So Chrissy had popped out of the woodwork, had she? Well, I'll be damned."

Liz glanced through Chrissy's profile. Her photo showed a woman with warm eyes and an enthusiastic smile. Shit, she looked almost the same as she had at school.

"A realtor living in LA, huh?"

She scrolled through the qualifications section and noted that Chrissy had a Master's degree in English Literature from USC.

"Maybe that's why she's in America? Makes sense. She was always talking about moving abroad."

Liz's interest was official piqued, and the thought of a school reunion didn't sound that horrific, so she shrugged and accepted the connection, hitting the 'reply' button and writing back to one of her oldest friends.

6

Emily swept the hand blender round and round in slow, rhythmic circles. She watched the mixture dance and swirl in the bowl, oil and water churning against each other in a yin yang of contradictory connection. Although the elements fought against it, soon they would combine and emulsify, and the soap would trace.

Emily loved this stage of the soap making process. The alchemy of creation. The inevitability of the joining, so hard fought against, but with a surrender that offered something new and wonderful.

This was her meditation, watching for the trace in the quiet of her kitchen, and she was blissfully happy and content in this moment.

She'd set up all the tools and ingredients she would need. Carrot puree from the vegetable garden, and gentle oatmeal to soothe the skin. Orange and tangerine essential oils, and fresh raw honey from her neighbor Pete, who had several hives at the end of his garden where the meadow met the stream.

As the mixture reached trace, Emily slowed and then stopped the blender. She added the turmeric, and as she did, the delicate scents of camomile and olive oil were overtaken by the more heady warmth of the spice.

Next came the carrot puree, honey, and essential oils, and she blended again, looking for a medium trace.

The exquisite smells rose and washed over her in a delicious wave of sensory exhilaration, making her skin tingle and glow as a shiver ran through her body.

Emily remembered reading somewhere that smell was the most potent and instinctual of all the senses, because the scent receptors are located deep in the base of the brain, giving smells a fast track to our deepest emotional center. It wasn't until she began making soap and distilling her own essential oils that she'd come to know the deep truth of this.

Satisfied with the thickness of the soap, Emily reached for a soap loaf mold, and in sweeping motions, she poured the mixture into it. She banged the mould on the table to remove any air bubbles, and finished it with a sprinkle of dried camomile.

"*Done*," she thought to herself, with a deep sense of satisfaction.

Heading through the kitchen carrying her new creation, she turned and pushed open the side door with a swing of her hip. She walked around to the garden and down the path to her soap shed. Ed had laughed and gently teased her when she first started referring to it as 'her soap shed'.

"So you've laid claim to it, eh?" he'd said with a chuckle, and told her he was proud that she'd made a home for creations.

Emily had tried to explain that the soap needed a cool place to cure for six weeks, and the old potting shed was the most sensible place to store it so that it was out of the way. Ed just grinned and winked, and said that she needed no explanation. He'd added that when she became a soap mogul, he would retire and go fishing every day.

As she reached the shed door, her mobile phone rang. Frowning, she tucked the soap into the crook of her arm, opened the door and stepped through into the darkness.

Once inside, she reached for her back pocket. The screen glowed in the dimness of the shed, and she saw Ed's name illuminated.

"Hey you. What's up?" she answered with a smile.

"Hi lovely. Nothing much, just checking in. What are you up to?" Ed's voice was soft and warm.

"I'm good. I just made some more honey and oatmeal soap. We were running low."

"Oh nice! That reminds me, Claire was asking if you had any more of the Avocado and Spearmint? She loved it, and she wants to get some for her mum."

"Um, I think so. Let me check. Hang on a sec. Yes, I have some back here. Tell her you'll bring her some tomorrow."

"OK, will do. And she said that she wants to pay you for it this time. I said that you'd say no, but she insisted."

Emily squirmed. She had never been comfortable charging people for her soap. She made it with a grateful heart, and it felt kinda icky to charge for something that gave her so much joy.

"Well, OK. But tell her she really doesn't have to."

"I know. I said that, but she was having none of it. Anyway, gotta go. The boss is in a foul mood again today, so I should probably go and look like I'm doing something productive, eh? Love you, baby. See you later."

"OK, hun. See you later," They both rang off.

Ed was a funny one, and Emily smiled as she thought about his endearing mixture of mischievous schoolboy and steadfast patriarch.

He was the Accounting Director for a local printing company, and one of the most senior managers in the business, and yet he still talked about work like he was the new intern, likely to get kicked to the curb at any moment. Everyone at work respected and adored him. In fact, everyone who knew Ed adored him. He was one of the best people Emily had ever met, and she thanked her lucky stars that he had fallen for her, of all people.

She was still smiling to herself as she walked back to the house, when she felt her phone ring again.

She reached for it, assuming Ed had forgotten to tell her something, but her smile fell away as she saw her mother's name on the screen.

Emily took a deep breath and answered in a bright tone.

"Hi Mum. How lovely to hear from you. How are things?"

"Hi darling. I'm just wonderful, thank you. I was wondering if you still needed me to pick up Jack from football practice tonight?"

"Oh yes, that would be great. Thank you so much Mum, I appreciate it."

"No problem at all. 7.30pm at the football ground, correct?"

"Yes, that's right. And thank you again for your help. I would do it, but I need to finish getting everything ready for bake sale tomorrow."

"I understand. You're a busy lady, Emily and I'm more than happy to lend a helping hand."

"OK, well, I'll see you tomorrow night then? Thanks Mum," Emily heard the click of her mother ringing off.

Back in the kitchen she hurried about, tidying away the soap making paraphernalia as she waited for the kettle to boil. One last cup of tea and a quick sit down before heading out to pick up Harry from preschool. It would be nice to spend some time with him alone while Sophie did homework at a friend's house, and Jack played football.

She poured the tea and sat, sinking into the peace of the empty house.

Leaning back in her chair, she pulled her hair from its messy bun and shook it as it unfurled down her back.

She considered brushing it out, but as always, she thought better of it. She'd needed a haircut for so long that her hair had lost all its shape and grace. It had now reached the stage where a high bun was her only option.

There was no love lost between Emily and her hair, and hadn't been for some time. When she was younger, it had been a striking auburn, with gorgeous natural curls that made her an obvious casting for the lead in 'Annie'.

As she had grown, however, it had become a more undecided color. I was as if her hair didn't feel brave enough to be outright red anymore and had pulled itself back to a nondescript off-brown color. 'Strawberry brunette,' her mother had called it for a while. And then she had stopped mentioning it altogether.

Emily spun her hair back into a high bun and reached for her phone, scrolling through updates and emails as she finished her tea.

There was a friend request on Facebook, which was unusual because Emily's circle of friends was pretty stable, consisting of mums from the kids' school, and some old friends she rarely spoke to anymore. The invitation was from someone called Chrissy Miller, and she looked familiar.

"Oh my god, that's Chrissy from school!" Emily laughed at the realization of it. Chrissy looked the same as she had at sixteen. No surprise there, Emily thought with a wry smile.

"I wonder if she's going to Rachel's Memorial Ceremony?" Emily thought, her chest tightened at the sudden memory of Rachel.

She accepted the invitation and scrolled through Chrissy's

profile.

Lots of radiant smiles from Chrissy and what looked like a husband and two children as well. Emily guessed their ages at about twelve and sixteen, an older boy and younger girl. The boy was handsome and sporty, with the confident look of someone who had always gotten what he wanted in life. The girl had a strong, determined, uncompromising look about her, and Emily smiled, thinking of her own turbulent daughter. The husband was handsome in a 'classic superhero' kind of way, and Emily could tell from the many photos of beaches and swimming pools that these guys lived somewhere abroad, in the United States, Emily guessed.

"*Yup,*" she thought to herself as she saw 'lives in Pasadena, California' on Chrissy's info section.

Emily smiled with amused contentment to think of Chrissy living in California. She had always known that her friend would move abroad.

Chrissy had been defined by her wanderlust, and she'd never felt at home in England. As Emily washed up her mug and set it on the drying rack, she pictured her old friend sitting on a beach as the sun sank below a crimson horizon.

She imagined her listening to the crashing waves, feeling the warm sand between her toes and the ocean lapping at her feet, as she bid farewell to another perfect Californian day.

"*Good for you, Chrissy. I hope you've finally found where you truly belong.*" Emily thought to herself with a smile.

7

Gatsby
Monday, April 15th - Pasadena

"What the hell are you guys doing in there?" Chrissy yelled towards the open front door of her home. "You need to get in this goddam car right now, or we're going to be late for school, again!"

She stood in the driveway next to her car, driver door ajar, jaw clenched, trying to control the rising exasperation she felt for her casually disrespectful kids.

"You know, you won't get away with this with your father next week. He'll just leave you here, and you'll have to find your own way to school."

"Sounds good. I'll just stay home instead," answered Josh with a winning smile as he slid into the passenger seat of the car.

"Hey! How come he gets to ride shotgun again!" bellowed Jackie, swinging the front door shut with a slam it made the glass rattle.

"My God, Jackie! You'll take the entire house down if you crash around like that! Show a little respect, please." Chrissy felt the telltale stab of a tension headache as she stepped into the car. She pulled the door shut and shoved the gear stick into reverse.

"Who's slamming doors now, eh?" said Jackie with a devilish grin.

"Watch it, young lady. I've had quite enough from you already this morning. I have a lot to organize today and I don't need any more of your sass, OK?"

They rode the rest of the way in silence while the kids looked at their phones and Chrissy thought through her 'To Do' list.

By the drop-off line, the atmosphere was jovial again, and they shouted their farewells with waves and smiles. Chrissy was grateful that, although her family could be combative, they forgave as quickly as they attacked, and all was forgotten in a moment.

This was Scott's influence, of course. He had always been a forthright, 'say what you feel' kind of guy who could have a stand up row one minute, and be joking and laughing the next. It had taken Chrissy quite some time to adjust to this wild roller coaster of emotional interaction, particularly as she and her mother had always operated on a comparatively even keel.

This was somewhat ironic, because her mother was almost always furious with the government regarding one issue or another, and could spit poison for hours on topics such as homelessness and nuclear weapons. But together they were always loving and peaceful. On the rare occasion when Chrissy attempted to pick a fight, her mother would smile and say, "Let's keep our indignation for the bourgeoisie, shall we?"

Chrissy watched her children walking away and, drumming her fingers on the steering wheel, she waited for the line of cars to move forward. She sighed with exasperation as various mothers in the cars ahead of her shared extended farewells with their precious offspring.

"Come on, come on!" she thought to herself.

Just as she reached the exit, her phone buzzed. She grabbed it and saw a text flash up from Jessie, an old friend and fellow school mom.

> *Hi there. Did you drop off already? If not, then do you have 5 mins to spare? Vanessa wants to speak to us all about last-minute logistics for the Ball.*

Chrissy's heart sank, and for a moment she considered just swinging her car out of the exit and claiming ignorance later. But she couldn't leave Jessie in the clutches of the terrible Vanessa. *"No man left behind,"* she said to herself and parked up.

She texted back,

> *Just walking in now. Where are you?*

> *At the picnic tables under the oak trees.*

As Chrissy walked towards the tables, she could see Vanessa handing out papers and jabbing a sharp finger towards each member of the group.

Vanessa was petite and ferocious, an attorney, and insanely competitive when it came to her children.

She was the mother of three daughters, two of whom still attended the school, the eldest having graduated last year. Her eldest daughter had been on the shortlist to be crowned Rose Queen for the Rose Parade several years ago, but the judges had awarded the title to someone else, and Vanessa was still smarting from the snub.

This year she was overseeing the annual fundraiser, and

she was determined it would be the most opulent and successful event in the history of the school.

The theme of the evening was 'The Great Gatsby', and Vanessa had spent hundreds of hours over the past six months sourcing just the right decor, auditioning multiple bands, and taste testing hors d'oeuvres from all the most reputable caterers this side of Hollywood.

The event was now a mere two weeks away. The countdown clock had started, and God help anyone who risked the perfection of Vanessa's masterpiece.

She was issuing orders as Chrissy slipped onto the bench next to Jessie.

"Janice, you will need to arrive at the venue at 5pm sharp to check the tables are set up correctly. You will see the correct configuration on page 7. Janice, please turn to page 7 so I'm confident that you understand."

Janice dropped her eyes, flicking through her stapled sheets to the required page.

Vanessa continued. "You must check that the tablecloths are spotless, and that the chairs have been dressed correctly. The bows need to be straight. I want them uniform, understand?"

Janice nodded.

Then Vanessa turned her gaze to Preeti. "Preeti, you are in charge of table decorations. Please arrive at the venue no later than 5.30pm. On page 8 you will see a photograph of how I want the table decorations to look. I want this followed exactly. The event coordinator also has a copy, but I won't have time to make adjustments on the night, so I am trusting you to manage it, yes?"

Preeti nodded.

And so it went on. The set up of the Art Deco photo booth, the background lighting, instructions for the band, and an exhaustive list of requirements involving large white feathers, gold and black party decor, and towers of champagne glasses.

As the meeting concluded, Chrissy stood and said, "I'm sure I speak for everyone when I say thank you so much for all your hard work and dedication, Vanessa. This event is going to be spectacular, and it's all down to you." There was a ripple of polite applause.

Vanessa gave Chrissy a withering smile and turned back to her papers.

Instructions having been given, the troops were dismissed, and Chrissy and Jessica walked back to their cars.

Jessie shook herself and said, "Wow, that woman is scary"

Chrissy laughed and said, "Tell me about it!"

"Did you hear that she's been campaigning to raise the bar even higher for the school's entrance exam? She's concerned about the school's academic reputation, which is ridiculous because our kids get some of the highest grades in the State."

Chrissy glowered. "I know. I've already spoken to the Principal about it. I'm concerned that we're becoming too elitist. One of Jackie's friends applied last year and didn't get in because they wouldn't offer her the right accommodations for her dyslexia. Vanessa and her cronies are trying to turn this place into 'baby Harvard Law School', and I'm not sure that's what the kids need. There's enough pressure as it is."

Jessie shrugged. "I'm pretty sure the only reason she tolerates me is because we're one of the school's very few Black families. You can speak to the Principal all you want, but you know who calls the shots around here. Money talks after all."

Chrissy raised her eyes to heaven, knowing it was true.

Back in her car, Chrissy threw the gear stick into drive and peeled away from the curb. On the drive home, she pondered the indomitable Vanessa and how uncomfortable she made her feel.

Chrissy had sensed that Vanessa disliked her from the start, but she was never able to work out why.

She had discussed it at length with Jessie, but Jessie reassured her, saying, "Vanessa is like that with everyone, just don't get on her bad side and you'll be fine."

But over the years it became somewhat of an obsession for Chrissy. She'd joined various school committees that Vanessa headed up, and had brought homemade, gluten-free, vegan treats for the other committee members to snack on during meetings. But no matter how much she tried to please her, Chrissy always felt like she was being endured. It was as if Vanessa had somehow judged her and found her wanting, and it drove Chrissy mad.

"Why do you even care what that tight faced bitch thinks, anyway?" Scott said in an exasperated tone one night after listening to Chrissy agonize over yet another Vanessa encounter. "She's the worst kind of snob. You know what, I'd be more concerned if she *did* like you. She's just a mean girl, and you aren't. Maybe she's jealous? You ever thought of that?"

He'd pulled her to him, wrapping her in a fierce hug, born from both frustration and the need to protect his wild, delicate girl.

To others, his wife always seemed so in control and enthusiastic, but he knew a deeper side of her. A sensitive, almost fragile spirit, empathetic by nature with a wistful yearning to belong.

This was the girl he'd fallen in love with all those years ago, and the girl that he worried about more than he cared to admit.

As Chrissy pulled into the driveway, her mind snapped back to the present moment. Crap, there was so much she needed to organize before she flew out tomorrow.

She went to the kitchen, grabbed a glass, and pushed it up

against the filter on the fridge door. Sipping the cool water, she sat down and opened the 'To Do' app on her phone.

"OK. Pool guy, done. I've told him he needs to check the chlorine levels again. Gardeners, done. I've mailed them a check, so they should get that before they arrive on Friday. Maid, done. I paid her double last week, so that will cover us until I get back. Yoga coach, done. I've told her I'll be away for a week and that we'll start again on the 25th."

What else? What was she forgetting?

Scott had agreed to finish work early while she was away, so he could take the kids to their extra-curricular activities. Chrissy had already emailed him a copy of the schedule and made him promise to look at it every morning.

She had tried to simplify the ride shares for that week by calling in favors from the other moms.

Josh would be at track practice after school every day except Thursday, and he also had debate class on Tuesdays and Fridays at a different location.

Jackie had gymnastics every day after school, apart from Wednesdays when she would walk home with Audrey to do homework and study at her house.

At least they both owned cell phones so if Scott messed up they could always call him to go get them from wherever they're stranded.

She had already packed most of what she needed, and she could finish the rest tomorrow morning after the school run. It was a late afternoon flight, so she would have some time at home before she needed to get an Uber to the airport.

For a moment she wondered if this whole thing was a terrible idea, and whether she should just stay home instead.

No, she wanted to pay her respects to Rachel and her family, and she was looking forward to seeing Liz and Emily again. Plus, her mum was expecting her as well, and she couldn't let her down again.

"I'm sure that it'll be fun once I'm there," she thought to herself, and turned her focus back to her packing.

8

G&T's
Friday, April 19th - Gloucestershire

Chrissy: *You ready? See you in the bar in 10 mins?*

Emily heard the vibration that signaled the text arriving and reached for her phone on the bedside table. She hadn't realized she had been drifting off to sleep, and she was glad of the nudge from Chrissy. She texted back.

Emily: *Sure. See you there.*

Hauling herself off the bed, she shuffled to the bathroom.
"*Wow. When did I get so old?*" she thought to herself, as she realized she would much rather be taking a long bath and snuggling down with a book than heading down to a bar to meet her friends.
She checked her makeup one last time. A brush of mascara and some lip gloss were all she wore nowadays.

She'd considered trying to style her hair for the evening, but it all seemed like far too much effort, so instead she'd wound it round and secured it in her signature high bun.

Slipping on her shoes, she examined herself in the full-length mirror. It wasn't an inspiring sight. She was the epitome of everything she had always been; sensible, unadventurous, and plain, which was a little frustrating, as she had bought this outfit especially for tonight. When she'd tried it on in the store, it had looked elegant and sophisticated.

"Maybe it's not the clothes, maybe it's the wearer," she thought to herself with a frustrated sigh. She had hoped that when Chrissy and Liz saw her after such a long time they would have exclaimed with amazement, saying how vibrant and gorgeous she looked. But that would never happen.

She had always been and would always be the dowdy wallflower.

With a resigned shrug, she grabbed her clutch bag and headed downstairs.

The hotel was incredible. A Victorian gothic mansion with elaborate turrets and baroque curlicues. It loomed over the surrounding grounds like the set of a classic Hollywood horror movie.

When Emily arrived earlier that day, she had marveled at the manicured grounds and had felt quite grand as she drove up the wide, sweeping driveway to the entrance hall. As she entered, the vaulted church-like ceilings and intricate mosaic floor had taken her breath away. And when she saw the sweeping wooden staircase, she felt for a moment like Scarlett O'Hara in 'Gone With the Wind'. She had turned, hoping that Rhett would be behind her, ready to roughly embrace her and carry her upstairs for a night of passion.

But there had been no Rhett, only her luggage, and she'd schlepped it to her room.

Now, as the sun set over the beautiful rolling hills, the Lodge took on an eery quality, as if ghosts from the past were watching from the shadows.

Emily was relieved to find that the atrium bar was warm and welcoming.

The place had an airy, sophisticated feel, with high ceilings and honey-colored stone walls. The room was narrow, but the arched windows on either side and the glass ceiling above, paired with the soft lighting, made it feel spacious. Trees and plants were placed with expert care to create the ambiance of an outdoor space. The resulting effect was that of a piazza in Italy, rather than in a hotel in Gloucestershire.

She waited.

The barmaid made eye contact and smiled at her with an expectant expression. Emily smiled back, blushed, and looked at her watch.

When Chrissy had said *'10 minutes'* Emily had thought she actually meant 10 minutes. But then, when had Chrissy ever been on time for anything?

"Why am I even surprised?" Emily thought to herself with an ironic smile.

After a few minutes, the barmaid made her way over to the table, and Emily ordered herself a gin and tonic. Just as it was delivered, a beautiful and exuberant Chrissy came round the corner and greeted Emily with a squeal of glee and a flutter of tiny claps.

"Oh my God! Oh my God! It's so amazing to see you!" Chrissy exclaimed as she bounded across the room.

Chrissy was effervescent with excitement, and Emily couldn't help but laugh out loud and allow herself to be dragged into a bear hug while straddling the coffee table.

"OK, calm down, you crazy woman, or you'll have both me and the table over on our sides," Emily said, beaming at her old friend.

"Wow, it's been so long, and I've missed you so much. I feel awful that I haven't been in touch," said Chrissy, releasing her childhood comrade and taking the seat next to her.

The smile dropped from Chrissy's face, replaced with a flash of desperate yearning so intense it stabbed at Emily's heart. Tears welled in Chrissy's eyes.

"Oh, no" said Emily, "Don't be upset. We've all been terrible about keeping in contact, but we're back together now. Well, kind of."

Her voice drifted off as they both looked at each other, the shadow of Rachel forming in the air between them.

"I'm gonna grab a drink," said Chrissy with a forced brightness in her voice. "Is that a G&T? Yum. I'll get one too. Want another?" she asked Emily.

"Gosh no, not yet. I've only just started on this one," Emily said with a broad smile.

"OK. Back in a sec," Chrissy said, as she headed off to the bar.

She ordered a drink, and on her return to the table she stopped dead in her tracks, releasing another squeal and peal of claps. Emily looked round to see her jumping on a tall, blonde, elegant lady in an expensive pantsuit.

Chrissy jumped up and down like a toddler on a sugar high as Liz pushed her away and laughed.

They both headed over to the table, and Emily stood to hug Liz.

They squeezed each other tight in a long-overdue embrace, and then grinned over their shoulders at Chrissy, both raising an eyebrow that spoke volumes, and taking them back to their teenage years.

"Fucking hell, this place is creepy, isn't it?" Liz exclaimed. "I only had time to dump my stuff in my room and come down, but I made sure to check the wardrobe for vampires first." The others laughed. Liz's swearing was the same as always, so incongruous against her aristocratic looks.

By the time Chrissy's drink arrived, they were already deep in conversation, only punctuated by the ordering of a G&T for Liz, and a second drink for the others, against all Emily's protestations.

"So, you live in America now?" Liz asked Chrissy. "You like it?"

"Yes, it's fantastic. I love California so much. I think it's where I was always meant to be." Chrissy said with a genuine smile of contentment.

"You went there for college, right?" Liz asked. "I remember you got that scholarship. Although you could have gone anywhere, you were such a brain-box," she said with a smile of pride.

"I considered Cambridge, but I liked the English Lit course at USC more because the professors were a bit more progressive." Chrissy explained. "And then I met my husband, so I never came home."

"Still married?" Liz said, always one to cut to the chase.

Chrissy laughed. "Yes, still married. He's a great guy, and we have two kids as well."

"Well, how disgustingly Hallmark of you," Liz said with an impish grin, and Chrissy flicked her arm and poked out her tongue in a playful manner.

"What about you, Emily? You married?" Liz asked.

"Yes, and he's lovely. His name is Ed, and we met in college as well. He works in finance for a local printing company. We have three kids, two boys and a girl," Emily beamed.

"Ha!" exclaimed Liz. "Hey Chrissy, Emily sees your two kids, and raises you one. Now that's one game of poker I'll never play" Liz snorted, and the friends laughed and smiled at each other. It was delicious to be back together again.

Pretty soon the phones were out, and photos were being displayed. Chrissy shared photos of Josh's last track meet, and they all commented on how handsome and grown up he looked. Then she showed them photos of Jackie at gymnastics, and they were amazed at how good she was.

"She's in the competitive team and trains for eighteen hours a week. The rest of the time she's with friends, I don't feel like I get to see her very much anymore," bemoaned Chrissy.

Next was Emily's turn, and she passed around photos of Philip, Sophie, and Harry.

"Wow," Liz said "Those kids are redheads, aren't they? They look like mini Kate Winslets."

Chrissy added, "Well, you always had gorgeous auburn hair when you were younger, didn't you, Emily? They must get it from you. Is your husband a redhead, too?"

"No, he's got brown hair, so that's all me," said Emily with a proud smirk.

Chrissy put her head on one side and studied Emily.

"Would you consider going back to that color again? I think it would suit you, and it would make your complexion shine."

Emily sighed. "I never left it, it left me. I'm not sure what color this is. I think I'm just waiting for it to go grey," she said with a smile and a shrug.

Liz took a sharp inhale of breath. "Young lady! We do not speak of such things. Now hush your mouth," she said, breaking into a terrible southern accent.

Chrissy raised her eyes to heaven and chuckled. "Well, I think your kids are adorable. And how about you, Liz? I'm gathering that you don't have kids, but do you have anyone special in your life?"

"I have a no-good boyfriend. He's gorgeous, but he knows it," Liz said, in a sardonic tone.

"Ooh, let's see a photo," Chrissy said, her eyes shining.

Liz pulled out her phone and showed them a recent photo of Xander.

"Bloody hell, Liz, he *is* gorgeous" Chrissy exclaimed, her jaw dropping.

"Yeah. He's a looker alright. He gets away with a lot because of it. Not with me, but with pretty much any other female within striking distance, and a lot of men too," Liz said with a raised eyebrow. "His name is Xander. It's short for Alexander. He's Greek, that's why he looks like Billy Zane's younger brother."

"What does he do?" Chrissy asked, intrigued.

"He's a fund manager at a hedge fund in London. He used to work at Goldman Sachs, that's where I met him."

"And bloody hell again," Chrissy said, her eyebrows raised. "You've hit the jackpot with that one, Liz."

"Yeah, maybe," Liz replied, looking rather wan. "We never seem to spend any time together anymore. We're always so exhausted from work. At least the sex is still amazing, though," she added, grinning and wiggling her eyebrows.

"That's not be all and end all of a relationship, though, is it?" Emily said as she sipped her G&T.

"Now there speaks a woman who hasn't had sex in a *long* time, am I wrong?" Liz chuckled and lent forward to prod Emily in the ribs.

"Hey, stop it!" Emily protested. "That's none of your business. And anyway, I'm not about to discuss my sex life with two people I haven't seen in decades." She raised her head high, trying to look sophisticated, before collapsing into a fit of giggles.

"By the way," Chrissy said to Emily, "You smell gorgeous. What perfume are you wearing?"

Emily smiled and said, "It's not perfume, it's moisturizer. It's wild rose and honey. I made it myself."

"No way!" Chrissy said with amazement. "It smells delicious. When did you start making your own moisturizer?"

"My youngest boy Harry has terrible eczema, and when he was tiny, I was beside myself trying to find something to wash him with that wouldn't make his skin flare up. I tried some eczema products that were on the market and they were OK, but in the end I started making my own soaps and moisturizers, just so I knew exactly what ingredients were in them."

"That's so impressive. I wouldn't even know where to begin." Chrissy said. "What type of soap do you make?"

"Well," Emily said, and listed them on her fingers. "I still make the basics like honey and oatmeal and other combinations that are good for eczema, but I've also branched out into other soaps like, let me think now, there's tee tree oil with charcoal, pink Himalayan salt with grapefruit, coconut and lime, and my new favorite, a coffee cocoa salt soap."

"Wow!" Exclaimed Chrissy "You have a whole cottage industry going there. So, when is Ed going to retire?" She said with a wink.

"Oh, don't," replied Emily, tutting. "He keeps making that joke too, and I've told him I only make them for fun, it's not a proper business."

"Whatever, girl," said Chrissy in her best American accent while making a playful 'talk to the hand,' sign. "I reckon you're sitting on a goldmine there, if you played your cards right." Then, with a furrowed her brow, she asked, "In fact, could I have some to take home?"

"Sure!" said Emily, her face lighting up with pride. "I'll give you some on Sunday before we leave." She beamed at Chrissy, and Chrissy gave her a conspiratorial wink.

"Anyway," said Liz, who had been studying her phone, "Enough about soap. I'm parched, let's get another drink."

* * *
*****

They ordered another round of drinks, and a selection of bar nibbles. Chrissy yawned and stretched her arms above her head.

"Sorry, it's not a comment on the company. I just didn't sleep very well last night," she explained.

"Is it jet lag? When did you fly in?" Liz asked.

"No, I got into Heathrow on Wednesday and stayed at a hotel near the airport. It was lovely, and the spa was amazing, but then I Ubered down to Bathampton yesterday to see my mum and I stayed with her last night. Let's just say that the accommodation wasn't what I'm used to."

Emily looked quizzical. "When did your mum move to Bathampton? I always thought she'd stay in that little house in Windsor. It was so cute."

Chrissy sighed. "She doesn't exactly live in Bathampton. She's there right now, but it's not permanent. Sorry, I'm not explaining myself very well, am I? Mum bought a narrow boat, and it's on the Kennet and Avon canal. It's docked at Bathampton right now, but she moves it every two weeks to avoid paying mooring fees. The canal runs from Bristol to Reading, and then in theory she could join the Thames and chug right up into London if she wanted to, so she could be anywhere on that stretch. It's kinda hard to tie her down, if you know what I mean," Chrissy said with a raised eyebrow and a knowing look.

Emily stared at her, agog. "Wow, that's amazing. Your mum is so cool. I can't imagine my parents ever selling up and buying a boat. Trish is the best." She beamed.

"Hmm," replied Chrissy in a sardonic tone. Emily had always adored Trish, Chrissy's impulsive, mercurial mother, but Chrissy had grown up being buffeted by her spontaneous and carefree ways, and as a result, she didn't share Emily's romantic views on the 'wild and free' lifestyle. She hadn't had a terrible childhood, far from it, but her mother had taken 'free range parenting' to a whole new level.

People often asked her how she had been brave enough to go to university in a different country and didn't her mother miss her? Chrissy never had the heart to tell them she wasn't sure her mum would even notice her absence. When they were together, Trish was loving and fun, but Chrissy never felt that she was high on Trish's agenda. There were so many other causes she was involved in that Chrissy only ever got a small slice of her mother's attention.

It was fine, though. It had led her to California and to Scott, and she wouldn't change that for the world.

Liz nudged Chrissy. "Hey you. You asleep already? Sleeping on a boat obviously doesn't suit you, you're more of a 5-star hotel girl, right?" Liz joked and waved to the barmaid for the check. "It's getting late. Maybe we should all head to bed? I'm not sure what tomorrow will hold," she said with a suddenly sober expression.

They all exchanged weighted looks and agreed it was time to turn in.

They paid the check and headed up to their rooms, hugging each other tightly as they said their good nights.

They each felt a tug as they walked away, as if a gossamer thread, long since dropped, had been pulled taut once more, and they knew they never wanted to drop it again.

9

Memorial
Saturday, April 20th - Gloucestershire

Soft classical music drifted through the imposing double doors as Chrissy entered the ballroom of the hotel. The memorial decorations were both elegant and modest, classical in an understated way. Vases of lilies placed on stands about the room enveloped the mourners in a delicate fragrance, the melancholic scent of a thousand tears.

Rachel's mother greeted Chrissy with a gentle smile and a murmur of appreciation. As she handed her the Order Of Service, Chrissy saw the lines around her eyes, and a deep sadness that seemed to haunt her face.

She looked so much older than Chrissy remembered, and Chrissy wondered how much of it was due to time, and how much because of her daughter's untimely death.

She leaned in to Chrissy and said, "Thank you so much for coming. I know Rachel thought of you often. In fact, she was talking about the three of you the very last time we saw her. She loved you all so much."

"I know. We loved her too. I'm so sorry for your loss, Mrs.

Sullivan," Chrissy whispered back.

As Rachel's parents greeted the other guests, Chrissy moved toward the rows of seats facing the front of the room. She scanned to see if either of her friends had arrived and was relieved to see Emily in the middle of a row towards the front.

Emily gave a small wave and motioned to the seat next to her.

Chrissy walked down the center isle and slipped into Emily's row, passing the other chairs until she reached her friend.

"Hi" she whispered.

"Hi" responded Emily, smiling back at her friend.

Chrissy settled in the chair and placed her clutch bag on the floor beneath her. Although the mood was solemn, the room had a cheery color scheme that felt somewhat inappropriate for the occasion.

The thick, peach colored carpet was warm and cosy, if a little challenging to walk across in high heels. Chrissy realized how unused she was to seeing carpet on the floor in a public place, having lived in a hot climate for so long.

The walls were a golden yellow with matching heavy drapes framing the floor to ceiling windows along the left-hand side of the room. The high ceiling was ornate and covered with bright blue and gold designs. A chandelier hung at its center, and Chrissy thought of the grand balls of bygone times. She smiled despite herself.

The room filled with mourners, adorned in dignified black clothing. They each offered their condolences to the grieving parents, and then took their seats.

Chrissy noticed that most of the attendees were of Rachel's parents' age, and she wondered where all Rachel's friends were. Surely she had other friends who would come to show their respects? It couldn't just be the three of them, could it?

Looking down at the Order Of Service, Chrissy noticed the photograph of Rachel on the front cover. It showed her at age eleven or twelve, smiling while sitting atop a fence with rolling fields behind her. It represented the epitome of bucolic perfection and, Chrissy felt, was a little out of step with the Rachel she remembered.

Rachel had been far more at home in urban settings, capturing images of rusted railings, crumbling buildings, and the waifs and strays on the edge of society.

Rachel had seen beauty in their imperfections where others had only seen only decay and degradation. That had been her gift, and the reason she had become such a celebrated photographer.

Also, Rachel only ever took photographs in black and white, and the image on the Order Of Service was in color.

As she pondered this, Chrissy caught sight of Liz entering the room, looking exquisite as always, in a classic black fitted dress with a single strand of pearls. Liz's mother would have been so proud of her, but of course Chrissy would never dare say anything of the sort to Liz. She signaled to her, and Liz acknowledged with a quick smile.

She walked down the rows towards the front, making her excuses as she squeezed along the row to join her friends. They whispered their hellos and then fell quiet as somebody at the back of the room pulled the double doors shut, and a hush descended over the room.

Rachel's father stood and cleared his throat. He thanked everyone for coming, and said how touched he felt to see so many close friends in attendance, all of them there to celebrate his precious Rachel. He asked everyone to refer to their Order Of Service and then gestured to his wife, who stood to read a poem.

Rachel's mother stood, and in a clear voice read, 'Do Not Stand at my Grave and Weep' by Mary Elizabeth Frye. It was beautiful, and promised that loved ones are not dead, but surround us for eternity in the beauty of nature.

A silence descended on the room as she gathered herself, and others dabbed their eyes with tissues. Then she raised her head and addressed the gathering.

"I believe Rachel will always be with us, because she lives on in our hearts, and in the exquisite photographs she left for us. Our daughter will always be a young, vibrant expression of beauty, taken from this world too soon."

The Memorial continued with a 'Life Tribute to Rachel', including a selection of memories recounted by her parents of Rachel's younger years.

Her parents spoke with love and longing about idyllic vacations by the beach, and a family dog with which she could now be reunited. They played a piece of music that Rachel had learned for a piano recital, and its beautiful haunting notes created delicate currents of sorrow sweeping around the room.

At the end of the Tribute, Rachel's father asked that everyone move to the adjacent room. He explained that Rachel had bequeathed her parents a selection of her most famous photographs, asking that after her death they be auctioned off and the proceeds given to an animal sanctuary she had supported for many years.

However, before the public auction, the family wanted to share the collection in a private showing with the attendees of Rachel's memorial.

"Please stay as long as you wish, and afterwards join us for refreshments in the atrium bar." Rachel's father said, gesturing to the adjoining doors.

*****

The three friends walked around the room, pausing in front

of each of Rachel's photographs.

The large prints, displayed on simple wooden easels, showed humanity in all its fragile beauty and desperation. Black and white testaments to the places nobody wanted to go, and the people nobody wanted to acknowledge.

It was stark, raw, and haunting.

An abandoned railway bridge covered in graffiti, the tracks beneath it overgrown, silent and forgotten by the bustling world above.

The face of a young homeless man with bright, shining eyes full of life and warmth, framed by filthy, disheveled hair.

A homeless disabled woman in a wheelchair, her possessions hung about her in plastic bags. The pride shining in her eyes as she held up an intricate pencil sketch of a running horse she had drawn.

A group of sex workers dressed in provocative clothing, laughing together, content in each others' company.

Rachel had titled each photograph with one word. She followed it with a sentence, explaining where and when the photograph had been taken.

****

Emily stopped in front of one particular print that made her heart quicken.

It showed a group of grimy young girls, only seven or eight years old, the same age as her Sophie. They were grinning and laughing at the camera as they dragged on their cigarettes. They leaned on a metal handrail that separated a concrete path from a dusty scrub of playing field. Behind them loomed a large utilitarian apartment block, a concrete, desolate building pecked with hundreds of tiny dark windows. Some girls wore summer tops, others hooded jackets. One girl wore a short skirt and another, sweatpants. It was hard to tell what season it was, but the heavy clouds in the background suggested a chill in the air.

Rachel had titled the piece 'Mischief', and the description read, 'The children of the condemned Sighthill tower block, Glasgow 2010.'

As Emily looked into their filthy, precious faces, a mixture of sadness and rage welled up in her. They were so young, and it seemed like such a waste. What could this life possibly offer them? How could they ever break free from this cycle of poverty and deprivation? And how could Rachel have called this heartbreaking scene 'Mischief'? It seemed so trite and frivolous, and Emily's jaw clenched in reaction to it.

Her breathing deepened as she tried to suppress her rising anger.

As she looked closer at the girls however, she noticed that yes, their clothes were worn thin and their hands and faces smeared with dirt, but they each had the joyous, impish expression of a small child up to no good, and loving it. They knew they were breaking a rule set forth by adults, and they seemed delighted to find that they were being observed, but not reprimanded, by this strange lady and her camera. They rejoiced in their rebellion, and for a moment Emily saw the shadow of her own Harry, caught stealing a cookie from the kitchen table, running through the kitchen with giggles of glee before she could catch him and take it away.

These girls, in their own way, were happy, triumphant, and free.

****

Meanwhile, Chrissy stood in front of a different print.

She felt her chest sinking into itself, her lips tightening as she fought back the tears.

The print showed a small girl dressed in her school

uniform, backpack on her shoulders and head held low, waiting alone by the edge of a train platform. She wore tiny white ankle socks and black shoes. The muted shades of her pleated skirt and matching suit jacket seemed strangely formal, such adult clothing for such a small child. Her toes touched the faded 'do not cross' line, as she stood uncomfortably close to the edge of the platform.

Chrissy felt a desperate urge to reach into the photograph and pull her back from the edge. To hold her close as the train approached. To protect her from this unforgiving adult world. Rachel had titled the piece 'Resilience', and the description read, 'A young girl makes her way home after school.'

Chrissy's fists clenched as she hissed the words, *"this isn't resilience. It's not resilience when she doesn't have a choice. She's only a baby. How can she be asked to grow up so fast?"*

Bitter feelings rose from deep inside her as she questioned Rachel's understanding of the situation.

If Rachel had been a mother, then she would have understood. She would have seen the truth of it. This wasn't resilience. There was nothing noble here. This was neglect.

Chrissy couldn't bear to look at the photograph any longer, so she turned and walked briskly out of the room to get some fresh air.

Chrissy passed Liz on her way out, but she was oblivious.

****

Liz stood silent and still, staring into the eyes of a woman in one of Rachel's prints.

The woman's elderly face held a troubled, faraway expression, as if she were trying to recall something that eluded her, the echo of a distant memory too faint for her to hear. Her eyes appeared washed out, blue once maybe, but now they held a misty opal quality.

Her white hair fell in waves, cut into a neat bob. She wore a hospital gown, and next to her sat an elderly gentleman holding a hairbrush in one hand, and a strand of her hair in the other. He seemed to be brushing her hair with love and reverence, talking to her all the while. Liz imagined him in that hospital room, the love in his eyes as he brushed and talked, his wife sitting, staring into the distance.

The photograph was titled, 'Promises', and the caption read 'Milly and Stan, St Mary's Hospital Dementia Ward.'

Liz looked at the old woman's face, at the deep set lines in her cheeks, her chin, around her mouth and on her forehead.

She tried to imagine what she might have looked like in her twenties, or her early forties, as Liz was now.

Had she been beautiful?

Would she have smiled at her own reflection in the mirror?

Liz wondered who she had been back then when she was young.

Was she vibrant and determined?

Capricious? Or polite and demure?

It was hard to tell now, as if her soul had already left, leaving only footprints in wet sand.

Liz turned and walked out of the room.

10

Running
Saturday April 20th - Gloucestershire

"I need a cigarette," said Liz as she past her friends in the foyer. Chrissy had been holding back the tears as she walked past Emily a few minutes earlier, and Emily had followed her into the hallway to comfort her. They were both standing by a tall grandfather clock as Liz walked past them, heading towards the front entrance of the hotel.

The three of them stood outside, arms crossed, hugging themselves tight to fend off the brisk April chill. Clouds skittered across the sky and the light was low and brooding. Rain was on its way.

Liz dragged hard on her cigarette as she poked the gravel with the toe of her elegant black mule.

"Well, that was a fucking joke, wasn't it?" she stated in an icy tone.

"What the hell, Liz? Show a little respect, please," said Emily, horrified.

"Oh, come on, Emily," Liz replied. "What the fuck was all that 'taken too soon' bullshit? Rachel didn't die of cancer, or in an accident, she killed herself, and not one of them had the guts to acknowledge it. Rachel was suffering from clinical depression and her parents were always too uncomfortable to face that fact."

Emily's eyes dropped to the ground.

"Maybe they were scared. Or they didn't know what to do. I don't think they did it intentionally, maybe they just didn't understand it. And what's more," she said, now with an edge to her voice, "I don't think you should judge them Liz, they just lost their only daughter."

Chrissy turned on Emily and said in an icy tone,

"What the hell do you know, Emily. Liz is right. If Rachel's parents had ever a*cknowledged* their daughter's mental illness, then maybe she wouldn't have killed herself. Wow, you haven't changed at all have you? Stop pretending to be such a saint and admit it. You make me sick with your 'holier than thou' bullshit. You're not a fucking nun and you never were!"

Emily turned to Chrissy. Her eyes were wide, but her jaw was set in defiance.

"How *dare* you speak to me like that," she said in a low, venomous tone. "Who the hell are you to judge me? You don't even *know* me anymore. You are obviously upset by something, but don't take it out on me, OK? I'm not your whipping boy, and I can't help it if I have more self-control than you do, that's *your* problem, not mine. Grow up, Chrissy."

They squared off against each other, looking like they might come to blows. Liz stepped in.

"Bloody hell, you two. What's with the cage match? Calm down, you crazy bitches," she said with a laugh that defused the situation. "OK, tensions are running high, and I know that we're all very emotional, but let's not rip each other to shreds on the doorstep of this beautiful building, shall we? How about we all take a break to calm down, and then we can get back together for dinner? It's 2pm now. Shall we meet in the bar at 6pm?"

They agreed and headed to their rooms.

****

Thirty minutes later, Liz stood on the covered porch of the hotel, dressed in her running gear. Stretching, she waited for a break in the weather so she could feel her body come alive as she ran. She watched as the rain came down in sheets, but before long the dark clouds cleared and a feeble sun peeked out.

She stepped out onto the driveway, the gravel crunching under her running shoes. Breathing in the fresh, cool, delicious air, she started out.

She ran down the driveway and turned left into the lane. It was overgrown on both sides, and only just wide enough for two cars to pass.

She ran under a canopy of ancient oak trees, dodging the puddles and reveling in the sweet aroma of nature, a welcome break from the acrid air of central London.

As she hit her stride, her breathing slowed to match the rhythmic pounding of her feet on the tarmac.

Undulating fields of new grass flanked her on both sides, while mature oak and hawthorn trees dotting the horizon showing the first signs of Spring leaves. Warped wooden fences and thick hedges marked long established boundaries, while clouds of daffodils swayed in the soft breeze.

Once or twice she spied an ancient stone wall, almost hidden under a tangle of bramble bushes. The stillness of the English countryside seeped into her soul, calming her as she ran.

As she rounded a bend in the narrow road, she caught sight of a cow chewing its cud. It watched her with disinterest as she ran past, before dropping its head once more.

Breathing hard, Liz stopped by a wooden gate to admire the view that stretched out before her. She leaned on the decrepit fence post, catching her breath as she marveled at the quiet elegance of the hills rolling away into the distance. A thousand delicate shades of green. A living watercolor, both simple and infinitely complex.

This London girl, who lived for the vibrance of the city, had always been scornful of the countryside. But now recognized the beauty that surrounded her.

For the first time, she saw the countryside of Constable and Blake, and she understood their lifelong passion for sharing this delicate perfection.

In the soft light of the afternoon she could feel the history of the land, the silent echo of centuries past. These hills and valleys had borne witness to the lives of countless souls, of kings and beggars alike, and marked the passing of time with unchanging majesty.

She walked now, enjoying the peace that surrounded her. Normally she would listen to music while she ran, but today she craved the tranquility of the trees and hillsides. She needed to think about Rachel, about her friends, and about herself.

Liz was not a contemplative person by nature, and she loathed the 'narcissistic self-help types' as she called them. But the Memorial Celebration had raised some unexpected emotions in her, and she was not prepared to dismiss them out of hand.

She thought again about Rachel's photograph of the old lady with dementia, with her devoted husband by her side.

She remembered how, as she stood looking at it, she sensed a creeping loneliness, a hollow emptiness so black and deep that it made her catch her breath. The love and tenderness in the eyes of that old man had been undeniable, and she contrasted it with the way Xander looked at her.

At that moment a dull ache had risen inside her, and it wouldn't shift.

As she was pulling on her running shoes, she'd argued to herself that 'gooey sentimentality' wasn't for her. That she and Xander didn't have that kind of relationship because their relationship was based on strength and respect. Alpha meets Alpha. And that sappiness wasn't what she wanted in life.

But now she wasn't so sure.

Her ironclad belief that she was invulnerable was wavering, and it scared Liz. What did that mean for her future? For her relationship with Xander? Could they build the kind of love she had seen in that photograph?

As she walked back towards the hotel, she thought about the night they'd met.

Goldman Sachs had been hosting a fundraiser for some good cause, she couldn't remember which one. Her firm had made a generous donation, and Liz was making the most of the networking opportunity it afforded her.

She had been deep in conversation with one of the senior partners when Xander appeared at their side. He smiled at her, a fabulous, white, warm smile, as he held out his hand to introduce himself.

There was electricity between them as they shook hands. But she was also aware of the young female interns at the bar, watching them and grinning as they nudged each other. She knew Xander's type, and she wouldn't be taken in by him. Others would have been swept off their feet, but she'd seen this scenario play out before, and she knew better than to mix business with pleasure.

She'd been polite, if somewhat curt, and had excused herself at the earliest opportunity. She had expected him to pursue her, but he didn't.

They had crossed paths again several weeks later at another function. He smiled at her but did not approach, and she was surprised by her disappointment.

Six months later, at a Christmas party, he appeared at her side once more.

He made a joke about a certain politician who had been involved in a recent scandal, and they began a conversation. She'd been surprised by his effortless charm and obvious intelligence, and by the end of the night when he suggested they share a cab, she'd found herself agreeing.

As the cab pulled up outside her apartment, Xander kissed her, soft and deep, and the heat rose between them. But then he had declined to come in.

The next week they went for dinner, and he stayed over at her place. Within weeks they were living together in his gorgeous penthouse apartment. That was almost eight years ago.

As Liz arrived back at the hotel lobby, she pulled out her mobile phone to check for messages.

Nothing.

She started a text to Xander.

> Hi there. I'm here. Drive was fine.
> Memorial was depressing. No surprise there, I guess.
> Miss you.

She sighed and deleted the text.

Back in her room, Liz stripped down and showered.

Sitting on her bed, her body and hair wrapped in towels, she called Xander's mobile phone.

No answer.

Irritation rose in her as she looked at the clock on the nightstand.

"What could he be doing at 4.30pm on a Saturday that he can't

answer his phone?"

She called his work mobile.

"Hey. What's up, babe?" Xander answered with an edge to his voice. There was music and muffled voices in the background.

"Hi" Liz said, a knot in her stomach.

"You OK? You still in Cornwall?"

"Gloucestershire. Yes. I'm here another night. I'll be home on Sunday."

"Great! You having fun?"

"It's a Memorial, so no, not really. It was an emotional day, I still feel kinda wiped out."

"Mmm-hmm."

"Xander, what are you doing?"

"Oh, sorry babe, I just finished playing golf with the boys. We're in the bar. David's getting a round of drinks. What were you saying?"

Liz sighed.

"I was thinking," she continued, "maybe we should go away sometime soon? Spend some time together? We haven't had a break for so long it might be nice to get away from work and just hang out a bit?"

"Sorry Liz, I missed that. Hang on a minute," she heard him hold his hand over the phone and shout into the distance that he wanted the cod and chips. "Sorry, babe, I can't really talk now. I'm glad you're having a good time. Let's catch up tomorrow when you're back, OK?"

"Ok. I love…" she heard the phone disconnect.

11

Spark
Saturday, April 20th - Gloucestershire

As Liz ran through the woods surrounding the hotel, Emily sat on her bed talking to Ed.

She was fuming when she got back to her room, and she punched the unlock code into her phone so hard and fast that she needed to retry it several times before it complied.

Ed had been taken aback by the anger in Emily's voice and, very wisely, he had decided to let her talk and talk until she was finished.

Once she was done venting her frustration, Emily paused and said;

"So? She's a bitch, isn't she? Do you think I should just leave? After all, I only came here for Rachel, and I've said my goodbyes, so now I could just pack up and leave. Screw the fact that I've booked for two nights, and screw both of them, they're the worst."

There was another pause while Emily waited for Ed to agree with everything she'd said and tell her they didn't deserve her friendship.

When his response wasn't forthcoming, she snapped, "Ed? Are you even listening to what I'm saying?"

"Yes, I am, and you sound furious. I get it, and you're right, Chrissy shouldn't have spoken to you in that way, but do you really want to leave? You've missed your friends so much, and I think you'll regret it if you storm off now."

"I'm not *storming off*, Ed," Emily said with venom. "You make me sound like a petulant teenager. She was out of line and she's a bitch and I don't have to take it, right?"

Ed replied in a measured tone, "Well, yes, she was out of line, but from the sound of it, everyone was distressed. Maybe those photographs triggered something in Chrissy and she unintentionally took it out on you? But Emily, you can't punish her for one mistake. Aren't best friends the ones who have your back, even when you're lashing out and acting badly? I'm not saying that she should be allowed to treat you like that all the time, not at all, but can you let her have this one, and give her a chance to redeem herself?"

Emily huffed. "I suppose so. But if she speaks to me like that again, I'm done."

"Fair enough," said Ed, a smile creeping into his voice as he said, "And if you need me to, I'll ride over there on my white horse and punch her on the nose for you."

"You're such a fool," said Emily, grinning despite herself. "I really miss you, you know? I wish you were here."

Ed snorted, "God, I'm glad I'm not! You she-wolves are terrifying," he said with a chuckle. "But I wonder if this isn't exactly what you needed? I haven't heard you sound this sparky in the longest time. What time are you guys meeting up?"

"Liz said 6pm, so I'm going to chill out on the bed and read my book for a bit, then I'll have a shower and get ready. Thank you, baby. I love you. Speak to you later," and they said their goodbyes.

She felt steadier now, but as she leaned back on the pillows, she knew Ed had been right. It felt exhilarating to argue again, and she realized with a start that she was hungry for more. She checked herself; the guilt creeping upon her as she chided herself for being so immature.

She thought back to her childhood and remembered with fondness the epic, blazing rows she would have with her sister. Fights that would often culminate in physical blows, much to the consternation of their mother.

Once, when Emily and her sister were arguing, Emily had pushed her off the top of their slide set, resulting in a fractured wrist. The girls kissed and made up within the hour and Emily had been the first to sign her baby sisters cast, but Jennifer, their mother, was furious for a week, making barbed comments long after the sisters had forgiven and forgotten.

One evening Jennifer said to Emily in a cool tone,

"You need to learn to control your temper, young lady. No man is ever going to want to marry a willful, reckless tomboy. Understand?"

Emily raised her eyes to heaven at the memory.

And yet, against all the odds, and to her mother's surprise, she had managed to find a man to marry her after all. A wonderful, considerate, funny man. A man who worshiped her and loved and cared for their babies.

But she and Ed never argued. They disagreed and discussed things, and often they saw things from different perspectives, but they never fought.

Emily tried to recall if they ever had.

They'd been friends at college, and Emily had always felt safe with Ed. Her friends adored him and so had her parents, so when he proposed, it seemed like the most natural thing in the world to accept.

She had been studying law and planned to practice, maybe even pass the bar, but life had taken a different course.

As she thought back to those days, she remembered what it had been like to argue a case, and she yearned for that fire and passion again.

A cold lump formed in the pit of her stomach, and she quickly picked up her book to distract herself.

Settling back into the pillows, she scanned the pages to find her place. It was a light-hearted romantic comedy about a twenty-something girl in New York.

She tried to read, but a sudden anger overtook her.

"God, this book is utter shit," she thought to herself, slamming it down on the floral bedspread.

Standing, she walked to the window and looked out over the grounds of the hotel. She opened it a crack to let in some fresh air, suddenly claustrophobic in the hot, stuffy room.

The air had a damp, fresh smell, and the grass and flowerbeds glistened from the earlier rain. The birds had not yet begun their songs, and a melancholic silence hung in the air that soothed Emily's troubled mind.

She sighed the tension away and, feeling renewed, she went to grab her phone.

Leaning against the old radiator on the wall, she listened to its rusty clunks and rumbles as she scrolled through her emails.

She filed away stationary coupons and ideas for new soap recipes. She skim read news articles and deleted home improvement ideas.

Then her jaw tightened as she saw an email from Helen. It was, of course, yet another passive aggressive complaint about the 'disappointing lack of parent participation' at a recent school sports day.

Helen was a fellow school parent who took it upon herself to 'improve' the school by making all the other parents feel inadequate at every opportunity. Emily had once called her a weasel, and Ed, while stifling a laugh, had told her not to be so mean. But she was a weasel, and she took pleasure in other people's discomfort.

"I wouldn't mind it so much," she had complained to Ed, "if she would just say what she meant. Have the guts to *say* it, rather than hinting and implying all the bloody time! If you need ten volunteers for something, then just say 'we need 10 volunteers' instead of lecturing us about our responsibility as a wider bloody community!"

She continued to read on, as Helen pronounced that, "those parents who understand the value of a rounded education will carve out the time needed to attend next weekend's Spring Festival where we prepare the schools gardens for our new spring crops. Please join us as we plant the seeds of our children's future. Also, please remember to wear appropriate footwear."

It would be funny if it weren't so bloody irritating.

"Oh fuck off Helen, you sanctimonious cow."

Emily was shocked.

What the hell was wrong with her? Was it hormones? Where was all this anger coming from?

Ed had been right. There was a spark in her now that had been missing for a long time, and it scared Emily a little. Even a tiny spark like this could smolder and grow and turn into an uncontrollable forest fire, if left unchecked. She felt both excited and terrified by the possibility.

A quiet realization crept upon her.

She wanted more. So much more.

She became aware of an itchy discontentment, and a rising feeling of anger. She had never acknowledged it until now, but she was angry. Deeply angry.

She shook herself and breathed a deep, shaky breath.

"Get a hold of yourself! You have nothing to be discontent about. You have an amazing life. You have everything. Some people would kill for what you have, how dare you be so selfish as to complain."

She sat back down on the bed, shaking as the shame engulf her. What would Ed think if he could see her like this? What would her children think?

She took a deep breath and looked at the clock. It was 4pm.

"OK. A couple of hours until I meet up with the others. I'll read my book for a bit and then I'll get ready," she thought to herself, as she picked up her book again and settled herself into the pillows.

12

Adrift
Saturday, April 20th - Gloucestershire

Chrissy sat on her bed, flicking through the room service menu. She wasn't particularly hungry, but she'd only picked at her breakfast and it was almost 3pm, so she knew she should probably eat something.

"God, I hate jet lag," she thought, her stomach turning at the thought of a greasy grilled cheese sandwich.

Although she'd arrived in the UK days ago, her body clock still hadn't adjusted. She wondered if it was her age, and she groaned at the thought.

She ordered a BLT with chips, keeping her expectations low.

Some time later, a surly server knocked on her door and presented her with an ostentatious silver platter covered with a domed lid. She took it and thanked him. He grunted before heading back down the corridor.

Underneath the dome, she found a sandwich and a soggy pile of French fries. She stared at them in a confusion, before saying to herself,

"Oh God. Of course. 'Chips.'"

The sandwich was two pieces of cheap white bread containing one limp lettuce leaf, a watery slice of tomato, and some very salty bacon. As she picked the sandwich up, the bread sank beneath her fingers like a memory foam mattress. She took a bite, and with a grimace, put it back on the plate. Something was greasy in it, and she soon discovered that the bread had a layer of butter on it, something she was no longer used to.

She turned her attention to the fries instead. They were thick and stodgy and covered in salt and vinegar, and they tasted like heaven.

She finished them, and wished she'd ordered more, but at least it would see her through till dinner.

She wondered what time it was in Pasadena, and a wave of homesickness washed over her.

Sighing, she looked around the room.

It was decorated it in the usual style of hotel rooms the world over; a bland, unobtrusive color scheme with functional, replaceable fixtures. But there was something distinctly English about this room that she couldn't quite put her finger on. The color scheme was cream and green, with decorative pillows dotted about her on the bed and on the armchair. Matching, nondescript artwork of flowers and leaves created a safe if uninspiring ambiance, and the bedspread and curtains shared the same subtle paisley print.

It was elegant and classic, if somewhat sterile. The thick, brown shag pile carpet felt luxurious under her naked feet, so different from the hardwood floors of home.

As she was freshening up in the bathroom earlier, she had stopped as she dried her face, breathing in a familiar smell that caused distant memories to flit about her, too faint to take any recognizable shape.

Chrissy lay back on the bed, her body aching with

weariness.

She thought about the events of the day, and the photograph that had disturbed her so much.

She cringed as she recalled the way she had spoken to Emily; it was unjustified and so out of character for her. What had she been thinking? What a bitch she had been, and for no real reason. Was it just jet lag? Was she exhausted? She would apologize to Emily as soon as she saw her, if Emily would even accept an apology from her.

Again came the stab of guilt.

She looked at the clock on the bedside table and thought of her family back home.

Doing the math, she counted back eight hours from 2.30pm. It was only 6.30 in the morning in Pasadena and no one would be up yet.

Josh had track practice at 8.30am but he wouldn't heave himself out of bed until the last minute, and Jackie had gymnastics at 9am but she wouldn't be awake until 8am at the earliest. Scott would either be in bed or out for a run, so there was no point in calling the house.

Chrissy smiled as she imagined Josh swigging orange juice from the fridge, while Jackie yelled at him in disgust. "Ew, Josh, gross! Thanks so much, now no one else can drink it."

She pictured her son shouting up the stairs to his father, asking where his running kit was. And Scott shouting back to say that he had no idea.

In that moment she was transported to her warm kitchen on a Saturday morning, the California light streaming through the windows, and she felt a sharp pang of homesickness.

Five thousand miles from home, and aching for her family, she wondered how much they were missing her.

Over the last couple of years, they had drifted apart, their relationships becoming transactional, never stopping to take the time to connect or talk to each other anymore.

At that moment Chrissy felt a desperate urge to catch a cab to the airport, to get back to them and hold them tight against her, before she lost them forever.

Shaking off the feeling, she reasoned with herself that this was jet lag, nothing more significant, and nothing that a couple of hours of sleep wouldn't fix. She had three and a half hours until she was due to meet up with the others, so she would try to get some rest and no doubt things would seem more stable and less dramatic after that.

She closed the blackout blind and the curtains and settled back onto the bed, pulling the top sheet over her legs.

She drifted off into a fitful sleep filled with vivid, disturbing dreams.

She dreamed she was back on her mother's narrowboat, the rhythmic rocking of the water moving beneath her like the ticking of an ancient clock.

It was nighttime, and she lay in the darkness on the uncomfortable guest bed, narrow and hard as a navy cot, listening to the unfamiliar sounds around her.

The wide river beneath was powerful and threatening, the swift, unforgiving currents pulling them away from the bank.

The mooring rope snapped from its post, and the boat began to drift down the river at the mercy of the current.

A cold stab of alarm ran through her as she stiffened, the hairs on the back of her neck standing up.

She tried to move, but she was paralyzed, lying helpless and terrified as the boat swung from side to side.

With a huge effort, she dragged herself off the bed, her body heavy as lead as she struggled down the length of the galley and out into the icy night air.

The boat jolted to a stop; grounded on a muddy riverbank.

Straining to see further down the river, she could make out only blurry shapes, but the roar and churn of a steep waterfall not far from where they had stopped was unmistakable.

She inched along the side of the boat until she could make out the edge of the bank. Jumping off the side of the boat, she landed in the black, sticky mud the boat had lodged in.

She fought to pull each leg out of the sucking, clawing mud, desperate to get to the shore.

Ahead of her she could see a dark forest, the trees so close together they blocked out even the faintest moonlight.

She knew this forest from her childhood nightmares, and the dread swirled about her, wisps of fear stroking her like long dead fingers.

Now she found herself deep in the forest, standing barefoot, wearing nothing but a nightdress, her feet cut and bleeding, burning with the cold.

A noise behind her made her turn, swiveling her head, blinking and straining, trying to find even the faintest light in the all-consuming darkness. She sensed shapes moving about her, whispering that she did not belong, that she should not be there, and she knew it was true.

She ran, stumbling and screaming as she went, crashing into trees and tripping into unseen holes, trying to find a way out.

Chrissy dreamed fitfully. Stumbling and searching, until her alarm brought her back to reality with a start.

Her heart was pumping and her breath ragged.

She sat up, disoriented for a moment, until the room came into focus. Then she lay back on the bed, filling her lungs with the cool air of the room as she tried to calm her turbulent thoughts.

13

Pact
Saturday, April 20th - Gloucestershire

When Chrissy arrived at the atrium bar, she spied Emily seated on a stool, smiling and chatting with the barman.

Her long hair, curled into soft delicate ringlets, fell down her back almost to her waist, tousling together in a soft waterfall of shine. Chrissy admired Emily's long, flowing chiffon dress. It had a light blue floral print that not only complimented her figure, but accentuated her height.

Chrissy had always considered Liz to be the tall one of the group, but as Emily sat at the bar, unaware that she was being observed, Chrissy realized how elegant and commanding she could be, even if Emily never saw it herself.

She approached the bar.

"Hi Emily," she said in a small, apologetic voice, "I wanted to say how sorry…"

Emily smiled and held out her hand. "Honestly, it's fine. It was a tough day with a lot of emotion. I get it, and after all, if you can't scream at your best friend then who *can* you scream at, eh?"

Chrissy's eyes welled up with tears.

"Oh good grief, girl, come here," Emily said, smiling and pulling Chrissy in for a maternal hug.

"I'm so sorry," Chrissy sniffed. "I'm hoping this is all just a bad case of jet lag, otherwise I can only assume it's the beginning of a complete mental breakdown. So basically, I'm really, *really* hoping it's just jet lag."

As Emily laughed and Chrissy wiped her eyes, they heard a familiar, gravelly voice by their side.

"I brought a taser just in case, but it looks like you guys kissed and made up already," Liz drawled as she pulled up a seat next to the bar. "I need a *bucket* of wine, and make it quick!" she said, gesticulating to the barman.

Several glasses of wine later, they were laughing and joking again. The years seemed to roll away, and they found themselves back in their late teens, with all the angst and possibility that the future offered. They gossiped about the girls from their school year, laughing at memories of boys and alcohol, and situations that were both humiliating and, with hindsight, wildly comical.

Emily sighed. "It was tantalizing back then, wasn't it?"

"What? What are you talking about, woman?" said Liz.

"The future. When we were eighteen and there was nothing we couldn't do, nowhere we couldn't go. Yes, we were all under confident in our own ways, but we had the belief that the future was limitless, if we could only find the courage to reach for it."

"You're a nutter," Liz replied with a grin and a dismissive wave of her hand.

Chrissy turned to Emily and nodded vigorously. "No, you're right, Emily. I left England and moved to America and never looked back. I didn't realize how brave it was at the time, but now I think about it, it was kinda crazy, wasn't it? And you! You went off to study law. Everyone thought you were so quiet and sensible, but you were always kind of kick-ass, weren't you?" Chrissy beamed at Emily.

Liz, who had been looking at her phone, looked up and said, "Yeah, Emily, did you ever practice law after you qualified?"

Emily sighed. "No, I never did. I met Ed, and he was studying for his accountancy qualifications, and before I knew it, we were married and buying a house. I was busy with homemaking, and then I fell pregnant with Philip. So that was that, I suppose."

Chrissy raised an eyebrow. "Yup. I know all about the 'before I knew it' feeling. Scott and I weren't even married when I found out I was pregnant with Josh. I was on my way to completing my PhD in literature, but that never happened. I had Josh a couple of months after I turned twenty-five. He's fifteen now."

"Wow," Emily said, reaching out to put her hand on Chrissy's arm. "He's so handsome, though. He looks so sporty and all-American. If that's not a bad thing to say?" she said, looking nervous.

Chrissy laughed. "No, you're right. He has the 'all-American jock' look, exactly like his father. It totally put me off when I first met Scott," she said, smiling, before the sinking feeling returned.

Chrissy looked at her friends. "Actually, this memorial service has made me think I need to make some changes in my own life. I've realized that my kids are getting older and we don't spend enough time together talking about things that matter. I want to reconnect with them and understand who they are, after all they are becoming adults in their own right, now."

She paused, looking at her old friends. "I know this sounds kind of corny, but I was wondering if we could make a pact to improve something in our lives, in honor of Rachel? And then maybe we can stay in touch and hold each other accountable for the promises we've made? I'd love to keep in contact, and it seems like a good way to make sure it happens. What do you think?"

Emily beamed. "That sounds like an amazing idea! I would love to stay in touch with the both of you, and you're right, Chrissy; this weekend has made me realize I need to spend a little more time on myself and not just see myself solely as a mother and wife. I mean, I love my life and I wouldn't change anything for the world, but I feel like I've lost myself a little since the kids were born."

Liz looked at the other two, one eyebrow raised incredulously. "Really? We're doing this? Oh ok, why the hell not?"

"Yay!" squealed Chrissy with a little trill of claps.

"What's your pact, Liz? What do you want to change?" asked Emily.

Liz tutted and frowned. "I think I need to spend some more time with Xander. We've been together for years and we're going nowhere. I feel like we need to make this whole thing less of a fuck-fest, and more of a lasting relationship,"

Emily raised her eyes to heaven. "Wow Liz, how eloquent."

"OK, it's a deal," said Chrissy with conviction, putting her hand into the circle. "The musketeers are reunited, and we swear to support each other with our goals here forward."

The others laughed and put their hands on top of hers.

They broke, and Chrissy raised her glass to make a toast. "To old friends, and new goals. To never losing each other again. And to Rachel, who will always be with us in spirit. Thank you, Rachel, for bringing us back to each other."

"To Rachel," they said in unison, and clinked their glasses.

14

Greece
Friday, May 10th - London

Liz sat on the marble countertop, drinking her pinot noir and watching Xander cooking their dinner. It was a long time since they'd eaten together, and he had been surprisingly enthusiastic when she'd suggested it.

"Shall I make my famous steak with creamed spinach and garlic fries?" he'd asked, and she'd agreed with a flutter in her stomach, as this was the dish he used to cook when they were first dating.

She watched him as he studied the sizzling steak. He waited until just the right moment before flipping it over onto the other side. He knew the perfect moment to take it off the heat and let it rest, in order to produce the most juicy sirloin. It would melt in her mouth and transport her to carnivore heaven, and her mouth watered in anticipation.

As he cooked, he moved about the kitchen, smiling and chatting in a happy, carefree manner about the lads from his running group and various people at work.

Liz nodded and listened, and thought to herself how

utterly gorgeous he was.

He was wearing his casual lounging clothes; a pair of light blue board shorts and a plain white t-shirt. His calves were tan and muscular, toned from running, his shoulders broad and powerful, an echo of his previous life as a competitive swimmer in school. The hair on his forearms was blonde, bleached by the sun.

She once joked with him that he was the least hairy Greek she had ever encountered, and he'd responded with a laugh, saying it was because he was 'the runt of the litter'.

She thought of his firm torso under that shirt, his perfect abs, his strength and gentleness when they made love, and a warm tingle ran through her body.

Xander was more relaxed than she'd seen him in a long time. He loved to cook, although he rarely did anymore. He came alive in the kitchen, and he smiled at her, his eyes twinkling as he reached into the oven to shake the tray of fries.

Coming from a large Greek family, Xander had grown up in the family kitchen, surrounded by a constant cacophony of noise and smells and family drama. He claimed he hated the intensity of the Greek culture, but he'd never lost his love of food, and he was in his element in the kitchen, cooking for himself and others.

Liz wondered why they didn't have friends over more often. The apartment was big enough to entertain, and Xander's cooking was sublime. Maybe she could suggest that they host a get-together sometime soon? Although, who would they invite? They didn't have any shared friends.

"It smells amazing," Liz said, jumping down from the countertop to fetch the bottle of wine. "You want another glass?"

"Definitely. Thanks, babe," replied Xander, grinning at her and winking as he stirred the creamed spinach.

"So, I was thinking we should take some time off work and go away somewhere? In June, maybe?" Liz broached as she leaned against the doorframe. "I sent you an email yesterday about it, but I'm assuming you haven't seen it yet."

"Ah, yeah. I'm not sure that June will work for me, sorry. If I'm going to make partner this year, I kinda need to be around over the summer."

"What the hell, Xander? They can't have a problem with you taking a week off. You're a human, not a machine, and we haven't been on holiday for over three years."

Cursing herself, Liz took a deep breath and tried again in a warmer, more relaxed tone.

"All I'm saying is that it would be nice for us to have some time for ourselves and decompress. I was looking at all-inclusive breaks in the Maldives. The islands are gorgeous, and the water is crystal clear. They said on the website that the scuba diving is some of the best in the world. You said you wanted to go diving again, didn't you? Maybe you could teach me?"

"Yeah, that sounds great, but I don't know that I can take the time off. Giles is breathing down my neck about these new portfolios, and the next three to six months are critical for the fund."

Liz shifted her footing and cleared her throat, trying not to let her exasperation show.

She hadn't told Xander about the pact she'd made with the girls, afraid that he might find it all too contrived. She had tried a couple of different tacks over the last couple of weeks to bring them closer together, but Xander had seemed distracted and remote since she got back from the Memorial.

She tried again; "OK then, how about just a long weekend away? We could visit your family on Spetses? I'd love to get to know them better, and your auntie said we are always welcome. How would we do that, though? Do you fly to

Athens and then get an island hopper to Spetses? Or would we need to get a ferry?"

"I'm not going to Spetses," Xander said in a flat tone. "Everyone would make a massive deal of it, and I can't handle my family right now."

Liz felt a stab of anger and a twinge of insecurity.

She'd met Xander's family only three times in the eight years they had been together.

They had been wonderful. Exhausting, incredibly loud and intrusive, and completely insane, but wonderful all the same.

Liz loved the openness and warmth she felt when enveloped by Xander's huge Greek family, and she had hoped they could all spend more time together, but Xander was always against it.

Liz tried not to take it personally, and Xander insisted it had nothing to do with her. He said it was because they would try to pressure him into joining the family shipping business, and he had no intention of doing so. His older brother ran operations out of New York, and Xander had always been pegged as the heir apparent here in London, but he'd railed against their expectations and gone into the world of finance instead. Xander said that his family made him feel claustrophobic, and that he needed space away from them.

"Fine. Let's just go to Paris for a weekend. Or Brussels, maybe?" Liz reached into her back pocket for her phone and cursed, remembering that it was charging on her nightstand in the bedroom. "Give me your phone and I'll look up how much Eurostar tickets would be from London to Paris."

For a brief second, Xander looked guarded. It was almost imperceptible, but after a career in headhunting Liz read body language better than most, and she had seen it.

"Um, I'll look it up in a minute. The steaks are ready and I'm about to plate up."

Liz frowned.

"Just give me your phone and I'll check while you plate up. It's in your pocket, right?"

"Jesus Christ, Liz. Just give me a second and let me do this, OK?" Xander's voice was sharp, and Liz was suddenly on edge. "I'm sorry to snap," Xander said a moment later. "I just don't want to talk about vacations right now. Let's enjoy dinner together, it's so nice to spend time with you, I don't want to spend it talking about something else."

The tension subsided as they sat at the kitchen table and ate the delicious meal.

They talked and laughed. Liz poured more wine and told Xander about an awful client she had been managing, while Xander chuckled at her vitriolic description of the poor guy.

With dinner consumed and another bottle of wine opened, the two of them sat on the sofa and watched TV. Xander put his arm around Liz and said how lovely it was to spend time just doing nothing together, and Liz, sated and content, snuggled into the crook of his arm and breathed in his delicious smell.

She slipped her hand under Xander's T-shirt and stroked his chest. She reached lower, but Xander caught her hand and held it.

"I'm exhausted, babe. I'm sorry, I might just need to sleep, if that's OK? In fact, I'm going to head to bed."

Taken aback, she said, 'of course it was OK,' but Xander had never rejected her advances before. She'd noticed over the last couple of months he hadn't wanted sex as often, but she'd put it down to exhaustion.

This was different, though. She felt awkward and a little embarrassed. Was she getting old? Was she not as attractive as when they had met?

She sat in front of the TV for a while, half-heartedly flicking through various shows.

When at last she crept into the bedroom, she could hear

Xander's slow, deep breathing, a sure sign he was asleep.

Liz slipped into bed and lay in the darkness, staring at the ceiling, trying to brush aside the feeling of foreboding that was building in her.

After about an hour, she turned and looked at Xander, his beautiful dark hair framing his face. She pulled back the covers and slipped out of bed.

Tiptoeing around to his side of the bed, she picked up his phone.

Padding to the bathroom, she shut the door and switched on the light.

She sat on the toilet seat, holding Xander's phone and wondering what the hell she was doing.

"Do I honestly believe that there's something going on? Could he be hiding something from me? And wouldn't I know if he was?" She questioned. *"How ridiculous. I would be livid if Xander ever looked through my phone while I was asleep."*

Despite her protestations, she keyed in his security code and scrolled through the apps.

"I hope its porn." She thought to herself. *"That I could handle. In fact, I'd be totally fine with that. God, I really hope its porn."*

She clicked on the 'messages' icon and scrolled through the names.

There was her name, Xander's running team, a buddy from work, and an old jock friend from his school whom Liz loathed. Not much of interest there.

She clicked the 'mail' icon, and scrolled through reams of subscription emails for sports equipment and upscale restaurant's, most of which remained unread.

"Good to know that Xander gets as much shit delivered to his In Box as I do," she thought with a smile.

She clicked on the green messaging app that Xander used to group message his drinking and running buddies. She had no desire to read through their incessant neanderthal banter about sports and women, so she scrolled down through the names, but stopped when she saw a name she didn't recognize.

Laura Patterson

Who was that?

Xander had typed the first line of the last message, and it was visible on the front screen. As she read it, Liz's stomach lurched and dropped. She opened the full message and read the contents.

"I'm not interested in your attempted blackmail, and you are despicable for messaging me something like this. I never want to hear from you again, and if you try to contact me, I will use the full force of my legal team to annihilate you. You have picked the wrong person to fuck with, and you will regret it if you continue with this pitiful scheme. DO NOT CONTACT ME AGAIN."

Stunned, Liz scrolled down to the sender's message.

"Xander, I need to speak to you. If you won't take my calls or respond to my messages, I guess I'm going to have to do this here. I'm sorry, but when I said I was going to have an abortion, I lied. I had the baby. I don't expect you to have any contact or play any role in her life, but I do expect you to pay child support. I haven't asked you for anything until now because I've been managing on my own, but my circumstances have changed, and now I need the financial contributions you are legally obliged to provide for your child. Again, I'm sorry to land this on you right here, but you have left me no choice. If you don't respond to this message, then I will have to get my attorney involved. Please respond ASAP."

* * *

Liz sat and stared ahead for a long time, trying to process what she had read.

After a couple of minutes, she looked at the phone again. The date of the sender's message was April 18th. Xander had responded at 5.30pm on April 19th. This had happened three weeks ago, and he had said nothing to her. Nothing about receiving a message from a woman claiming to be the mother of his child.

After a long time, Liz stood up. She walked back to the bedroom and placed Xander's phone back on his nightstand. She walked to the linen closet, took out a woolen blanket, and carried it to the living room.

She couldn't lie next to Xander right now. She couldn't be near him.

Lying still under the blanket, she stared at the ceiling and listened to the clock ticking on the wall.

Tick, tick, like the gentle but insistent march of time, pulling her life in a direction that she did not understand, and was not willing to accept.

15

Lauren
Saturday, May 11th - London

At 5.30am, Liz pulled on her workout clothes and running shoes and slipped out of the front door of the apartment.

She hadn't slept, and she was ready to sweat away the haunting feelings that permeated her body.

She stepped into the chilly morning air and began to run.

The sun was rising above London, brushing the tops of the buildings with a delicate pink light, bringing color to an otherwise grey skyline. The streets were slick from last night's rain, and the air had a fresh earthy smell, so different to the usual car fumes that enveloped the city.

Liz could see her breath, and she sucked in the bitingly cold air. Her lungs struggled, fighting for oxygen, until she hit her stride and relaxed into a steady pace.

As the city stirred, waking from last night's slumber, she ran past the Northbank Restaurant and on to St Paul's Walk.

In front of her the Thames snaked through the half-light, ancient and imposing as always, the primary artery of this incredible, ancient metropolis. She stopped to appreciate its quiet, rushing, sinuous beauty.

The early morning light glinted off the water, creating shimmering ripples of gold. Although the surface looked calm and inviting, Liz knew there were strong currents and undertows running beneath it, ready to drag any swimmer down into its freezing depths.

There was very little river traffic at this hour; the glass sided leisure boats bulging with tourists wouldn't set out for another couple of hours, and the commuter ferry that chugged across the river during the week was nowhere to be seen. Liz spotted a squat tug boat making its way up the river, no doubt transporting lumber or materials for one of the many commercial building projects underway in the ever-changing city.

She ran down St Paul's Walk with the river on her left. Reaching the steps that led up to the Millennium Bridge, she pumped her legs, hitting each step like a drum.

She headed across the bridge, over the river and towards the Tate Modern on the South Bank. On the other side she turned towards the ferry pier, pushing herself into a full sprint until she stopped, panting, at the entrance to the Globe Theatre.

Breathing hard, her entire body tingling with the exertion, she waited for her heart to slow to a steadier pace. A sense of peace fell over her, and her sanity returned.

She stretched her arms above her head, inhaling deeply and steeling herself, finding the strength to turn towards home and face whatever would come next.

Reaching the steps to the bridge, she bounded up them with renewed vigor. She turned, preparing to run back towards the city, but she stopped in awe, stunned by the panorama in front of her.

The dome of St Paul's Cathedral glowed with an iridescent light. A delicate, opalescent beauty that took her breath away.

Ribbons of pink and purple lit the sky, pushing back the rich blue of the fading darkness. The dawn was bringing the sky to life before her eyes, growing to a crescendo of color that took her breath away.

She turned, looking around her, wanting to share this moment with someone, wanting to see the wonder in their eyes and to feel the precious connection of shared exhilaration.

But there was nobody there.

There was never anybody there.

*****

She unlocked the front door, not sure if Xander would be awake yet, but as the door swung open, she heard his voice coming from the kitchen.

"Is that you, Liz? Where the hell have you been?"

She took a deep breath, walked into the kitchen, and headed straight to the fridge.

Reaching in, she grabbed the orange juice and took a large swig straight from the bottle.

Then she turned to look at Xander, who was staring at her, frowning.

There was a long silence. Liz took another long swig, returned the bottle to the fridge and turned to face Xander again, her eyes squarely on him.

"Who's Lauren?" Liz asked in a calm, controlled tone.

The color drained from Xander's face as he leaned back against the countertop.

"What do you mean?"

"I asked you a simple question, didn't I? Who. Is. Lauren?"

There was a long pause while myriad of expressions passed over Xander's face. Horror, anger, discomfort. He looked like a cornered animal. Liz had never seen him like this. She'd only ever known him to be suave and confident. Or passionate. Or caustic. But never panicked. Never hunted.

She waited, staring at him with her jaw set, the distance growing between them.

Xander's face crumpled, and he sat down heavily on one of the kitchen chairs.

"Oh God, Liz. It's awful. I'm so sorry I didn't tell you, it's been a nightmare, I can't even believe it myself."

"Go on." said Liz in an icy tone.

"Lauren was an intern I worked with ages ago, well, four years ago, to be precise. I didn't even know her, we'd never spoken, then one night at a work event I was drinking too much, and she was all over me. I should have said no, but the guys were goading me on. Anyway, I ended up sleeping with her. Oh God, Liz, I'm so sorry, I don't know why I did it, and it only happened once. I swear I'd never cheated on you before, and I never will again. I'm so ashamed of myself. I tried to tell you, but I just couldn't bear it. Anyway she quit, and just before she left she told me she was pregnant. I'd heard that she was sleeping around with all the guys at work, and that night we'd used protection, so I told her there was no way it could be mine. She kept insisting I was the father, so I told her I'd pay for her to get an abortion if she'd just leave me alone. I never believed it was mine, but I suppose I felt sorry for her, plus it seemed like the best way to get her off my back. I don't know why she picked me. Maybe she thought I'd be a soft touch or something? Anyway, she told me she'd sort it out herself, and I never heard from her again."

Xander's eyes dropped. He looked beaten. Mortified.

Liz watched him, waiting for the rest of the story.

"And then?" she said with venom.

Xander sighed, shifted in his chair, and continued.

"OK. So then out of the blue I get this message on my

voicemail at work. I mean, I haven't spoken to this girl in years, and now she's saying that she has to speak to me about something. Well, I knew she was trouble, and obviously I wanted nothing to do with her, so I ignored it, hoping she'd go away. Then she sends me a WhatsApp message with some bullshit about her having had the baby and wanting me to pay child support. She's fucking dreaming if she thinks she's going to hook me into paying for some bastard child that could be the offspring of at least a dozen guys in my office alone! There's no way, and I've told her that if she contacts me again, I'm going to get my attorney involved and she'll wish she never met me. I'm not taking this bullshit from a little cockney slut like her."

"Wow. So I'm adding 'arrogant snob' to my list of reasons why I hate you, right?" Liz thought to herself as her jaw set.

Xander sat slumped over the kitchen table, his forehead resting in his hand, looking up at Liz with a desperate, pleading expression.

"Please, baby, you *know* me. Yes, I can be an arrogant shit at times, but I love you, and I would *never* do anything to hurt you. I made one stupid mistake and I will regret it for the rest of my life, but I don't deserve this. I refuse to let this conniving piece of trash threaten everything that matters to me. But most importantly, I refuse to let her destroy the most precious thing I have - my relationship with you. You have to believe me baby, please don't let her win."

Liz stared at Xander for the longest time.

"How did she know your mobile phone number?"

Xander sighed and shook his head. "After, well, *that night*, she texted me a couple of times asking if she could see me again. I said no. I should have shut her down hard, but I was trying to be polite. I apologized and said I was in a serious relationship with someone else. I told her that what had happened between us would never happen again, and I asked her not to contact me in the future. I don't know how she got my number. I'm assuming one of the girls in the office gave it to her, or maybe one of the guys did it as a joke. She texted me a couple more times, but I ignored it and she stopped. I assumed she'd moved on to some other poor guy in the office. Seriously, Liz, she was a menace. In fact, I think they fired her in the end because the rumors got so bad. It's kinda sad. For someone so young, she was a mess."

Liz stared at the kitchen floor.

She felt old, as if she had aged a thousand years. She was exhausted, and at that moment she wished she could sink into the floor and be done with all of it.

She felt the rise and fall of her chest, a tightening and then a sob. And then another.

Her body shook despite her determination to hold it together. She couldn't stop it though, she couldn't contain the grief.

"Oh, baby. Oh God, I'm so sorry," said Xander, jumping to his feet and wrapping his arms around her.

She wanted to push him off, to hit him, to fight him, but she didn't have the will or the energy.

He held her as they both sobbed, their bodies shaking with grief.

Xander whispered apologies and promises as Liz drifted further and further away. She felt the chasm growing between them. Yes, they were holding each other, crying together, but she knew in her heart they were crying for different reasons.

She cried for something lost.

She mourned for the promise of something that would never be.

This was not shock, the shock had come and gone.

This was the pain of a truth she had always known, but had chosen to ignore.

16

Opportunity
Tuesday, May 14th - London

Liz heard the buzz of her cell phone and glanced down to see a text light up the screen.

> *Hi Liz, it's Emily. I hope you're well?*
> *I'm sorry to text you out of the blue like this,*
> *but I was wondering if we could talk?*

She was at her desk on a call with a client, and after a flash of irritation she picked up her phone and responded.

> *Sure. Call you in a bit.*

She finished up her call, grabbed her cell and her purse, and left the office for the relative calm of the London city streets.

She stood hunched over; her back to the wind, sheltering her cigarette and trying to catch the flickering flame of her lighter. Finally, the cigarette tip glowed red, and she stood upright, taking a big draw and sighing out the smoke into the wet London air.

It had been raining all night and although the rain had stopped; the air was still moist and the streets slick. The iconic red London buses swished through the puddles that lined the sidewalk edges as the occasional bedraggled tourist leaped out of the way of the spray.

She hesitated before making the call.

Rereading the text, she tutted to herself. She recognized that tone; it was the tone of someone who wanted something. Liz disliked being wanted. She found it intrusive, clawing, almost claustrophobic. Yes, they were friends, and it had been nice to see her again after all that time, but that didn't mean that she wanted to become embroiled in Emily's everyday dramas. Liz had too much to do and disliked the inanity of most people's comings and goings.

She heard her mother's voice saying,

"Now Liz, it is impolite not to respond to a friend. Think of your breeding and try to be gracious."

Liz's jaw tightened, and the swear words bubbled up like lava. She had to stop herself from swearing out loud, lest she look like some crazy old woman losing her mind on the side of the street.

She took another drag and dropped her shoulders.

No, this was her friend, and she would call her back. Not because it was the 'polite' thing to do, but because she wanted to. And it would be nice to hear a friendly voice right now, although she couldn't quite admit that even to herself.

"Hi Em, it's Liz. How's it going?"

"Oh my gosh, thank you so much for calling me. I'm so sorry to bother you at work, but I need your advice if that's OK? Am I disturbing you?"

"Yes," Liz thought, but she said, "No, not at all. What's up?"

"Well, we had some bad news yesterday," said Emily, her

voice fractured.

Liz's heart jumped with alarm. Was Emily sick? A cold dread ran through her, taking her quite by surprise. Maybe she cared more than she realized.

Emily continued in a hesitant voice, "Um, Ed found out yesterday that his company has been bought by a much larger competitor and, well, they told him they are letting him go."

"Oh. That sucks," Liz responded, not knowing what to say next.

"Yeah. Apparently his job crosses over with 'existing positions' and they are 'streamlining to remove duplication.' They said that he's an outstanding worker, so they're offering him redundancy pay and a good reference, but he's too senior to be considered for any of the open positions. They told him it's a 'great opportunity to explore other avenues', but I have to admit that right now it doesn't feel like a great opportunity." Emily's voice was small and muted.

There was a pause while Liz considered this news.

"Well, anyway," Emily continued, sounding flustered. "I promised Ed that I would call you and ask for your advice about how he should go about finding a new job. He's worked for the same company since he graduated, so both of us are a little out of our depth here. Can you offer any recommendations?"

Liz pulled a face. "Um, well, I'm happy to talk to him about how to find a good agency to work with, and how to network with potential employers. But I specialize in the banking sector, so unfortunately my clients wouldn't be interested in his experience. Didn't you say he worked in manufacturing or something?"

"Printing. Yes, I totally understand, and I don't want to be a bother." Emily sounded drained.

"No, honestly, I'm happy to help in any way I can. Maybe I

could come over for coffee sometime and we can talk about it?"

Liz stopped herself, shocked by such an uncharacteristic offer. What was she doing? She never volunteered her time to anyone!

"Oh wow, Liz! That would be amazing! Thank you so much. I know it's a pain and that you work so hard already, the last thing you want to do with your personal time is talk more about networking and interviews. I appreciate it though. I really do,"

Emily's voice caught in her throat, and Liz felt a twinge of pain for her. This must have come as a terrible shock to them. Such a stable, sensible family with a stable, sensible world, suddenly thrown upside down.

Hmm, she could relate to that at some level.

"It's my pleasure." Liz said, sounding positive. "I can tell by the way you talk about him that he's a really amazing guy, so they're idiots if they're willing to let such a good man go. We'll get him a better job, with *twice* the pay, and that'll show them," she said with a grin.

"You're amazing," Emily said, laughing in response. "What would I do without you. I've missed you so much!"

"So," Liz said as she ground out the stub of her cigarette beneath the ball of her stiletto. She wasn't quite ready to let Emily go yet. Talking with her made her feel warm and content.

"Would you consider getting a job yourself to tide you over if it was needed?"

"Well," Emily said with a hint of excitement in her voice, "Funny you should say that. I had an interesting conversation last week with a lady called Kolleen. From Los Angeles."

"Oh, yes?" Liz's eyebrows shot up. Now her curiosity was well and truly piqued.

"Yes, um, hang on, let me back up a bit. Remember when

we met up for the Memorial and Chrissy and I were talking about the soaps and moisturizers I make?"

"Mmm-hm" said Liz, who had no memory of this conversation.

"Chrissy took a couple of samples home with her and she shared them with this friend of hers called Kolleen. Kolleen has her own business making natural beauty products, and Chrissy said she loved my moisturizers so much she wants to sell them on her website! Chrissy asked me if I would be interested in speaking with her about shipping some of my product over to California and she'll be a distributor for me. Crazy, eh?"

"Seriously? Well bloody hell, Emily, that's amazing!" Liz exclaimed, pumped and elated by her friend's success.

"I suppose, yeah. I was a bit blown away at first, and a little uncomfortable about the whole thing. But Ed said I should at least speak with her, so we did a conference call last Monday. It really went well. We spoke for almost two hours. We started by talking about how I source my local organic ingredients, and then she asked me how I would expand the business to more of a going concern. I shared some of my ideas on strategic sourcing, cost control and quality assurance. I was surprised how easily the answers came to me. I had put together something of a business plan a year or so ago, and I've obviously been thinking about it more than I realized."

"That sounds fantastic. So, what are the next steps?" said Liz, still beaming with pride.

"I said I would do some videos of how I made the product, and shots of me walking around my herb garden. But now it's all a bit of a moot point because of Ed's news." Emily sounded deflated.

"Why should that matter? You should still do it. It could be an amazing opportunity," Liz said, frustrated on behalf of her old friend.

"Hmm. My mum says that I should put it aside for now and focus on supporting Ed in finding a new job. Plus, she says I have my hands full already looking after the kids and the house."

Liz's eyes narrowed. "Tell your Mum to go fuck herself."

Emily exploded with laughter.

"Um, no Liz. That's more your style than mine! I might come back to the whole idea some time in the future, but for now I'm going to need to shelve it. Anyway, what's new with you?"

Liz hesitated and sighed. She'd been walking down the road as they talked, trying to keep herself warm against the chill wind. She hadn't expected to be talking for this long, so she hadn't brought her heavy coat with her. She pulled her suit jacket tight around her, but it offered little protection against the damp air.

Now she found herself alongside the railings of the old church. She looked up at the ornate spires, standing silently against the skidding grey clouds.

"Actually, something happened to me too, as we're sharing shitty news," she said, incredulous that she was about to share this news with anyone. "I'm considering leaving Xander."

"What?" Emily sounded stunned. "Why? What happened?"

"I found something out, and I'm not sure what to do about it. I found a message on his mobile phone from a girl he used to work with. She had a baby, and she's saying that he is the father. He denies everything of course, but, I don't know, I just don't trust him."

Silence.

"Oh my God, Liz, I'm so sorry," Emily stuttered. "I can't even imagine how you are feeling right now."

"Emily, you studied law. Can she make him take a DNA test or something? How would she prove that he's the father? He's threatened her with legal action if she even contacts him again, but can she get a court order to force him to do a paternity test?"

"Oh Liz, I'm so sorry, I never studied family law so I'm the wrong person to ask. But it seems a little strange that he's refusing to do a paternity test if he's so sure he's not the father, no?"

Liz drew a manicured finger down the length of an iron railing.

"I'm considering contacting her," she said to Emily.

"Who?"

"The girl from the message. The girl with the baby."

"Why would you do that?" said Emily with horror.

"I just want to know for sure. I want the truth, and I want to hear it from her."

Emily blew out and tutted with concern. "Well, be careful Liz, you might be getting yourself into dangerous waters with that one. I know we haven't been close friends for a long time, and even when we were I would never have told you how to live your life, but this might not be a path you want to walk down."

"I don't think I have a choice," replied Liz, as her hand closed around the ice cold metal of the railing.

17

Xanax
Thursday, May 16th - Pasadena

"Thanks so much Gabriella, today was super fun, as always." Chrissy smiled at her barre instructor as she threw her hair forward to re-tie the messy bun on top of her head.

She exchanged pleasantries with her fellow classmates as they re-stacked their hand weights and wiped their mats down with the complimentary, lemon scented antibacterial wipes. Then she grabbed her water bottle and her wrap and headed out to the changing room.

Vanessa was opening her locker as Chrissy approached, and they made eye contact.

"That was a hard one today, no?" Chrissy said in a bright, enthusiastic tone.

"Mm-hmm" replied Vanessa.

"I love your top by the way, is it Lululemon?"

"Yes," replied Vanessa, pursing her lips.

Chrissy smiled and shifted her weight.

"Oh, and congratulations again on the Ball. It was incredible! Of course we all knew it would be. And we raised so much money! You must be so pleased. Do you think you'll chair again next year? Or is it too early to make a commitment? It's a tremendous amount of work, I know."

Vanessa zipped up her bag and flashed Chrissy a polite yet icy smile, saying, "I'm so sorry, I'd love to stay and chat, but I'm late for a meeting."

Chrissy watched as Vanessa turned and smiled pleasantly at the receptionist before heading out the glass front doors.

She turned back to her locker, her color rising. *"What the hell, Chrissy?"* She berated herself. *"What is your problem? Just leave it alone!"*

Still smarting and humiliated, she reached in to her purse to grab her cell phone.

She glanced at the screen and stopped short, feeling the blood run out of her.

8 missed calls. 3 from the school and 5 from Scott.

What could possibly have happened in the hour she had been in her barre class that would require that number of calls?

She felt her legs go weak beneath her, and she sat down heavily onto the bench.

There were voicemails. One from school and one from Scott.

Her mind raced. Had there been an accident? Had one of the kids been seriously hurt? She felt tears of guilt welling up already. What kind of mother was she if one of her children had been hurt and scared and she hadn't been there for them? What if they had been crying and calling for her as she stood at that barre toning her calf muscles, oblivious to their suffering?

She tried to control her breathing as she listened to the voicemail from the school.

It was the Principal speaking in a hard, cold tone, asking her to, 'Contact him as soon as possible. There was a situation they needed to discuss urgently.'

Chrissy was confused.

This wasn't the panicked voice of someone dealing with an accident involving one of their pupils.

What could have happened that would require such an immediate response if not an accident?

Chrissy hit the link to the voicemail from Scott. What she heard floored her like a locomotive.

Scott's voice came, shaky and hesitant, almost unrecognizable.

"Hi Chrissy. It's Scott. You need to call me. Call me as soon as you get this, OK? There's a problem. We have a problem. Josh has been arrested at school. The school just called me. They couldn't reach you, so they called me. I was in surgery and I only just got their message, so I called them back. They told me the police came to the school and arrested him. They took him to the station. He's at the police station right now. They told me he was caught selling drugs. I'm in the car on the way to the station. I had an elective scheduled for this afternoon, but they cancelled it for me. Can you call me? Where are you, anyway? Call me as soon as you get this, OK? I suppose we should meet at the station then, yes? It's the one just down the road from the school. You know where I mean, right? So meet me there and we can work out what's going on, OK? Oh Christ, how could this have happened? Chrissy, I...."

There was a pause, and Chrissy could hear Scott's voice almost break.

"I love you, baby." He said in a faltering tone. "We'll sort this out, I promise. I'll see you there, OK?"

Chrissy was cold. Numb and shivering.

She stared into space. Lost in time. Outside reality.

"I need to stand up now," she told herself. *"I need to put my shoes on and go to the car. I need to drive to the police station."*

Shaking, she inhaled a slow breath, trying to steady both her nerves and her mind.

"First things first," she told herself. *"Put on your sneakers and put your barre socks away so you can find them next time."*

She checked the time. It was 9.42am.

"The traffic won't be bad. I can make it there in 20 minutes or so," she thought to herself.

She moved as if in a dream.

She walked through the changing room and said goodbye to the receptionist before heading out into the parking lot.

She unlocked her car and stepped in, placing her workout bag on the passenger seat next to her. She put the car into reverse and checked her reversing camera to make sure there were no obstacles in her way, before pulling out of the parking space.

In silence, she drove along the quiet streets to the police station.

She had driven this route so many times for school pick ups and drop offs, the little town so familiar with its quaint restaurants and steepled churches.

A man was walking his dog on the opposite side of the road, and as she past he stopped to chat with an acquaintance who bent to say good morning to the little furry companion.

When she arrived at the station, she wasn't sure where to park. She'd only been here once or twice before, when the children were younger and they'd dropped off Holiday cookies to the brave and noble first responders. On those occasions they had parked next to the kids' play park and walked up. And afterwards the children had played on the swings.

But where should you park when your son is being held as a criminal?

Is there a specific parking space for that?

How long would she be, she wondered? Should she park

in the '20 minutes or less' space, or would it take longer than that?

She parked on a side street and walked up.

As she pushed open the door, the air conditioning blew over her, offering a pleasant respite from the growing heat outside. Chrissy realized she was still hot and sweaty from her workout. She must look awful, but she couldn't care less.

Scott was sitting on a flimsy blue plastic chair in the waiting room. He looked ashen. Chrissy had only ever seen him look this way once before, when his father had been rushed to hospital with a heart attack. Yes, Scott was a surgeon, and he was calm under pressure, but that had rattled him to his core, as had this it appeared.

"What's going on?" whispered Chrissy, sitting next to him. "Where's Josh?"

"They have him in a holding cell. The officer has gone to get him. The traffic on the freeway was awful so I only just got here myself. Where were you?" He looked at her with frightened, questioning eyes.

"I'm so sorry, I was at my barre class. I go every Thursday morning at 8.30am. Tell me what's going on. What happened?"

Scott sighed raggedly, rubbing his forehead.

"I'm still trying to figure it all out myself. The Sergeant told me that some kid collapsed in the boys' locker room, and they had to call an ambulance. The hospital confirmed that he was having a bad reaction to some drugs he'd taken, and someone told the teacher that he'd gotten them from Josh."

Chrissy was both incredulous and defensive.

"That's ridiculous. It can't be our Josh. The kid must have it wrong."

"That's what I thought. But the Principal called the police, and when they searched Josh's locker they found Xanax. He had a plastic bag of pills stashed in the back of his locker, and a couple of kids came forward to say that he'd been selling them for a couple of weeks now."

Chrissy stared at Scott. She couldn't believe what she was hearing.

"Are they sure it's him? It *can't* be him. Why would he do that? It's insane to even *think* he would do something like that. He's on the track team, he's an athlete for God's sake," she said, her heart pounding.

"Apparently he admitted it," Scott said, stupefied. "He said he'd bought a bag of them from a guy he met at a party a couple of months back. At first he was just selling them to the other guys on the track team, but then word got around and he sold to another couple of kids, including the boy that got sick. Oh, and the kid that collapsed is OK, by the way. So that's good, I suppose."

Scott looked at his shoes.

"My son is a drug dealer," Chrissy thought to herself. *"My son, the star of the track and field team, the head of the debate team and the light of my life, is a goddam drug dealer."* She felt hollow.

They both glanced up as Josh came down the corridor, flanked by two officers.

Although her boy was almost six feet tall, he looked small between them. Shrunken. His head was low and his shoulders slumped forward. He looked up at his parents, and the guilt, and grief, and fear in his eyes stabbed at Chrissy's heart.

"I'm sorry. I'm so sorry," he said in a desperate, trembling voice.

The Sergeant cleared his throat and said, "Well, we don't need to hold him any longer, and as he's a minor we can release him into your custody, if's that's agreeable? You'll be hearing from the probation officer regarding next steps."

"Oh, OK, Sergeant. Thank you so much, and I'm so sorry

for all of this." Scott said and, faltering, he held out his hand to shake.

After a moment's pause the sergeant took Scott's hand in his own, shook it, and said, "He's not a bad kid, he just made some bad choices."

They nodded at each other, and Scott turned to put his arm around his son.

Scott and Chrissy walked out of the station with their son between them.

As they walked in silence, Chrissy remembered the times she and Scott had swung him between them, lifting his little legs high in front as he squealed with delight.

Their boy was all grown up now, and things were different.

"Can I ride in mom's car?" Josh asked in a small voice.

"Of course," replied Scott. "Jackie just texted me asking if I can come and pick her up from school, so we'll see you both at home, OK?" he said, looking at Chrissy with concern in his eyes.

They rode in silence all the way home. It wasn't an angry silence; it was a silence that offered them the space they needed to process what had happened.

When they got home, Josh asked if he could go to his room until lunch, and Chrissy nodded in agreement.

"Do you want a snack or anything?" she asked as he headed through the living room.

"No, thank you," he replied, and Chrissy's heart broke to hear the small, vulnerable voice of her baby coming from the body of the man he'd become.

Jackie was livid when she got home. She slammed her bag down in the hallway and screamed up the stairs.

"What the fuck were you thinking, you asshole? Congratulations - you've ruined my life as well as your own!"

"Jackie!" Shouted Chrissy from the kitchen. "Stop it!

Things are bad enough."

Scott shut the front door behind him and headed to the lounge.

"I need a drink," he said, pouring himself a large whiskey.

"Really?" Chrissy asked. "Isn't it a little early for hard liquor?"

"I'll make an exception," he said in a caustic tone. "You want one?"

"Actually, I think I will. Thanks."

Grimly they drank as Jackie slammed her bedroom door above them.

"What happens now?" Chrissy asked in a hushed tone.

"I did a bit of research and it looks like they'll charge him with delinquency. We'll need to get a lawyer, and he'll have to appear in juvenile drug court, but for a first offense and for such a small amount it looks like he'll just have to go through some drug counseling, and maybe do some community service."

"How can you be so calm and rational about this?"

Scott shrugged. "What else can I do?"

Chrissy put her glass down and went back into the kitchen. She looked out of the window, watching the sunlight pouring through the tree branches onto the grass below, leaving intricate dappled patterns.

She took out her phone and scrolled through her emails. There was a message from the school principal.

"Scott?" she said towards the living room door. "The Principal wants to meet with us and Josh tomorrow morning. Can you make it?"

Scott appeared in the doorway, his jaw set, a steely expression on his face.

"And so it begins," he said bitterly.

18

Best Wishes
Friday, May 17th - Pasadena

Chrissy sat in a comfortable chair in the reception area outside the Principal's office, flanked by the two men she loved most in the entire world.

She looked at Scott's profile as he stared ahead, his strong square jawline and thick, dark hair, and smiled to herself as she remembered the night she'd fallen in love with him.

She reached out and squeezed his hand, smiling encouragement. He responded with a flicker of a smile, but his eyes were guarded and serious. He had been quiet all night and all this morning, but Chrissy was feeling determined and positive about the situation.

Waking early, before the sun was up, she had brainstormed ideas to help turn this near-tragedy into an opportunity, not only for her son, but for the entire school.

She'd been excited to share her ideas with Scott. Maybe they could invite guest speakers to the school to talk about healthy ways to deal with stress? Or how to cope with peer pressure? Scott hugged her, and she'd seen the love in his eyes, but he had not shared her enthusiasm for seeing the opportunities this situation presented.

Now they waited to meet with the Principal, while the administrative assistant eyed them from behind her computer.

She sipped her coffee and typed; her manicured fingers pecking at the keyboard like irritated birds. She did not offer them any refreshments.

Chrissy remembered the first time they'd sat in these chairs waiting to see the Principal. They'd been there for Josh's entrance interview, nervous and excited, brimming with expectation and pride for their boy.

Josh sat like a little businessman in his suit and tie, hair combed and styled, with a serious expression on his face. He was still a boy though, and before long he was swinging his legs and pulling on his collar and tie, trying to loosen their restrictive grip on his neck. He'd looked like he was dressed for a wedding, and she'd been concerned about whether he could handle himself in such a high-pressure situation.

But as they entered the Principal's office he'd transformed into a suave, confident, smaller version of his father, holding out his hand to shake the Principal's, and introducing both himself and his parents.

He'd killed it in the interview, and they had all gone out for barbecue afterwards to celebrate. He seemed more confident after that, more sure of himself, as if something had shifted in him. Their little boy had begun his transition into adulthood, and Chrissy and Scott shone with pride.

Things were different now.

Chrissy leaned over to Josh and squeezed his hand, saying, "It's going to be OK baby, you'll see."

He looked at her with a haunted expression, his eyes searching her face, desperate for the reassurance he needed. Gradually he relaxed, and an uncertain smile flickered across his wan face.

Just then the door to the office opened, and Josh's smile vanished.

Chrissy looked up, and her heart froze.

There in the doorway was Vanessa, laughing with the Principal as she took her leave.

As she saw Chrissy, the warmth evaporated from her eyes, replaced with a look of contempt and derision.

She looked from Chrissy to the boys, and a cold, poisonous smirk appeared on her lips.

In silence, she turned and headed for the exit. Chrissy felt Scott tense in his seat, and for a moment she considered putting an arm across him. But he had the self-control not to react, even to that bitch Vanessa. They both knew why she had been here, and they hated her all the more for it.

The Principal called them in, and they filed into his office, taking their places in the soft leather chairs opposite his heavy wooden desk.

He cleared his throat and began.

"Thank you all for coming. We need to discuss the events of yesterday. Thankfully, the boy who was taken to hospital is recovering, and his parents don't intend to take legal action, so there will be no further ramifications in that regard."

"Oh, that's such good news." Chrissy broke in. "It must have been terrifying for all of them. Again, we are all so sorry for what happened, and we intend to do everything we can to make amends. Isn't that right Josh?"

Josh nodded, his eyes on the floor.

Chrissy opened her purse and took out her notebook. "In fact, I have some ideas that I want to share with you about ways in which we could..."

"Let me stop you there, Mrs Miller," said the Principal. "I'm afraid that the situation is far more serious than you seem to realize. We simply cannot risk the reputation of the entire school in the pursuit of rehabilitating one young man. Yes, Josh has been an exemplary student and an invaluable member of our community until now, but these charges are not something we can just overlook. Behavior like this strikes at the very bedrock of what this school stands for, and it cannot be tolerated."

"I understand that," Chrissy replied, "and it was foolish and reckless of him to do it. But doesn't this school also believe in forgiveness and understanding? Would it not forgive a member of its community for making a mistake, as long as they learned from it? Surely Josh has earned the right to correct this wrong and become a stronger person because of it?" Her voice trembled.

Scott sat forward in his chair.

"Principal Lewis. What are you proposing?"

The Principal took a deep breath and cleared his throat again.

"Mr and Mrs Miller. The administration and the parents both feel it would be best if Josh left the school. We thank you for your generous contributions over the years, and we wish Josh all the best for the future, but we cannot in all good conscience continue to have him as a student in our community. Jackie, of course, is still welcome to attend the school, if that is your wish."

There was a stunned silence.

"So, you're kicking me out?" said Josh in a timid, broken voice.

The Principal cleared his throat again.

Chrissy's mind raced. *The parents,* eh? She knew exactly who he meant by 'the parents'.

She could rip that vindictive bitch's throat clear out.

Scott took a deep breath and stood up.

"Well thank you, Principal Lewis. I expected nothing less from this fine establishment. Good luck with your fundraising next year, you will need it. You'll forgive me if I don't shake your hand."

He turned to Chrissy and Josh. "Let's go, folks."

They headed to the car in silence.

On the drive home, Chrissy was livid.

"That fucking bitch Vanessa was in there pouring poison into his ear. How *dare* she masquerade as *'the parents?'* She doesn't represent anyone or anything other than her own fucking elitist aspirations! I'm sorry for swearing, but it's justified under the circumstances."

There was a sob from the backseat. Chrissy turned to see Josh, his head in his hands.

"Oh, baby, it's OK. This isn't over. I'm going to fight this - just you watch me!"

"But mom," he sobbed. "They won't listen. And Jackie's going to go ape shit when she hears what happened." His shoulders trembled as he held his head low.

Chrissy wheeled back around, her heart pounding with rage.

"Those fuckers. They'll be sorry. The minute we get home, I'm calling Jessie and we're going to start a coup! They can't get away with this!"

Scott frowned, a weary expression in his eyes as he said,

"Just tread carefully, baby. If you draw a line in the sand and make people choose, you might be disappointed by the results."

"Oh, whatever Scott. You don't know the other moms, they will never put up with this."

Scott raised an eyebrow, but kept quiet.

Josh had been right about Jackie's reaction. She did indeed go ape shit.

"What the hell! Oh, my God! Now what?"

"Now Jackie, calm down," Chrissy had said, trying to pacify her enraged daughter. "This isn't a done deal yet. And anyway, you can still go to the school if that's what we decide we all want."

Jackie looked horrified.

"No fucking way! Why would I want to go to a school that treated my brother like this? Yes, he's a clueless idiot who messed up big time, but outside of this incident he's a genuinely good guy, and they should have his back. It makes me sick to think that they're kicking him to the curb to save their own precious reputation! I wouldn't go back to that school if you paid me."

Chrissy, Scott, and Josh all stared at Jackie, open-mouthed.

"What?" she said, shrugging. "He's my brother, and I love him." She waved away their looks of astonishment. "I still hate you, though," she snarled in a venomous tone towards Josh.

"Well, I'm not giving up that easily," declared Chrissy. "I'm going to text Jessie, and then we'll see what happens. The good guys will triumph!" she exclaimed, striding through the kitchen.

She sat in the living room and constructed a text;

"Hi there! I'm sure you heard what happened yesterday. It's been a nightmare. Anyway, we met with the Principal today and he suggested it was best if Josh left the school. I know, right? It's crazy! I'll tell you who's behind all of this, it's that bitch Vanessa. I saw her coming out of his office just before we went in. She's obviously bullying him into saying things he doesn't mean, so I'm thinking that you and I should have coffee tomorrow and make a plan. Maybe we can petition the rest of the school and make him take Josh back? What do you think? Can't wait to catch up tomorrow."

Chrissy waited over an hour for a response. She was beginning to worry when the phone finally chimed. With relief, she grabbed it and read the text from Jessie.

"Hi there. Yes, I heard what happened. I'm really glad Josh is OK. It must have been so scary for all of you. I didn't realize the Principal would come down on him so hard. Expulsion? Yikes, that's rough. I'd love to help, but Darnell thinks it would be best if we didn't get involved. Also, he said he'd prefer it if the kids spent some time apart, just until this whole thing blows over. Maybe we could get together over the summer? We're thinking of you, and we wish you all the best. I can't wait until we can put this all behind us."

Chrissy sat on her bed, rocking back and forth, cradling her phone, the tears rolling down her face.

She pictured Darnell and Scott grilling together last weekend, swigging beers while they laughed and talked about the game. She and Jessie had been chatting in the kitchen, holding glasses of wine while their kids shot hoops and played together in the pool.

She thought back to last summer, when Josh had admitted to having a secret crush on Jessie's daughter. The moms had squealed with joy when they found out, and had schemed about a future wedding, talking about what a happy ending it would be for everyone.

Scott was right. That line in the sand had told her more than she ever wanted to know, and now her heart was broken.

19

Coffee
Saturday, May 18th - London

The rain-washed streets looked grimy and unkempt as the Uber pulled up outside Costa Coffee on Station Parade.

Liz stepped out of the car, stretching her leg far out toward to curb. There was no way she would risk stepping into the dark, oil slicked rainwater that flowed down the gutter between the street and the sidewalk.

She paused, despite the rain and her lack of an umbrella, to consider whether this was the right course of action.

She'd never been to Barking before, and as she looked around her, she decided she hadn't missed much. Apart from a couple of weary looking people hunched over in rain jackets at the bus stop, the sidewalk appeared bleak and empty. The occasional car swooshed past her, while a red double-decker bus stopped on the other side of the road to offload a catch of damp travelers and scoop up a few new ones.

The coffee shop was squeezed in on both sides by a terrace of dreary little stores. On one side, a run down fried chicken takeout that looked like it would fail most health codes, on the other, a dusty liquor store.

Liz found her nose wrinkling in displeasure, and she checked herself, realizing how much like her mother she must look in this moment.

"The apple doesn't fall far from the tree," she could hear her mother sneering.

"Fuck off," she replied to the voice in her head.

As she pushed open the door of the coffee shop, a blast of hot air hit her in the face. Why did shops and restaurants in England insist on blowing stifling air straight at you as you entered their establishment? Liz had never understood this uniquely British welcome. It felt like being greeted by an overenthusiastic hairdryer, and it did nothing to enhance your sense of comfort. Thankfully, the heater positioned over the doorway proved only a momentary affair, and the rest of the establishment had a warm, cozy atmosphere.

Liz looked around, ruffled and nervous. For a moment, a surge of panic rose in her. Why the hell had she organized to meet this woman? A woman who claimed to be the mother of her boyfriend's child. Someone Xander described as a 'manipulative psycho.' Was she pouring gas on a fire here? Surely this was, at best, unwise, and at worst, fucking nuts!

Just as Liz considered leaving, a young woman sitting in the corner caught her eye. The woman raised her hand in a brief, uncomfortable wave of acknowledgement.

Liz walked over and, after flashing an awkward smile, said, "Hi. Are you Lauren?"

"Yeah," the woman responded.

Then, an awkward pause.

"Um. OK, I'm going to grab a coffee," said Liz. "You want anything?"

Lauren shook her head and looked down at her folded hands.

Liz walked over to the bored-looking barista and ordered a latte.

She returned with her drink and sat opposite her.

Lauren was not at all what she'd expected. But then, Liz didn't know what she'd expected. She looked no more than twenty-five years old with an oval face, full cheeks and wide set almond-shaped eyes. Her shoulder length brunette hair was pulled back into a ponytail, and she has a competent, sensible, no-nonsense manner about her. She wore no visible jewelry other than small stud earrings, and her tank top, rain jacket, jeans and boots were nondescript.

She did not seem at all like the shallow airhead Liz had imagined, or the calculating bitch Xander had made her out to be.

"Thanks for coming," Liz said, not knowing where to start.

"No problem," Lauren replied. "I have to admit I was surprised when you contacted me."

"I bet!" Liz said, grinning despite herself. "I'm still not sure why I did."

"Maybe because you want answers?" Lauren replied, looking up and holding Liz's gaze.

Liz paused.

"I read the messages between you and Xander, and I confronted him about it."

"And what did he have to say about it?" Lauren asked.

Another pause.

"Well, he told me you're a manipulative bitch who's after his money," Liz stated in a matter-of-fact tone.

"And yet, here you are," Lauren said, tilting her head to one side in an inquiring manner.

Liz was impressed. Lauren conveyed a quiet dignity far beyond her years, and Liz couldn't help but be intrigued by her.

"So, you want to give me your version of it?" Liz asked.

Lauren flashed her a look of defiance before saying,

"Bloody hell, you've got a cheek. You are aware that I owe you nothing, right? I don't have to justify myself to you, or anyone else."

Liz shifted in her seat. "I know, and I'm sorry. That came out all wrong. You're right, I do want the truth, and I don't believe I'm getting it from Xander. I should be furious right now. I should hate you for ruining my life, but when Xander told me what happened, I wasn't shocked. I realized that deep down I'd seen this coming all along. I don't hate you, and I'm not here to judge you, I swear. I just want to understand what happened."

Lauren sighed, and after a moment she began.

"Fine, here you go, then. I met Xander five years ago when I was working at Goldman Sachs. We worked in different departments, but he and his colleagues would always joke around and flirt with me, just harmless fun, nothing serious. But then Xander started asking for my number and suggesting that we grab a drink after work sometime. I told him no because I didn't want to jeopardize my internship. What a bloody cliche, eh? Screwing the intern. Anyway, he persisted for a while. He even got my mobile phone number from one of the other interns, and he started texting me. I ignored the texts and avoided him as much as I could, and then one day he walked past me in the corridor and ignored me. The texts stopped, and I assumed he'd lost interest. I kinda forgot about it, but then in December at the Christmas party everyone was drinking too much, and I ended up dancing with Xander. I don't know what I was thinking, but he seemed so charming and everything, and I was all dressed up and feeling special. He told me he had booked a room at the hotel for the night, and we ended up going upstairs together."

Lauren reddened a little as she looked at Liz.

An echo of anger and betrayal rumbled through Liz's heart, but it was overtaken by the need to hear Lauren's side of the story.

Lauren took a deep breath and continued.

"After that night, he acted like I didn't exist. He'd conquered me and moved on to the next girl. I was relieved because, although my ego was a little bruised, I didn't want to risk losing my internship over it. Plus, I knew he had a girlfriend, and they'd been together for like, *forever*."

Again Lauren looked chagrin, but Liz only shrugged in a 'water under the bridge' kind of way.

"So, all's well that ends well, right?" Lauren said, "except that come January I missed my period. I did a test and realized I was pregnant, bloody pregnant, at eighteen, with no money, no partner, nothing. What a nightmare, right? I cornered Xander at work and told him, and he went fucking crazy. He told me that if I tried to pin it on him, he'd destroy me and my career. He got aggressive, he scared me. He made me promise to have an abortion and said that he'd pay for everything if I kept my mouth shut. I was really messed up. I still didn't know what I wanted to do about the pregnancy, but he kept hounding me, so I agreed to do it so that he would stop pressuring me."

Lauren's face was drawn and pale, with deep lines furrowing her forehead. She looked haunted as she recounted her experience, and Liz's heart went out to her. This wasn't the carefully constructed story of a master criminal. Liz had been around bullshitters all her life, and she recognized honesty when she saw it.

She wasn't surprised, either. Deep down, she'd known all along that Xander was lying. She'd always known he was a narcissistic piece of shit, and she'd still built her castle on the sand of his lies. More fool her, eh? More fool her.

Lauren explained that she and her little girl Naomi lived

with Lauren's grandmother, but that things were tough financially, and she needed child support in order to make ends meet.

"I'm in nursing school now, you see?" Lauren explained. "I switched degrees after Naomi was born, my priorities shifted and I didn't want a high-powered job in the city anymore. I only have one year left until I'm qualified, and then I can work flexible shifts so I can look after Naomi, but right now I can't get a job and study full time, so money is tight. My nan looks after Naomi while I'm at school, but she's getting on a bit and she has bad arthritis so I can't ask her to watch a crazy four-year-old for more than five hours a day. Naomi is amazing, but she can also be exhausting to look after."

Liz looked into Lauren's worried face and saw the weight of responsibility, the deep love and a passionate need to protect her baby that outweighed anything else. This was motherhood, and Liz felt a flicker of longing, something she had never experienced before.

"Do you have a photo of her?" Liz asked, and then instantly regretted the imposition. "Oh God, I'm so sorry. I don't know why I even asked. That's too weird, isn't it? It's just that you light up when you talk about her."

Lauren smiled. "Yeah, it's totally weird. But for some reason I reckon you're alright. Hang on." She grinned and fished around in the beaten up purse hanging on the back of her chair. She pulled out an old mobile phone.

"Here," she said. "This is her."

Liz looked at the child in the photograph. Naomi had the same wide-set almond-shaped eyes as her mother, but her face was more heart-shaped, with a little chin and dimples in her cheeks. She seemed more dainty and feminine than her mother, and she had a cheeky twinkle in her huge brown eyes that reminded Liz of Xander. Her hair was brunette, but lighter than Lauren's, and it was pulled up in a high ponytail.

"Wow. She's beautiful. You must be so proud."

Lauren beamed, and Liz found it refreshing to be genuinely interested in somebody's offspring for a change.

Lauren's eyes darkened again, and she said, "Now what?"

For a moment Liz wasn't sure what she meant. Then she sighed and said, "Hmm. Don't worry about it. We're going to get this sorted out, OK?"

Lauren's face hardened. "You know this isn't your problem, right? I can manage this on my own, I don't need your charity."

"Oh, I have no doubt about that," replied Liz with a chuckle, "but I want to help, if you're open to it?"

The tension slipped from Lauren's face, and she looked relaxed again. "OK. Thanks, I guess. I gotta go now, but it was nice to meet you"

"It was lovely to meet you, too," said Liz, smiling back at Lauren.

In the Uber on her way home, Liz texted Xander.

> *I met up with Lauren.*
> *I'm moving out.*
> *I'll find an apartment in town somewhere.*
> *In the meantime I'm going to stay in a hotel.*
> *I'll be at the apartment tomorrow between 10am*
> *and 2pm to collect my things.*
> *Please don't be there.*
> *Don't call me.*
> *There is nothing to discuss.*

20

The Grapevine
Saturday, May 25th - California

"Guys, we should be in Patterson in about twenty minutes," Chrissy said, looking over her shoulder to catch Jackie's eye.

Jackie pulled an earbud from her ear. "What?"

"Not much longer until we're in Patterson."

"Oh, Ok. Cool," Jackie said, replacing her earbud and staring out of the window again.

Chrissy looked towards Josh, sitting in the passenger seat.

"You hungry?" she asked.

"Sorry, what?"

"Are you looking forward to lunch? I'm hungry already just thinking about it."

"Um, yeah. Sure," he said, closing his eyes again and leaning back against the headrest.

Chrissy raised her eyes to heaven.

"Wow, such stimulating company my kids provide on road trips these days," she thought to herself with a smirk.

The journey had indeed been quiet, but it had been a comfortable silence, and it gave Chrissy time to unwind and reflect upon the events of the last week. Was it really only a week since their world had fallen apart?

Chrissy thought back to the day of Josh's arrest, and then to the meeting at the school. Her heart ached and raged at the memory. She'd been distraught after her text exchange with Jessie, and although she'd reached out to several other school moms, she'd received the same cold, formal response from them as well. Apparently, no one wanted to be associated with a young drug dealer and his family.

Over the next couple of days Chrissy retreated into herself. Shock was replaced by a deep, pervasive shame, and it oozed into every corner of her being.

Things had come to a head yesterday in the grocery store when a sour faced lady snapped "excuse me" as she past her in the isle and Chrissy flinched, almost bursting into tears.

It was an over-reaction, but in that moment she'd felt a desperate, overwhelming urge to run. Run away from all of this and hide somewhere safe.

Last night, through tears, she'd suggested to Scott that she and the kids visit his parents for a couple of weeks. Then maybe he could come up and join them? He had some vacation time to use, so why not take advantage of the cooler climate of Northern California before the heat of the summer engulfed the LA area? They had always loved Scott's quaint little home town of Ferndale, and Chrissy yearned for the comforting arms of Scott's mom Bonnie to hold her tight.

Scott had agreed, and Chrissy packed her bags.

She and the kids started out early this morning as Chrissy planned to do the drive in just one day.

Normally when they drove up to visit Bonnie and Walter, or Nana and Papa as the kids called them, they would split the drive into a two-day affair. They would drive the six hours up the I-5 from Pasadena to San Francisco, and stay overnight in the city.

They would have dinner at their favorite seafood restaurant, then wander down to Fisherman's Wharf to watch the sunset before heading back to a cozy family-run hotel just off the bay.

The next day, refreshed and in the vacation mood, they would drive the final four hours over to Ferndale.

Occasionally, rather than taking the I-5, they would take the longer, more scenic route on the 101, cruising along the beautiful coastal roads through Santa Barbara and San Luis Obispo.

Each time they did this Chrissy would insist that they sing 'Do You Know the Way to San Jose' all the way from Salinas to San Jose itself. Although Scott and the kids would groan and feign protest, they always ended up joining in with her, and it became a fond tradition for them all.

Chrissy had wonderful memories of these road trips where the four of them would chat and laugh and sing together.

Not so on this journey, it seemed.

Josh sat in the passenger seat, silent and distant, looking out the window.

He'd been like this since the arrest. As if his former jubilant, confident self had been wiped away, leaving only a void, and Chrissy mourned the loss.

She prayed that somewhere deep down inside this monochromatic shell, her little boy still existed. She hoped that Ferndale would provide the balm they all needed to heal from this ordeal.

*****

The first leg of today's journey was dull and monotonous. They drove for hours up the I-5 or, as the Angelenos called it, 'The Grapevine'. It offered nothing but miles and miles of rolling golden mountain ranges and diesel trucks. The road stretched out ahead into the distance, winding up and up, unattractive and functional but the fastest route across the state.

They were all grateful when they pulled into the parking lot of the restaurant in Patterson.   As soon as they stepped out of the car, they could smell the alluring wood-smoke of the BBQ joint, and it made their mouths water. There weren't many options for decent food on this truck route, but Scott, being the foodie he was, had found this little gem and it was always a reliable stopping off point on the journey.

Chrissy ordered with enthusiasm. "Hi! Can I get the taco salad with pulled pork, please? Thank you so much." The kids ordered ribs and brisket, with garlic fries to share, and they all sipped their iced teas as they waited for their food to arrive.

"Are you excited to see Nana and Papa?" Chrissy asked the kids.

Jackie beamed, "Totally! Do you think it'll be warm enough to take the dogs down to the beach?" she wiggled with excitement at the thought.

Chrissy laughed and said, "I'm sure it'll be lovely in the afternoons, once the marine layer has lifted. We usually visit later in the summer, so the mornings will be cooler than you're used to, but still fresh and wonderful. Those poor dogs won't know what hit them," she smiled in anticipation, and Jackie winked and chuckled at the thought.

Chrissy glanced at Josh and saw what she hoped was the glimmer of a smile. He had always loved racing up and down the beach with Bonnie and Walter's golden retrievers. They would splash together in the cold ocean waters, barking and squealing with delight, until they were shivering with the cold and glowing with happiness. Then Chrissy would wrap both children and dogs in huge fluffy towels and rub them down vigorously, before everyone piled back into Walter's jeep and headed home for delicious food and warm hugs.

Just then the food arrived and enveloped them in its delicious smoky aroma. Silence descended as everyone chewed and made appreciative noises. The Millers loved their food with a passion, and BBQ was one of their favorites.

Chrissy thought of Scott and how amusing it was to watch him revel in the joy of food.

Coming from a farming family and being one of four strapping lads, he had learned to fight for his fair share. He ate like he was in a scrum, unless of course they were at an elegant restaurant, then he would force himself slow down so he could appreciate the flavors and textures.

At family dinnertime his plate would be empty long before anyone else's, but nobody was permitted to leave the table until the meal was finished. Although Scott's family ate like it might be taken away from them at any moment, they had a reverent respect and love for food, as if life itself was measured in meals. They treated food like some families treat religion; it was the most important thing in the world to them, but they were respectful of others who did not feel the same way.

Chrissy had often wondered how Scott stayed so slim considering the amount he ate, thought, and talked about food. But somehow he still retained the same sleek, toned body he'd had when they met. She assumed it must be because of his early morning runs before heading in to work.

She smiled at the thought of him, and felt a stab of longing, wishing he could be there with them to enjoy this meal.

Pretty soon they were satisfied, and they sat back in their chairs to give their bellies the necessary room to expand.

Full and happy, Chrissy and Jackie shared memories of Ferndale and their plans for the coming weeks, while Josh listened to their expectant joy.

Soon they were loading themselves back into the car for the second leg of the journey. This was the longer leg, but a far more beautiful one.

The 580 was clear, and pretty soon they were cruising on the 101 through the idyllic countryside.

It had always amazed Chrissy how different the scenery was across the state of California. You could drive from the hard-edged tourist traps of Venice Beach, to the isolated beauty of the Sierra mountains, to the bucolic peace of rural farming communities in the north. It seemed like different worlds rolling into one another.

By 7pm they were driving through the majesty of the Humboldt Redwoods State Park.

The huge, ancient trees that towered above them had always mesmerized Chrissy, and she had never shaken the sense of wonder she felt the first time she saw them.

Scott had brought her up to meet his parents and on the way they had stopped in the Avenue of Giants. Chrissy had been chatting and laughing the entire journey, but now she fell silent and stared, wide-eyed, at these incredible edifices of nature.

She'd stood and let the silence envelop her, savoring the tranquility of the forest, the slowing of time, the deep connection with a natural law outside her own reality of busy freeways and fast-paced life. She'd breathed in the rich, earthy aroma, and felt, for just a moment, a deep sense of peace. Since then, every time they drove through this forest, she could feel the echo of that calm.

The sun was setting as they arrived at the little town of Ferndale, its fading light bathing the fields in a warm peach glow and stretching long shadows from the ancient oak trees.

The travelers were weary in so many ways, and as Bonnie, her dark soft eyes full of love, wrapped them each in a warm embrace, it was all Chrissy could do to stop herself from crying.

Bonnie was solid and safe, and Chrissy adored her. She was so different from Chrissy's own mother, and her calm presence was the safety Chrissy so desperately needed right now.

Behind her stood Walter, Scott's father, with his wide shoulders, and gentle, serious smile.

He put his arm around Chrissy and gave her a quick squeeze. Then he said in his low, gravelly voice,

"Come on Josh, let's grab the luggage."

As Walter and Josh carried the travel bags upstairs to the guest rooms, Bonnie ushered the others into the kitchen.

It was warm and cozy as always, with the table set for dinner. Delicious smells curled about them like ribbons of comfort, and Bonnie set everyone to work pouring wine for the adults and iced water from a pitcher for the kids.

Before long they were enjoying large helpings of Bonnie's famous meatloaf served with fresh green beans from the garden and mounds of fluffy, buttery mashed potatoes.

The atmosphere was light and jovial, and even Josh flickered a smile at Bonnie's animated tales of the latest small town drama unfolding around the sponsors of this year's County Fair.

Chrissy exhaled, the weight of worry dropping from her shoulders. They had made it, and she breathed a sigh of relief that the worst was now behind them.

21

Ferndale
Friday, June 7th - Ferndale

The bell jingled as Chrissy pushed open the door. The smells of freshly baked pastries filled her senses, making her stomach grumble.

"Morning April," she said. "What's good today?"

"Morning Chrissy." April greeted her with a beaming smile, and then added in a conspiratorial tone, "Don't tell anyone, but I just took some incredible orange and chocolate chip scones out of the oven. They're still warm, wanna try one?"

Chrissy gave a peel of tiny claps.

"Yum! They sound delicious. No need to try them. Give me two of those and two almond croissants as well. Josh can't get enough of them. Thank you so much, you're amazing."

April handed her the goodies in a paper bag, and Chrissy took it with reverence, determined to protect its delicious contents.

"When is Scott arriving?" April asked.

"He'll be here next weekend. He needs a vacation so I'm

glad he's taking the time away from work. He'll be here for a couple of weeks, Bonnie and Walter can't wait to see him."

"Well, give him my love. We miss having him around here. Bye then Chrissy, I'll see you tomorrow." April smiled as she waved her goodbyes.

Chrissy pushed open the door and tucked the paper bag into the basket on the handlebars of the old bike before swinging it toward home.

She cycled down Main Street, enjoying the early morning peace before the town came to life for another day.

She past the post office and the old theater, admiring their beautiful Victorian facades with the bright colors and ornate features. Ferndale was a close-knit dairy farming community, but it was also renowned for its stunning Victorian architecture, including the magnificent 'painted ladies' of Main Street. When Chrissy first visited, she had laughed out loud at how charming it all was.

She'd turned to Scott and said,

"Wow, no wonder you're the perfect all-American boy, you grew up in the perfect all-American town!"

He had tried to argue, but it was true. Ferndale was like something from the movies, with the freedom and small-town values of a bygone age.

As she cycled down the country lanes, she breathed in the cool, crisp country air and the occasional waft of deliciousness from the pastries.

The wheels of the old bicycle squeaked melodically, echoed in delicate chorus by the distant lowing of the cows in the fields next to her. The rhythm of the bicycle and the sights and sounds around her seemed to create a kind of bucolic meditation that both calmed her and lifted her soul with joy.

Refreshed and exhilarated, she kicked the stand on the bike and headed into the old farmhouse.

She could hear Bonnie's lilting voice, chatting and

laughing with the kids in the kitchen. They were all busy making apple pie, and Chrissy felt her stomach rumble again as she breathed in the smell of fresh lemons, crisp apples, and cinnamon.

Josh was peeling the fruit while Jackie mixed the dough. Jackie looked flushed and animated and blissfully happy, and Chrissy realized she hadn't seen her like this in the longest time.

"Yay! Breakfast! I'm starving," Jackie exclaimed with enthusiasm, eyeing the paper bag voraciously.

Chrissy snorted. "How can you possibly be starving? You had an enormous plate of eggs and bacon with toast just before I left."

"You burn off a lot of calories when you have to go out and collect the eggs yourself. Besides, I'm a gymnast. I need fuel," retorted Jackie with a grin.

Bonnie chuckled and handed Chrissy a steaming cup of coffee.

"Ooh, thank you. It's still chilly out there, but oh so beautiful," Chrissy said with a contented sigh.

Bonnie gave her a wink before turning to say, "That'll do for now, Josh. Now grab some plates and let's eat these pastries while they're still warm."

Full and content and dusted with flour, they were putting the apple pie into the oven when the front door opened and Walter called a cheery greeting. Bonnie looked quizzically at Chrissy.

"Hey honey, you're home early, everything OK?" she shouted.

"Yeah, yeah. I decided to knock off early today. They can call me if they need me."

He kicked off his shoes in the hallway and strode into the kitchen. "Mmm, do I smell coffee?"

Bonnie raised an eyebrow and gave him a smile.

"You do indeed. *My* coffee. And Chrissy's. I take it you'd like one?"

He smiled and nodded, looking like a schoolboy asking for a cookie.

Bonnie grinned and turned to the cappuccino machine.

As the milk bubbled and frothed she said,

"Right, you kids, off with you now. Go and throw a ball for the dogs, and later you can pick some veggies for me for dinner, OK? Now shoo!" She waved a dishcloth at them, as if she were scattering hens in the coop. They laughed and headed to grab their shoes.

Chrissy perched herself on a stool by the counter and smiled. She loved seeing her babies so happy together. They had become comfortable in each other's company again, happy to lounge all over each other on the couch while they played on their phones or read their books.

She turned to Bonnie and said,

"They seem to have gotten so much closer over the last couple of weeks, don't they? Even Josh is beginning to act like his old self again."

Bonnie smiled and nodded in agreement. She turned to Walter and said,

"How was work, honey?"

Walter blew a raspberry and shrugged.

"It was OK. Nothing out of the ordinary. Julie sends her love, by the way. She said she wants to speak to you before the next council meeting. She called it a '*side bar.*' That woman is getting too big for her britches if you ask me."

Chrissy giggled. She had already heard much about the indomitable Julie.

Bonnie tutted and put Walter's coffee on the table in front of him.

"Oh Walter, she's harmless. She takes her position very seriously, that's all, and she's concerned about the new proposals from the design review committee. I know she can come across as a bit of a busybody, but her intentions are always good."

Walter gave Chrissy a sideways glance and a wink that suggested his opinion was different, but that he dare not say any more on the subject. He concluded with, "Well, the old coot wants you to call her. When's lunch? I'm starving!"

Bonnie huffed and chuckled.

"Of course you are, darling. It's already 11am after all, and you're practically wasting away where you sit. Give me fifteen minutes and I'll rustle you up a ham sandwich, OK?"

"Thank you, Bee," Walter said, and winked at his beloved wife.

Bee was Walter's pet name for Bonnie. Scott had explained that in high school Bonnie had been crowned Dairy Queen, and on their first date Walter had told her she would always be his 'queen bee.' The nickname had stuck.

Walter's brow furrowed.

"Oh, and I forgot. I met Charley at the market earlier. You won't believe this. That big corporation has been pressuring him to consider their buyout offer again. They won't leave our farmers alone, will they? Don't they understand how hard it is to make a living as a dairy farmer, even without the big companies encroaching on their margins and squeezing their profits? They're going to drive every farmer out of business at this rate, and *then* where will we be?"

Bonnie sighed as she dried the dishes.

"It's true. It's been a tough couple of years. I remember when dad was still farming, the work was hard, and he worried about sickness and yields, but it was nothing like today. Back then it was simpler. Folks put either milk or cream in their coffee, those were the only options. Now there are all these nut milks and oat milks and who knows what. It's hard for the farmers to keep up."

"Who the hell puts nuts in their coffee, I ask you?" Walter grumbled and sipped his coffee. "If things continue like this, people will move away, and the town will change so much. It won't be the same."

Bonnie nodded in agreement. "But, change is constant honey, and we can't stop it by wishing it away. It'll be sad if people leave, but maybe new families will move in and love the town as much as we all do?"

Walter grumbled again.

"Pfft." said Bonnie, swatting at his mood. "Oh, Walter, you've never been the best with change, you're just like your dad in that regard. You'll fight it all the way, even when it's good for you."

"That's not true," Walter said indignantly.

Bonnie put her hands on her hips and raised one eyebrow.

"Oh really? How about this cappuccino machine, eh? It took me three years to convince you to buy one, but you kept saying 'why do we need a fancy machine, I like my coffee just the way it is'. In the end I gave up and bought it for you for Christmas, and has there been a day since then that we haven't used it? I don't think so!"

Walter looked sheepish and grinned at Chrissy.

"Damn you, woman, you know me too well," he said with a resigned smile.

"Actually," Chrissy said, sitting upright as she remembered something. "Talking of people moving away, I saw a 'For Sale' sign outside the old rectory. I cycle past it every morning on the way to and from the bakery. I never thought I'd see it for sale though."

Bonnie nodded. "Yes, Dorothy who lived there died earlier this year, and her children live across the country, so they've no need for it. They cleared out the contents a couple of months ago, so now they must be ready to sell it. It's beautiful on the outside, isn't it? Like a doll's house. But I'd imagine it needs a lot of work inside. I wouldn't think it's been updated since the fifties, maybe even before."

"Hey Chrissy, you're a realtor now, aren't you? Maybe you could sell it for them?" Walter beamed with pride.

Chrissy reddened.

"Um, it doesn't really work like that. Plus, I'm not sure how long we'll be here before we need to head back to Pasadena."

"Well, they'd be lucky to have you," said Walter, giving Chrissy a big hug as he reached to take a delicious smelling sandwich from Bonnie.

Just then Chrissy's phone chimed. She grabbed it and saw a text from Emily.

> *Hi Chrissy.*
> *Everything good with you?*
> *Are you free to chat?*
> *I need to talk to you ASAP if that's OK?*
> *Sorry to bother you.*
> *Text me when you're free to talk.*
> *Thanks.*

Chrissy raised an eyebrow and responded.

> *Sure. I'll call you right now.*

She threw on her jacket and stood on the front doorstep, stamping her feet to keep warm.

She hit Emily's number and waited.

There was ringing, then the click of an answer, followed by Emily's teary, choked up voice blurting out.

"Oh thank you, Chrissy. I really need to talk to you."

22

Kolleen
Friday, June 7th - Ferndale

"What's the matter? Is everything OK?" said Chrissy with rising concern.

"Yes. Yes, I'm sorry. I'm just really emotional." Emily held back the sobs and tried to steady her voice.

"What's happened, Emily? What's going on?" Chrissy's mind raced.

"I just had a fight with my mum. Everything's OK, it got a bit heated, that's all, and I'm still a bit shaken."

Chrissy felt a stab of annoyance. Why the hell would Emily be making a transatlantic call to talk to someone she'd seen only once in the last twenty years, just to tell her she'd had a spat with her mother. I mean, who does that?

"Is that why you called?" Chrissy asked, a little curtly.

"No. I know this is weird, but I wanted your advice on something," Emily said, forcing herself to take long breaths to calm herself. "OK, I'm OK now. Let me start from the beginning. Remember that I spoke with Kolleen at the end of May? She was interested in selling some of my products on her website. Well, there's been a bit of a hiccup." There was an awkward pause. "Um, Ed was made redundant, so I put the whole Kolleen thing on the back burner for the time being until he can get himself a new job and get settled in. He's been contacting loads of people through LinkedIn and connecting with old friends to see what opportunities might be out there. Anyway, I had an email earlier today from Kolleen and some of her partners. Apparently she's been working with a venture capital group to grow her business and they are interested in developing a range of locally produced beauty products for people with sensitive skin and skin conditions like eczema. Kolleen showed them my website, and they were impressed with how I'd sourced my ingredients, and what I know about sensitive skin conditions."

Chrissy cleared her throat and shifted a little, waiting for Emily to get to the point.

"Anyway," Emily continued, "they want to talk to me about a position working for them to build their product range in California. But the role would be based in Santa Monica, so we'd have to relocate. I'd be spending my time talking to local producers to source organic products. I'm not sure I even have the skills to do it, but I'm so excited about the opportunity I can't even think straight. They've asked me if I would come over for a week some time at the end of June to talk through all the details and meet the team."

Chrissy was floored. A wave of exhilarating pride swelled in her chest.

"Oh my God, Emily, that's amazing! I'm so proud of you! You *have* to do it! Hey, we'll practically be neighbors!"

"Well." Emily's voice sounded shaky again. "I was still reeling from the email and dancing around the kitchen when my mum arrived. I didn't think it through, I just blurted it all out. I was so excited and, yes, I was a little proud of myself and too caught up in it all. Anyway, Mum was mad. She told me to get a hold of myself. She said that this is not the time to be flying off to America on a wild scheme, and that she was disappointed in me for being so selfish. Chrissy, I have to admit, I just lost control. I couldn't help myself. I shouted at her and told her I would make my own damn decisions, and it wasn't up to her whether or not I went to America. I might have even sworn, I can't remember, it's a blur. Well, that's when she stormed out. She's furious with me, and now I feel awful, but I wanted to ask your advice before I give it all up again."

Chrissy's mama-bear instinct was triggered, and her blood was boiling. She'd never liked Emily's controlling mother, and it was obvious that the old bitch hadn't changed much over the years.

From an outsider's perspective, Emily's mother, Jennifer, looked like the perfect wife and mother, but Chrissy knew the truth.

Jennifer was forever baking fresh cakes and pastries for the school fundraisers, helping in the classroom, and walking her daughters to and from school every day. She didn't work outside the home, and she kept the house pin-prick clean with fresh flowers in the kitchen and all the beds made by 10am. When Chrissy was younger, she had often been jealous of Emily; the bowl of fresh fruit on the table and a home cooked dinners every night. A mother who was always attentive, and who always put her family first. But later Chrissy came to see the darker side of Jennifer's affections.

As a young girl Emily had been a bright, articulate and insightful child, who showed a natural flair for argument and discourse. Before long she could hold her own in any disagreement, even against the likes of Liz, and the two of them would often verbally spar, seeing each other as equals in a fight.

But Chrissy watched as Jennifer dampened this natural strength with subtle criticisms and put downs. She would tell Emily that she was 'getting too arrogant' and sow the seeds of doubt in Emily's mind. Ever so gradually Emily lost her fire and became the quiet, sensible, placid girl that her mother expected and required her to be.

Emily had attempted a form of rebellion in her last year of school when she announced she wanted to study law at university. Her mother had shrugged and said it would do to 'while away the time until she found a husband'.

Chrissy had often wondered who Emily might have been if she'd been blessed with a different mother, maybe even Chrissy's own mother. Would she be a high-powered lawyer in the city? Or have her own multi-million dollar company?

Chrissy felt her bile rise as she thought of how divisive and manipulative Jennifer was. So subtle and yet so destructive.

"What are you going to do, then?" said Chrissy, trying not to let the anger bleed through into her voice.

"Well, I'll talk to Ed about it when he gets home. He's playing golf with his friend Brian today and I don't want to disturb them, he's had such a tough time he deserves a break. The more I think about it, the more I want to do it, though. Does that sound crazy? I want to at least *talk* to them about it some more and see if its even a viable opportunity. I doubt they'll offer it to me. I can't imagine why they would pick me when there must be *thousands* of people in America who are far more qualified than I am. Also, what about the kids? Is it fair to take them away from their school, and all their friends? I'm worried it might be too much of a disruption for them. Oh, I don't know. I don't want to be selfish, but this could be an amazing opportunity for all of us. What do you think, Chrissy? It's worth meeting them to talk about it, isn't it?"

In that moment, Emily sounded both defiant and pleading. And Chrissy's heart broke just a little.

"You should *definitely* fly over and talk to them. Where's the harm in that? Even if they offer it to you, you don't have to accept. And you'd be more than welcome to stay with me if you want?"

Chrissy had offered before she thought it through.

Would they be back at home by then?

Probably. Although, everything was so uncertain right now.

"Oh! I hadn't even thought that far ahead. That would be wonderful. Thank you so much, it's such a generous offer, and it would only be me, I wouldn't bring Ed and the kids over at such an early stage."

Chrissy hesitated.

She wanted to stand by the offer, but she felt it necessary to offer some context, too.

"You're totally welcome to come and visit, of course. And I'd love to have you, but we're going through some changes right now."

"Oh. OK," said Emily quietly. "I'm sorry if I've imposed. It's no problem if I don't come. I'll just..." and her voice trailed off.

Chrissy steeled herself.

"No, Emily. You are more than welcome to stay with me. We've had some troubles of our own, that's all." And before she knew it, she was telling her oldest and dearest friend everything that had happened over the last month.

It was only as she recounted her story, crying and finally allowing herself to release all the pain, that she realized how desperately she had missed her one and only Emily.

Her heart ached for her old friend, and she couldn't wait to throw her arms around her and squeeze her tight.

23

Cynthia
Sunday, June 16th - London

"Give them both a hug from me, OK?" said Liz into her phone, "Believe me, I'd much rather be with you guys than this old bitch, but she wants to stick her pointy beak into my business and she won't leave me alone until she's done so. I'll call you later. Bye Lauren."

She hung up, a pang of longing stabbing her heart as she thought of Lauren in that warm, happy household, and she wished she could be back there again.

The gravel crunched as the Uber pulled into the circular driveway.

"Wow. You live here?" the driver said in awe.

"No, my parents do." Liz replied as she climbed out of the car and slammed the door.

The front of the house was indeed imposing. A rich cream exterior with a huge entrance way, the center of which was a magnificent front door flanked by two marble columns. 'Sentinels of snobbery, ' as Liz had once described them to a friend.

The house was symmetrical and immaculate, with white hydrangeas running the length of the facade, their color chosen to match the white sash windows.

Liz set her jaw in anticipation and rang the doorbell.

Her mother, Cynthia, opened the door and cried, "Darling!" as she pulled Liz in for a brief, awkward embrace. "Come in, come in," she said, leading Liz through the expansive foyer and down the corridor towards the study.

"Thank you so much for coming. I've been meaning to get this paperwork up to date for the longest time, and then I thought to myself, let's just get it done today. Carpe diem, as they say, no?" she flashed Liz a tight-lipped smile and signaled for her to take a seat in a large leather chair.

"Would you like tea? I have English breakfast, or Earl Grey if you'd prefer?"

"English breakfast. Thanks," said Liz.

"No problem. Back in a jiffy," Cynthia replied in a jolly tone as she headed down the hallway to the kitchen.

Liz sat, flicking her nails in an agitated way, an old habit from her childhood.

"Come on, come on," she thought to herself. The sooner she got this over with, the sooner she could get the hell out of this awful place.

Liz looked around the familiar study with its leather armchairs and heavy mahogany furniture. Imposing book cabinets lined the walls, rising to meet the high vaulted ceilings. Each shelf was crammed with books, uniform rows of thick tan volumes that matched the thick tan carpet, creating a stuffy, claustrophobic atmosphere that Liz loathed. The room smelled somewhat musty, like old papers and cigar smoke, which perplexed Liz as no one in the house smoked cigars.

Shifting in the chair, Liz cleared her throat and stared at the study door. She knew the reason for Cynthia's invitation, and her stomach was in knots because of it. She still hadn't worked out her strategy, and that made her nervous.

Sighing with exasperation, she stood up and walked over to the window.

Although she'd grown up in this house, it had never felt like home. The atmosphere had always been tense because of her parents' strained relationship. Cynthia exuded a palpable contempt for her husband, despising him for his failed businesses and his laissez-faire attitude toward their finances. Liz disliked her father almost as much as her mother did. She found his bumbling ineptitude infuriating, but she also felt a deeper level of distrust that she could never fully explain.

As Liz turned to scan the room, her eyes rested on a set of black and white photographs displayed in ornate silver frames on the large study desk in front of her.

She'd looked at these photographs a thousand times as a child, but they still intrigued her.

One was a family portrait of Cynthia, her sisters and her parents. The three sisters stood in a neat line wearing matching frilly dresses and white ankle socks with black buckle shoes. Their parents stood behind them, father in a suit and tie, and mother in a slim, elegant pale dress with matching Juliet cap. They were at some elegant garden party, socializing with other equally elegant ex-pats.

The other photograph showed Cynthia's father in his formal capacity, addressing the troops. He looked handsome and regal in his elaborate uniform with the epaulettes and brass buttons, and the hat with all the plumage.

When Liz was younger, she had announced that she thought he looked just like a chicken, and demonstrated her point by parading around the study, clucking and crowing while making thrusting movements with her neck and arms. Her mother had been furious and didn't speak to her for three days afterwards.

Cynthia was from an aristocratic bloodline. 'Old money' as some people called it. Her father had been the Governor of Kenya in the 1950s, and Cynthia and her sisters had consequently been born in Nairobi. At a young age, they had been sent back to England to attend a boarding school, and Cynthia rarely mentioned anything about her life growing up in Africa.

Liz jumped as her mother returned with a tray.

"Daydreaming again, young lady?" Cynthia asked as she laid out the china tea set on a side table. "I brought chocolate biscuits for a treat if you'd like?" She smiled her pursed lip smile.

Liz loathed the way her mother smiled. It was cold and calculating, never quite reaching her eyes.

"No, I'm good. Thank you."

Liz returned to her chair as Cynthia poured the tea in silence. She handed Liz a cup and saucer and sat down in the chair opposite her daughter.

"So, Elizabeth, tell me how you've been? How's Xander?"

Liz's color rose.

"He's good."

"Hmm. You two must come over for dinner soon. We haven't seen you for *the longest time,* and it would be lovely to catch up. How's work? You look a little drawn. Have you been working too hard, darling?"

Liz shot her a withering stare. "OK, enough. What do you want, mother?"

"Now, Lizzy, that's not polite. We haven't seen each other for so long I just wanted to see how you're doing," Cynthia said in a voice dripping with sincerity.

"On the phone you said something about wanting me to sign some updated trust documents. Can we do that? I have other places I'd rather be."

Cynthia looked vexed. She put down her tea and walked to

the desk, shuffling papers into various piles and then straightening each pile with a series of sharp bangs on the desk that made Liz think of machine gun fire.

"Fine. Here you go then, come and sign them."

Liz lifted herself from the chair and walked around to her mother's side of the desk. She skim read the documents and signed each of them. It felt strange to stand so close to her mother. It made her skin creep a little, as if she were in the presence of a malevolent spirit.

"Oh, and I've been meaning to ask you," Cynthia said in an intentionally casual tone.

"Shit. Here we go," thought Liz.

"When I called yesterday, you sounded like you were outside somewhere. And I could hear a child's voice. Who were you with?"

Liz had known this was coming, and she had kicked herself for being so careless. Her guard had been down, and she had answered her phone without looking at the caller ID.

They had been at the park, Liz and Lauren sitting on a bench talking, while Naomi played in the sand. Lauren had been so animated, telling Liz all about her current nursing placement in the pediatric ward. It had been her dream for so long, and she was almost there. Only one year left and she would be qualified. Liz had smiled and hugged her, and shared in the excitement. She was proud of Lauren and for everything she had achieved, and she wanted the very best for her.

Just at that moment Naomi ran up, sandy and smiling, her huge beautiful dark eyes imploring as she grabbed Liz's hand and tried to drag her up.

"Chase me, Auntie Liz, chase me!" she shouted with glee, scampering off behind the climbing frame.

Liz had played 'fierce monster' much to Naomi's delight, and as they sat on the ground in a fit of giggles, her phone had rung.

She'd reached for her back pocket and answered it without thinking. Why had she done that? What a rookie mistake. Her mother never called, so she hadn't even considered it an option.

But now, here they were, and Cynthia could sense Liz's discomfort. She had smelled blood in the water and she was coming in for the kill.

Normally Liz could flick off her mother's intrusive questions with casual indifference, but today she felt defensive, combative. This was different, and they both knew it.

"I was with friends,"

"How nice. Which friends?"

"A mother and daughter. I know them through, um, a mutual friend."

"Wonderful. Was that the child I could hear speaking in the background? Her London accent is quite distinctive, isn't it? How old is she?"

"She's four."

"How sweet. And have you known them long?"

"About a month."

There was silence while Cynthia sipped her tea and signaled for Liz to continue.

Liz sighed and said, "the little girl's name is Naomi. Her mother's name is Lauren. We were at the park together."

"Well, that sounds lovely. And is there a father?"

Liz colored.

"Holy crap, Mum, really? No, if you must know, the father isn't in the picture. Lauren is a single mother. But she's amazing with Naomi. She's at college doing her nursing qualifications, she only has a year left and then she'll be qualified,"

Liz kicked herself again. *"Stop trying so hard. Why are you telling her all this?"* she thought to herself.

"Hmm. A nurse. And are you a mentor of sorts? I fail to see what the two of you could possibly have in common."

"Actually, we're friends. We get on really well and I respect her. Even though she's young, she's very mature and sensible, and Naomi is the sweetest kid," Liz said, smiling despite herself. "You want to see a photo?" she asked, and then regretted it.

"Oh yes, I'd love to."

Liz hesitated for a moment, then opened a photograph on her phone. It showed Lauren and Naomi smiling and hugging each other. She handed the phone to her mother.

A flicker of distaste flashed across her mother's face, replaced in an instant with calm, polite interest.

Liz's breathing quickened as the hatred rose in her chest.

"Problem?" she asked through gritted teeth.

"No. They seem lovely. What delightful earrings she's wearing. Not my taste of course, but everyone is different I suppose."

Liz stared at her teacup, trying to control herself. She bit down the tears of anger, wishing she could throw the cup across the room and watch it shatter.

She wanted to get away from here, but instead she did what she always did. She pushed the feelings down inside her and sat tall.

Cynthia handed her back the phone.

"Have you heard from your brother at all?" Cynthia asked pleasantly.

"No. Have you? He's your son after all," Liz spat back.

Cynthia raised her eyebrows.

"He hasn't called me since he moved in with that man."

"Billy. David's boyfriend's name is Billy, as you very well know, mother."

"Hm. Yes." said Cynthia, pursing her lips.

There was a heavy silence.

Liz broke it by saying, "Is Dad around?" She asked, not because she was interested in the whereabouts of her father, but more to punish her mother.

Cynthia cleared her throat and began to collect the cups and saucers.

"He's at an auction up in town. He's been following the work of an up-and-coming French artist he believes will be the 'next big thing'. He's spent quite a lot of money on her paintings, so let's see if his hunch pays off, shall we?" Cynthia smiled, but her eyes were like steel.

Liz stood.

"Well, if that's all you needed, I'll be going."

"I understand, darling. Would you like me to call you a taxi?"

"No. I'll get an Uber. But thank you."

"Oh, It's no problem. It's on our account."

They walked in silence to the front door.

As the taxi pulled up, Liz gave her mother a quick kiss on the cheek.

Her mother squeezed her tight, and then released her, saying in a low tone, "It's been lovely to see you, Lizzie. Please come again soon, will you? And, I hope I'm not overstepping the mark by saying this, but be careful who you get close to. You never know their true motives, if you know what I mean?" She gave Liz a knowing look, followed by a quick pat on the arm.

Liz slipped into the car and told the driver to "Just go."

They drove for fifteen minutes while she stared out of the window, sobbing.

When her breathing calmed, she pulled her phone out of her purse and sent a text.

The phone lit up with a response.

Liz leaned forward and said to the driver in a horse voice,

"OK, I have an address for you. It's in the city, if that's OK?"

"No problem," said the driver.

They pulled up to the front of the sleek, grey apartment building and Liz hauled herself out of the car, wiping her face.

She pressed the buzzer, and the door opened.

In the elevator, she stood, staring into space. Numb. Too tired and angry and hopeless to feel anything else.

She rang the doorbell, and Xander opened the door.

He was wearing a black silk dressing gown, untied, so she could see his toned body.

He pulled her to him, kissing her hungrily.

She did not resist.

He swung the door shut behind them as they tore at each other's clothes.

24

Retirement
Tuesday, June 18th - Ferndale

"And then Mom freaked out big time when she found out Jackie was planning on getting a tattoo. You remember that?" Josh was sharing stories across the dinner table, his eyes shining and his soul filled to the brim with joy and contentment.

Everyone laughed as Chrissy shook her head, shrugged her shoulders, and raised her wineglass to toast her rebellious daughter.

Jackie flushed. "Well, I was thinking about Trish's spiderweb tattoo, and I thought I might get one too. It's so cool because of the whole symbolism thing. 'Fragility and Resilience' you know? From when she was protesting."

Chrissy's mother had always been something of a hero to Jackie. While the kids called Bonnie and Walter Nana and Papa, they had always called Trish, well, just Trish.

When Chrissy had first told her mum she was pregnant and asked her what she wanted her grandchild to call her, Trish had looked confused and said, "Um, well, Trish, I suppose? That's my name after all."

Chrissy hadn't bothered to argue. Her mother had never been one for observing traditional roles, after all.

Chrissy smiled at her daughter, watching those dark eyes flash with both defiance and sincerity. God, she loved this girl to distraction. Her baby girl was almost an adult, and soon she would be gone, out into the world to make her own way and build her own life. 'Fragility and Resilience' was right.

In that moment, Chrissy could see Trish reflected in her daughter. Jackie had inherited Trish's fiery nature and her passion for justice. After all, Trish's spiderweb tattoo commemorated her own role in the anti-nuclear protests at the Greenham Common Peace Camps.

For a moment Chrissy's mind flashed back to Rachel's memorial service and the photograph of the little girl on the train platform entitled 'Resilience'.

She felt a pain in her heart as she turned her eyes on her beautiful son, his face lit up with pleasure as he talked and laughed with his Nana. Could it be that the fragility she'd been watching for so carefully in her daughter lay instead in her handsome, sporty son? Had she failed him? Had he asked for her help, and she'd been too busy to hear? She would try harder to give him everything he needed from now on.

"Want a top up?" asked Scott, leaning in and looking at her with concern in his eyes. He could see she was a million miles away, and he gave her an "I've got you" look to reassure her as he poured her another glass of wine.

She sighed and smiled at him. What would she do without this amazing man?

As she rejoined the conversation, she realized Walter was talking about his practice.

"The medical world is changing so fast, and babies I delivered are having babies of their own now. I'm wondering whether it's time to hang up my stethoscope and pass the torch to the next generation. Hey Scott, you want to take over my practice and become a small town family doctor?" Walter asked in a casual tone, but there was something in his voice that suggested it wasn't asked entirely in jest.

"Oh God, no! Thanks anyway, Dad," said Scott with a huge grin. "I don't have the patience to do what you do."

The conversation moved on, but Walter's question stuck in Chrissy's mind, growing from an ember into a flame.

What if Scott *did* take over the family practice? They could move here and be closer to Bonnie and Walter. They weren't getting any younger after all, and the local High School was small and friendly, both the kids could make a fresh start.

The old rectory was up for sale for the first time in generations - could it be fate? Chrissy's mind drifted to the beautiful two story Victorian building with its white and cream facade, immaculate and cute as a gingerbread house. Plus, it was bound to be cheaper than their house in Pasadena. If they bought it outright, they would have no mortgage to worry about.

Ideas whirred faster and faster through her head. Once Chrissy started on one of these trajectories, there was no stopping her. Scott had once laughed about it, describing her as a 'dark haired, freckled, freight train' while he rolled his eyes and indulged her in whatever crazy scheme she'd been cooking up on that particular occasion.

Chrissy was quiet for the rest of dinner, and as they washed the dishes and put the kitchen in order, Chrissy said to Scott,

"You wanna sit on the porch and get some fresh air together?"

The kids settled down in front of the TV, and Chrissy and Scott slipped out the back door into the fresh, chilly night air.

"You OK?" Scott said with genuine concern in his voice. "You seemed so far away at dinner. Are you feeling alright?

Wow, yikes, it's freezing out here. Let me grab us both a warm sweater. Hang on, I'll be back in a minute."

Chrissy sat distractedly on the porch swing. She had a sudden craving for a cigarette, which was bizarre as she hadn't smoked since high school, and even then she'd only smoked to look cool.

In their teens she and Liz would lean casually on railings and smoke their cigarettes, while Emily refused to, too scared of what her mother would say if she found out. Rachel rarely came out with them in the evenings, even though she was always welcome, and even if she had been there, it was doubtful she would have smoked cigarettes with them.

Scott came back with the sweaters. He pulled up a worn lattice chair that had seen better days and positioned himself in front of Chrissy. He leaned in to her, looking into her eyes.

"What's up baby?" He said with such tenderness that Chrissy wanted to kiss him.

"I was thinking about what your dad said about retiring and giving you the family practice. I know you always say that you wouldn't want to be a small town doctor, but maybe this is the fresh start we need?"

Scott's face fell, and he dropped his eyes to the ground. He was silent for a while. Then he looked up, his eyes reflecting both concern and frustration.

"Look, I know you're hurting and it's been a tough month, but I don't think this is the solution. We have a life in Pasadena, and it's a good life. Yes, things are going to change, but I'm not sure 'running away from home' is the right way to deal with this."

Chrissy's jaw set, her eyes now mirroring his frustration.

"It's all very well for you to say that, Scott, but everything is different now. Not so much for you because your job will be the same, you'll come home to the same house every day, and you'll have the same hobbies. But my life has been wiped away. I still have my job, but let's be honest, that was only ever a minor thing. I'd built my entire life around the kids' school, and now it's gone, and I don't know where I belong anymore. And what about the kids? Aren't you worried about Josh? Haven't you ever wondered what would make him do such a thing? Maybe he needs a fresh start? Somewhere where nobody knows him. Maybe we all do."

The back door swung open and Jackie stepped out.

"What are you guys talking about?" she said, looking wary.

"Your mother thinks we should move to Ferndale," Scott said flatly.

Chrissy shot him a horrified glance. *"God, Scott, really?"*

"What the fuck, Mom!" Jackie said, her eyes wide with alarm.

"Now, hang on a minute. Your father and I were having a *private* conversation about what our next move could be. And watch your language Jackie, what would Nana and Papa think if they heard you talking like that?"

"I think they would agree it was justified! I can't believe you're doing this, Mom. Just because you can't deal with losing your bitchy, snobby friends, doesn't mean you can turn all our lives upside down!"

"What's going on?" Josh stood in the doorway, looking from Jackie to Chrissy.

"Mom wants to move to Ferndale because you're a loser drug dealer," Jackie snapped, whirling around and glaring at Josh.

"Oh, shit!" said Josh, going pale. "Oh God, I'm so sorry. I didn't mean…" his voice faltered and faded.

"Everyone, just calm down," said Chrissy. "Nothing has been decided. And actually this isn't your decision, it's ours," she said, looking towards Scott. "I just thought it might be a chance for a fresh start. This is such a lovely small community, you guys could make some good friends here."

"I have good friends, in Pasadena," snarled Jackie, while Josh looked at his feet.

Bonnie put her head around the door and said with a twinkle in her eye,

"When you guys are done yelling at each other, there's hot chocolate in here."

Chrissy flushed with embarrassment.

They filed into the kitchen, and everyone was grateful for the warm drink before they went their separate ways to bed.

Chrissy looked mortified. "I'm so sorry, Bonnie. We shouldn't have been shouting at each other."

"Nonsense! It's good to get it all out in the open. Walter and I argue all the time. In fact, we've been known to wash the dishes right in the middle of an argument. I'll wash and rinse while he dries. To be honest, I'm surprised that it took you so long to talk about things properly."

Chrissy felt herself relax, and she loved Bonnie all the more for it.

Then Bonnie said in a more serious tone, "Of course, we'd *love* to have you move here, but darling, make sure you're doing it for the right reasons, yes?"

Chrissy couldn't sleep that night, and in the stillness of the early morning she crept downstairs to sit on the couch.

With her feet tucked under her and her cell phone in her hand, she looked up the details of the old rectory. It was described it as 'four bed, two bath, original Victorian features with modern day comfort'.

Before she knew it, she had emailed the realtor to express her interest. She then wrote an email to her boss in Pasadena. It began,

Hi Ryan,

We're thinking of putting our house on the market. Can I talk to you about it tomorrow when you're free?

25

Bibi
Sunday, June 23rd - Surrey

As Emily closed the dishwasher, she heard her phone ring.

Huffing with irritation, she answered it, squeezing it between her shoulder and her ear while she juggled with the carving tray and the gravy jug, all of which needed to be put away after the family's big Sunday roast dinner.

"Hi Liz, how you doing?"

"I'm good. You busy?" answered Liz.

"No, we just finished lunch, so I'm clearing everything away. What's up?"

Liz, also juggling her phone, was stripping off her workout gear and getting ready to take a shower.

"I'm sorry to interrupt you on a Sunday, I won't be long, I just wanted some advice."

"Sure! Ed's going to take the kids to the park to kick a ball around, so I'm free to talk."

"I was wondering if I could have, or I mean *buy*, some of your eczema products? I know a little girl who's having some problems with psoriasis and I said I would ask you for some of your cream and body wash and stuff."

"Of course!" said Emily. "Always happy to help. In fact, I just finished making a huge batch of soaps and moisturizers, you're welcome to come over and pick some up if you want to? And you don't have to pay me, you goofball," she said with a grin.

"Oh! OK, wow. That would be great, if you're sure you don't mind? I just got back from the gym so I'm going to jump in the shower and then I could come over to collect it, if that's OK?"

"Sure! I'll put the kettle on," said Emily, feeling elated and texting Liz her address.

Two hours later, the front doorbell rang. Emily opened the door to her tall, elegant pal, and they threw their arms around each other in a happy embrace.

"Come in! Come in!" said Emily, bubbling with excitement.

"Holy crap girl, this village is like something from a movie!" Liz said as she kicked off her pumps and followed Emily through to the kitchen.

Liz had Ubered from central London to Emily's home in the Surrey countryside. The urban sprawl of metal and concrete had faded out of view, replaced by rolling hills and trees, and Liz began to realize just how different Emily's life was from hers.

As they drove into Emily's village, Liz had marveled at the ancient gray stone buildings set on narrow, winding streets.

As the driver pulled over to let another car squeeze past, Liz spotted a stream running in parallel with the road. Long reeds nodded back and forth, and a duck swam past with a late brood of ducklings following faithfully behind her.

Emily's home was on an equally narrow lane, much to the consternation of the poor Uber driver, and Liz thanked him and jumped out before he could complain some more about the 'lack of turning circle'.

The house was a two story Victorian cottage with wide bay windows and tiny yellow roses winding their way around a red front door. Liz pushed open the gate in the white picket fence and walked up the stone path. The path was boarded on both sides by swathes of purple lupins and pink peonies, their delicate heads nodding politely as Liz passed by. She stood on the 'Welcome' mat and smiled to herself before ringing the doorbell.

"So what's it like living in such a pastoral paradise? I mean, you have sheep for neighbors for fuck's sake," Liz snorted with amusement as Emily cringed, grateful that Ed was still out at the ice cream shop with the kids.

"It's wonderful. I never would have thought we would live somewhere like this, but it's so peaceful and the herb garden is idyllic. You want to see?"

Emily looked so enthusiastic that Liz conceded and followed her on a tour.

The house was comfy and well kept, although far too fussy for Liz. Every surface was covered with pottery and knickknacks, and the pastel colored walls were adorned with watercolors and photographs of the children.

Liz had to admit that the garden was beautiful. Fragrant flowers bloomed in flowerbeds, and a small pond added to the sense of serenity.

Emily turned to see Liz looking into the pond.

She smiled and said, "The kids have been watching the tadpoles hatch. I think they've all become frogs by now. If you crouch down here and stay still and quiet, you might be able to see them."

Liz watched her friend kneeling in the grass, beckoning to her with excitement. God, she loved this crazy lady, and she'd missed her so much.

"You are nuts if you think I'm getting down there in the dirt with you to look for gross, slimy creatures," Liz said with an amused grin, and Emily laughed in acknowledgement.

After a tour of the herb garden and the famous soap shed, they wandered back to the kitchen where Liz settled herself at the heavy wooden table while Emily poured them both a mug of tea.

"So, who is it that needs the eczema products?" Emily asked, handing Liz her tea.

"Um. It's a little girl called Naomi. She's the daughter of, um, a friend."

Liz dropped her eyes to the table and cleared her throat. She looked sheepish, almost guilty, and Emily was taken aback. She had never seen Liz like this. It was so out of character that it was almost alarming.

"What's going on, Liz?"

Liz threw her head back and inhaled, sighing out the stress of the last month. She looked up and met Emily's eyes, realizing how much she needed to talk this through.

"Remember I asked you for your advice about that 'situation' with Xander and the girl from work?"

"The one with the baby?"

"Yeah. Well, I met up with her. It didn't go the way I thought it would. I thought I'd yell at her and call her a slut and storm out or something. But we ended up talking. She wasn't what I expected. I'm not sure what I expected. Anyway, we kept in touch."

Liz flashed Emily a strange look, one of defiance mixed with fear. Emily saw the vulnerability in her eyes. At this moment, Liz was more vulnerable than she had ever seen her. Emily nodded, signaling for Liz to go on.

"The little girl's name is Naomi. She's gorgeous. Beautiful and clever, and oh my God, she's so funny," Liz smiled with warm pride. Her eyes soft and loving, and Emily felt for a moment as if she was intruding on an intimate moment.

"Sorry," said Liz, shaking herself. "It's weird I know, but

I've grown so close to them over the last month. I can't explain it, but I think it started at the Memorial when I saw that photograph of the old woman and her husband. It made me realize just how much I wanted that kind of connection, and the pain caused a sort of fracture inside me. It hurt so much that I never thought I'd be whole again. I always thought I'd feel a deep emptiness because of it. But then I met Lauren and Naomi, I now I feel as if that fracture is filling with light and energy." Liz took a jagged breath. "And apparently I'm a fucking poet now as well, would you believe it?" she snorted, waving away the emotion that hung in the air.

"No, it's lovely," said Emily, leaning forward, reaching for Liz's hand and squeezing it.

There was a tiny bud stirring deep down inside Liz. Something Emily has never seen in her wise-cracking, ball-busting friend. A sense of nurturing, a fragility that comes when you begin to genuinely care for someone else. And Emily knew how much Liz needed a safe place to explore this.

"They live with Lauren's grandmother in Barking." Liz went on, relaxing a little as she eased into talking about this new adventure. "She's from Glasgow originally. Her name is Betty, but they call her Bibi. And now, so do I," she smiled as she thought about them. "It's only a small terrace house. Only two bedrooms, but it suits them. They're so happy. And so goddam loud!" said Liz, laughing at the recollection of the howls of merriment that would shake the house and fill every space with deafening joy.

Liz's face was glowing now, as she shared stories of Bibi and Lauren chasing Naomi around the tiny house while Naomi scrambled up the stairs, screaming with glee.

She smiled. "It's funny. Although Bibi was a little guarded at first, she trusted Lauren's judgement, and pretty soon she had opened her home and her heart to me. It blows me away how welcoming they are. I'm a stranger. A snobby rich girl with no business encroaching on their life. But I'm more at home in that tiny terrace house than I have been anywhere else in my life."

In that moment, Liz looked so fragile that Emily thought her heart would break.

Liz straightened in her chair, her jaw tightening as she said in a hard edged voice,

"Oh, and I was stupid enough to let my mother find out about it. Well, part of the story anyway. She called last Saturday when we were at the park and I answered my phone without checking the caller ID. I was out of breath and laughing, which made her suspicious, of course. Then Naomi barreled into me, shouting and laughing, and that was it. She wouldn't leave it alone. She called me the next morning asking me to come over on some pretext, but it was obvious what her real motive was. She was slithering all around me, sweet as sugar and hissing, 'Oh Lizzie dear, do tell?'" Liz made a disgusted face.

"Lizzie? Yeesh. She still calls you Lizzie?" said Emily, cringing.

"Yup. 'Like Lizzie Borden' I once said, but she didn't get the joke."

Emily grinned.

"I wasn't sure how to handle it, but then I thought, fuck it, I'm just going to lay it all out there. Apart from the Xander part, obviously. I told her we were connected through a 'mutual friend', which is kinda true. As soon as she'd confirmed they're from the East End she had her nose in the air, making all sorts of judgements and assumptions about them. God, she's such a bitch. She's an arrogant snob and I'm ashamed of her."

Liz was clenching her teeth and looked combative. Her

color was high and her eyes flashing with anger and hurt.

"And then, well..." Her eyes dropped, and she squirmed, leaning in to confide something to Emily. But before she could, the back door flew open and in tumbled three laughing, chattering children, followed by Ed.

Their arrival diffused the atmosphere in the kitchen, and Liz smiled and said hi to Emily's red headed babies and their long-suffering father.

"Hey there, you must be Liz. It's a pleasure," Ed said, shaking Liz's hand as Harry hung, limpet-like from his leg.

"Mummy!" Harry shouted, jumping at his mother, his smiling, freckled face covered in chocolate ice cream.

"Oh, Harry! Did you *eat* any of the ice cream, or just smear it all over your face," laughed Emily, holding her baby tight.

Liz smiled at the two of them. Happy to bask in their love.

"The kids are going to wash their hands, and then I've said that they can have some screen time if that's OK?" said Ed. "I'm off to watch the cricket. Nice to meet you, Liz," he said as he beat a hasty retreat to the living room.

Emily raised an eyebrow and smiled.

"Oh, actually, I have some news," Emily said, beaming with excitement. "Remember that woman in California who wanted to sell some of my products on her website? Well guess what, she connected to a venture capital firm, and they want to talk to me about a job sourcing ingredients for them. It's based in Santa Monica! They've asked me to fly out and meet with them to discuss it."

"What the f... I mean, wow, Emily!" said Liz, her eyes gleaming. "Are you going?"

"I am indeed. They want me to go to LA next week. I'm going to stay with Chrissy, so that will be lovely. Her husband Scott and the kids are visiting family up in Northern California so we'll have the place to ourselves. I'm so nervous about the meeting, though. Ed's excited for me, but my Mum is totally against it and she's putting a lot of pressure on me to give it up." The light had gone out of Emily's eyes, replaced by a look of nervous misgiving.

"That's amazing! What an incredible opportunity. Plus, it's a week in the California sun. Nothing bad about that! In fact..."

Liz looked mischievously at Emily.

"What?" Emily said, smiling in a questioning way at her friend, who was obviously scheming something.

"Well, I didn't tell you, but I quit my job."

"What?" Emily said in horror.

"No, it's fine. They were a bunch of assholes, and I was sick of their macho crap. Then a couple of weeks ago an old colleague reached out to me on LinkedIn. She's started her own recruitment firm, and she asked me if I wanted to join. There are four partners, all women, and they're amazing. They want me to head up some of their biggest accounts, and there's the opportunity to become a partner in a year or so. My old firm was super pissed and played the 'non-compete' card, so now I'm on gardening leave for three months until the agreement expires. Anyway, I'm thinking..." Liz wiggled her eyebrows up and down like an old-time comic.

"What?" Emily was lost.

"Oh, for Gods' sake, woman, learn to take a hint. I'm asking if I can tag along with you to LA?"

Emily leapt off her chair and screamed so loudly that Liz covered her ears.

"Oh Liz! That would be amazing! We can all spend time together. It'll be so fun!" Emily said, the tears welling up in her eyes.

Ed stepped into the kitchen. "You OK, ladies?" he asked in an amused tone.

The old friends laughed and explained their plan, and Ed wished them bon voyage.

Emily grabbed her phone and messaged Chrissy, who was ecstatic when she heard they would both be coming.

Emily beamed at Liz and hugged her.

She smiled and said, "We've got Rachel to thank for this. If it wasn't for her, we would still be strangers. It's so sad that she's gone, but she's left us a beautiful gift." Liz nodded and squeezed Emily's hand.

26

Xander
Thursday, June 27th - London

As the early morning sun streaked its golden beams through the blinds, Liz turned over to look at Xander's face. He was so peaceful. And so unbearably handsome.

Thick, espresso hair, tousled and wavy, framed his face like gentle ripples in a pool. His skin was clear and bright with an olive tint that would turn to a dark, rich honey in the summer months. Heavy brows that held the hint of a frown, as if he were puzzling something over in his faraway dreams. His lips, full and soft and kissable.

Here she was again, in his bed. In what used to be *their* bed.

Two weeks ago she had come here from her parents' house. She had been raw and vulnerable, and she'd fled to his arms. She needed to be held and loved. They made angry, desperate love. And then later, they made soft, gentle love. Xander had asked her to stay, but she had said no. She wasn't ready, and she'd caught a cab home in the early dawn.

Last Sunday, she'd texted Xander to tell him about her LA

plans. She didn't know why, but she wanted to share it with him. He'd begged her to come over and talk. She had agreed.

He'd made dinner, a delicious lasagna, and they drank wine and talked. She'd told him about Lauren and Naomi and Bibi, and he'd listened, patient and open, with no sign of judgement or defensiveness. That was a good sign, right? They had shared work stories and laughed, and later they had made love.

She had stayed over.

And now here she was again, watching him sleep.

She brushed a strand of hair from his face and he opened his dark eyes, smiling at her with his perfect white smile as he stretched languidly.

"Good morning, gorgeous," he whispered, as he lent in and kissed her.

Electric ripples ran up Liz's spine, and she shivered with arousal.

"Good morning to you, too," she smiled and pushed him.

"You want breakfast?" he asked.

"Maybe just a coffee. I'm going to jump in the shower first though, if that's ok?"

"Sure," Xander replied, reaching out to grab her hand and kiss it as she walked past him into the bathroom.

Liz wound her hair up into a high bun as she walked into the kitchen, kissing Xander on the neck as he plunged the French press. The room was full of the smell of rich, dark coffee, and she was content.

She jumped up to sit on the countertop as she had so many times before. It was strange to be falling back into comfortable habits in Xander's apartment, and she was cautiously optimistic about what this could mean for them.

He came over to her, and with his hands on her knees, he parted her legs and stepped in. She felt the heat rise, and she saw the look of hunger in his eyes.

"No way! I've only just had a shower, and anyway I have things I need to do today!" she laughed and pushed him away.

"I can't help it. I've missed you so much."

The smile dropped from Xander's face, and his brows furrowed.

"Seriously, baby, I can't tell you how much I missed you."

He looked serious now. It was so uncharacteristic for this charming playboy that Liz cleared her throat and shifted her weight a little, on edge for what might come next.

"What?" she said as he looked at her. He stared into her eyes, his expression so intent and searching that she felt exposed, naked in a way she'd never been with Xander, or with anyone.

"I've had a lot of time to think about this, Liz, and I think we should get married."

Liz stared at him, her eyes wide.

"I've never treated you the way you deserved, and when you left, it made me realize how much I love you. You know me - I've never been serious about anything in my life. I've charmed and bullshitted my way through, because I was too scared to get hurt. But I'm not scared anymore. I know what I want, and I want you. I want to get married."

Silence.

Xander reached for the French press and topped up both their coffee cups.

"We'll have to do it in Spetses though, I know my entire family will *insist* on being there. There's a little church in the center of town where my parents got married. It was built in the 1800s and it's stunning. My cousin got married there, and the bride arrived in a horse-drawn carriage. You need to be Greek Orthodox to get married there though, so you'll need to be baptized beforehand. Just go with it, they won't expect you to go again after the wedding, and it'll mean we can get some amazing photographs at the church."

He looked at Liz, waiting for a reaction.

When he got none, he continued.

"Or, we don't have to do the whole traditional wedding thing, if you don't want to? I suppose that isn't our style after all. We could do it on the beach? My uncle will manage the catering for us. He's a well-known chef, and his almond sweets are famous all over the island." Xander flashed Liz one of his trademark killer smiles.

The smile faded.

"Liz? Say something."

But Liz was in a fog. She couldn't think straight. This was everything she had wanted, secretly hoped and planned for, although she would never had admitted it to anyone.

She had yearned to be embraced by Xander's family. To be enveloped in their love and warmth, their joy and revelry. So why the hesitation? Why was she stalling?

"Well?" Xander said, a shadow of concern passing over his face.

Liz tried to reach for the words. Tried to form a response.

"OK, this isn't exactly the reaction I was expecting, Liz," said Xander, his voice short and cold.

"Sorry. It's just, sort of unexpected." Liz stuttered.

"Apparently," he said in an acerbic tone, turning his back on her to clear away the breakfast dishes.

"What about Lauren and Naomi?" she asked, not knowing where the question had come from.

Xander's back stiffened. "What do you mean, 'what about them'?"

"Well, if we got married, would they come to the wedding? Would they be part of our lives?"

Xander turned to look at Liz.

"Look, baby. It's sweet that you've been helping them out. You're a good person and you've got a lot of heart, that's one of the many things I love about you. But it wouldn't be appropriate to have them in our lives long term. What's the saying again? *'you can volunteer at the shelter, but you don't bring home the strays,'* if you know what I mean?"

Liz felt a cold stab in her chest.

"Lauren and Naomi aren't stray dogs, Xander. Naomi is your daughter."

"Yes, well, we all make mistakes. How about this, I'll set up a direct deposit into Lauren's bank account to help her out? Deal?"

"So, they wouldn't come to the wedding?"

"God, no, Liz. What are you thinking!" Xander said with a snort of derision. "Imagine having to explain that to everyone. The little cockney flower girl, living proof of the groom's one-night stand with the office slut. No, Liz, be sensible." Xander flashed her a look of impatience mixed with condescension.

Another silence.

Liz slipped down off the counter and walked to the bedroom.

She gathered her things.

"What are you doing?" Xander said, following her with alarm in his voice. "OK, I'm sorry. I know you're fond of them and I shouldn't have said that, but I'm thinking about our future. Liz. Liz! Stop! Just talk to me!"

He grabbed her, spinning her round. His face hard, and his muscles taught.

He held her arm tightly, his fingers digging into her skin.

She ripped herself away from him.

Liz turned to look at him, anger and defiance rushing through her body. Then her shoulders dropped, and she bent to pick up her purse. As she stood straight again, she looked at him, her eyes filled with sadness and resignation.

"I loved you, Xander. I really did. I thought we could make

it work. Even after I found out about Lauren, I hoped there might be a chance for us. A way we could all be happy. But this isn't going to work. I'm sorry."

Liz walked towards the front door.

"So that's it? What the fuck, Liz? What the fuck do you want from me? I'm giving you *everything* you ever fucking wanted and *still* you're not happy! I don't understand this obsession with Lauren and her kid. Why is it so fucking important to you? They're nothing to you. Two months ago you didn't even know they existed, and now they have to come to our wedding? I don't understand why you're jeopardizing *everything* for them. How long will this '*friendship*' even last? You've got nothing in common and pretty soon the shine will rub off on this whole 'Good Samaritan' act, especially when she starts asking for money, *which she will do*. And when you're looking like an idiot, realizing you've been played, you're going to feel pretty bloody stupid that you threw all of this away, aren't you? But by then it'll be too late."

"Goodbye, Xander."

"No, Liz. Wait," he said, blocking the front door, his hand on the handle. "Listen, I'm sorry. I'm just confused. I thought you wanted to get married. I *want* to marry you, Liz. Come on, I put myself out there, and you threw it back in my face. I'm just trying to understand. I promise, we can make this work."

Liz sighed.

"Please, Xander, let me leave."

"OK, but can we at least agree to talk about it when you get back from LA? You can take some time to think everything over and decide what you want to do, then we'll talk when you get back, agreed? I can see how much you care about these girls. Maybe we can find a way to make it all work out?" He flashed a smile.

173

Liz raised her eyes to heaven. "Fine. But let me go now."

Xander stepped aside and opened the door for Liz.

As she walked past, he whispered, "I love you, Liz. You believe me, don't you?"

The morning air hit her like a spray of sea foam, cold and refreshing.

She breathed long, shaky breaths as she tried to process what had happened.

The streets were humming with commuters, heading off for another day of corporate productivity. She stood like a spirit out of time, no longer belonging to this reality. She was both visible and invisible, inconsequential to all these busy worker bees that surrounded her.

She ordered an Uber and rode in silence back to her short-term rental apartment.

She put the key in the lock, turned it, and shut the door behind her.

She dropped her purse on the floor and walked to the bedroom.

She sat on the end of the bed and listened to the sound of distant activity. So many people living so many lives.

Then she began to sob.

27

Pasadena
Sunday, June 30th - Pasadena

Chrissy was awake and busying herself downstairs in the kitchen while the others slept upstairs. The morning sun streamed through the windows, and she was joyous. The coffee was brewing, and she'd asked Alexa to play music by 'Palace Winter' as she squeezed fresh orange juice and sliced strawberries. The soft melodies mingled with the rich coffee aroma, filling Chrissy's whole being with happiness.

Yesterday had been wonderful, and she smiled with contentment, thinking of her friends sleeping in the guest room above her.

She had picked them up from LAX, her arms full of sunflowers and her heart full of love. Although they had been weary from their flight, they had laughed and hugged her as she leapt on them with squeals and kisses.

That night they had sat in the Adirondack chairs on her manicured front lawn, sipping G&T's and marveling at the views.

Chrissy's house sat on a private road, the other side of

which plunged down into a steep gorge. Below them and beyond the gorge rolled the immaculate greens of Brookside golf course, and ahead of them, a stunning, unimpeded view of the San Gabriel Mountains.

They chatted and laughed, and then fell quiet as they watched the sunset paint the mountains pink, orange and red. The visitors whispered that it was one of the most beautiful things they had ever seen, and she'd loved them all the more for it.

Today they were venturing out into Pasadena, and Chrissy was giddy with excitement at the prospect of showing them around.

"Good morning," said a sleepy voice from the kitchen doorway, and Chrissy looked up to see a ruffled Liz, scratching her head and yawning.

"Morning! You want some coffee?"

"Yes, please. And stop being so cheery," Liz replied with a grin.

"You sleep ok?" Chrissy asked, handing her a steaming mug.

"Oh, yes! That bed is amazing, and there's plenty of room for both of us," Liz replied as she put the mug on the table in the breakfast nook and dropped herself into a chair.

"You guys are such good sports to share a bed. I'm just sorry that we've only got one guest room."

"Not at all! It's so much nicer to be staying here than in a hotel, plus it's kinda like the good old days at school when we all crashed together to save money. Thanks again for putting us up while we're here."

"No, it's wonderful! It's so amazing to have you here, and it was perfectly timed with Scott and the kids still up in Ferndale with his parents." Chrissy looked around her kitchen as a brief stab of discomfort touched her heart. "It's weird to think that everything will be packed away in storage next week."

"So, where are you taking us today?" asked Liz with a smile.

"Well, I thought we'd just hang out in Pasadena if that's OK? I'd love to show you around some more." Chrissy sat down opposite Liz, beaming. "I've cut up some fresh fruit to tide us over, and then we can go for brunch later. There's a place in town called Marston's that serves the *best* breakfasts. It's in a cute little converted cottage, and they make the most delicious French toast. They also do macadamia nut pancakes, and omelettes, and huevos rancheros, all sorts of things. And after we've eaten we can just wander around a bit and see where the day takes us, if that works for you guys?"

"Sounds great to me," said Liz, leaning back and stretching like a cat.

"Should we wake Emily?" asked Chrissy.

"Oh, she's up already and making herself look gorgeous. I swear, this new haircut has turned her into a whole new woman." Liz snorted with amusement.

"She looks amazing! I would never have thought a simple cut and color could make *that* much difference!" Chrissy said. "She's even holding herself differently now. She looks so gorgeous and confident."

"Our little girl is growing up," Liz said, putting her hand to her forehead and clutching at her breast.

Chrissy tutted and swatted at her through the air. "I'm just saying that I'm glad she's feeling so good about herself. It's about time."

"What's about time?" asked a voice from the doorway, and there stood Emily, looking radiant.

"We were just saying how much we love your new haircut," smiled Chrissy, standing up and walking to the coffeepot. "Want some?"

"Ooh, yes please!" said Emily, touching her beautifully bobbed hair. "And thank you, it's a big change I know, but I love it."

"The color is wonderful. It's such a rich auburn, and it brings out your freckles. And the length really suits you." Chrissy said. "Seriously, I couldn't believe it when I saw you at arrivals on Saturday. You looked like a different person!"

"Oh, stop" Emily said, beaming. "It's only a new haircut." She batted away the compliments, but secretly she was thrilled that her efforts had been so enthusiastically received.

"Yup, you scrub up well, old girl," said Liz, winking. "Here's to hairdressers, and all they do for us." She raised her coffee cup, and the others followed suit.

"So what's the plan, Chrissy? I can't wait to see Pasadena. I'm so excited I could burst!" Emily squeaked and released a peel of tiny claps.

"Oh God help me, now there's two of you," bemoaned Liz, raising her eyes to heaven and giving them a sideways grin.

*****

Before long, they had set off on an adventure of Chrissy's design.

First she drove them along the edge of the Arroyo Seco, with its secret dappled groves of oak trees, whispering a promise of cool and shaded paths.

Then they drove under the elegant sand colored arches of the Colorado Street Bridge, architecture better suited to a grand cathedral than a simple thoroughfare.

"The locals call it 'suicide bridge' because of all the people that jumped to their deaths during the Great Depression," Chrissy explained. "It's over 100 feet from the bridge into the river bed, which is normally dry. It's a sad history, but the bridge itself is beautiful, especially at night when the lamps light up all along it, twinkling like fairy-lights."

They wound their way through Pasadena, driving past the grand mansions near the Langham Hotel with their stately front lawns and immaculate hedges. They marveled at the size of the homes, and each of them picked out their dream house, only to change their mind again and again as they saw even more beautiful properties around each corner.

Chrissy drove past the famous Gamble House and explained the Greene & Greene architectural style of Craftsman homes for which Pasadena was so well known.

"So your house is a Craftsman then?" Emily asked.

"Yes. Well, it's in that style at least. Although the inside is far too modern to be considered a true Craftsman," Chrissy replied.

"Ed would love these Craftsman homes," Emily pondered out loud. "He's always gravitated to the comfortable cottage style, with lots of wood and stone. I think that's why he loves our house so much."

"Oh, in that case you *have* to see this!" Chrissy said with enthusiasm, and proceeded to drive them through the Pasadena district known as Bungalow Heaven.

They exclaimed in delight as they drove past the rows of charming 19th century Craftsman cottages, each different in its own way, some with tended roses in their front yards, others with orange trees, and others still with bikes, wagons and sneakers scattered on their front porches. It had a safe, all-American neighborhood feel that reminded the visitors of TV shows they had watched growing up.

"Ha," Liz said, "This whole place looks like the set from The Wonder Years. It's weird, I kinda feel like I've been here before."

Chrissy laughed. "Well, they've filmed so many shows and movies here that it does kinda feel that way. I'll do you a

'Hollywood style' tour sometime, if you want? But not right now, I'm starving! Let's go eat."

Marston's did not disappoint, and they tucked into a delicious array of pancakes, French toast, eggs and muffins.

Sated and content, they rolled out of the little restaurant and into the glorious heat of the early Pasadena afternoon.

Walking down Raymond Avenue, Liz and Emily admired the beautiful 1920s buildings. A mixture of white plaster and red brick, Art Deco and Spanish Colonial styles stood shoulder to shoulder, loved and preserved, clean and fresh.

As they walked past a lush green park studded with palm trees, Chrissy stopped to point out the city hall. Its crisp white columns and graceful red domed roof stood in stark contrast against the azure blue sky, giving it a Mediterranean feel.

"Everything is so beautiful," said Liz in a hushed tone.

"And everything smells so delicious. Like roses, and jasmine, and fresh bread," said Emily, inhaling. Savoring the moment.

They spent the next couple of hours wandering in and out of the little stores of Old Town Pasadena. Boutique clothing stores with soft flowing natural fabrics, and stores with delicious smelling beauty products. Smiling faces and warm greetings came from staff and customers alike. They tried on dresses and breathed in the scent of hand lotion. They laughed and teased and admired each other in equal measure.

As the sun dipped below the horizon, bathing everything in its warm golden glow, they realized how hungry they were.

Liz sighed and said, "Well, this has been amazing, but I'm ready for a drink and some food. Who's with me?"

The others agreed, and Chrissy suggested a casually elegant restaurant not far from where they were.

As they walked and chatted and laughed, a deep contentment filled her to the brim. This truly was her happy place, and this moment could not have been more perfect.

28

Cocktails
Sunday, June 30th - Pasadena

Bathed in the early evening light, they ordered cocktails; a Mojito for Emily, a Dark and Stormy for Chrissy, and a Martini for Liz. They raised their glasses and toasted to friendship, smiling and sitting back into their modern wicker chairs to admire their stylish surroundings.

The outdoor patio was exquisitely decorated, a perfect balance of neo-deco suave, and adobe comfort. The ocher walls and heavy brass fittings created a warm, welcoming ambience, while the fairy lights and rhythmic splashing of the clay fountains brought a cool relief to an otherwise warm evening.

"This has been an incredible day. Thank you so much, Chrissy," Emily said, reaching across the table and squeezing Chrissy's hand.

"We haven't really done much, but it's been so nice just to hang out with you guys," replied Chrissy, smiling at her friends. "It's so lovely to have everyone back together. Well, almost everyone."

Her face dropped, and a sadness passed over her. The others sensed it too, and for a moment there was silence as they each thought of Rachel.

"Why do you think she did it?" asked Emily, breaking the silence. "I mean, I know she suffered from depression, but why that night? What was it that finally pushed her over the edge? Oh God, what an awful choice of words, sorry." She flushed.

Liz sighed. "Well, she was on her way to that award ceremony, wasn't she? Maybe it was all too much? She never liked the spotlight after all."

Chrissy shifted in her chair. "But why kill herself? I don't understand. Maybe I won't ever be able to truly understand, but I feel like I need to try."

Emily sat forward and placed her drink on the table.

"I worry she could never really be herself. To freely speak her mind. I wonder if anyone ever truly listened to her. I know we didn't, we'd have to admit that if we were being brutally honest. We were all too busy, too wrapped up in our own teenage dramas. We never took the time to sit with her and properly listen."

"I'm not sure that would have made a difference, though," interjected Liz. "Clinical depression is a chemical imbalance, you can't fix it by lending a sympathetic ear."

"But did we try?" Emily asked pointedly. "Did we ever give her the airtime she needed to share her feelings? Her parents sure as hell never did. It made them uncomfortable, so they never wanted to hear it. I remember them saying that they 'didn't want to indulge her melancholy tendencies'. They assumed it was just teenage angst, and that it would pass. Maybe that's why she turned to photography? It gave her a way to express herself when no one else would listen. Maybe if we'd listened more..." Emily gave a short, ragged sigh.

After a moment, Liz said, "Actually, you're right, Emily. If I'm honest, I never wanted to hear what she had to say. On the rare occasions when I opened myself up, it was so sad it felt like I was being sucked down into blackness. Like I was suffocating, listening to her soft voice. It was like she was a siren, leading you down and down, and all I wanted to do is to kick and scratch and claw my way back to the light and the air. But she lived down there, in the blackness. How did she stand it? I felt awful for her, but at the same time, I couldn't bear to join her, even for a couple of minutes. Maybe it would be different now that I'm older, but as a teenager it was just too much."

"It wasn't always like that, though. She could be fun too." Chrissy broke in. "I remember she had a wicked sense of humor, and she would laugh along with the rest of us. She was so clever, she made connections that one one else could see. Her humor was playful, but also surprisingly caustic. She was hilarious."

Emily's eyes brightened.

"You're right! And she did the *best* impressions of people. They were uncanny. Do you remember her impression of that creepy old history teacher with the protruding blue lips? She nailed him so well we'd all be crying with laughter."

"God, yes! I'd forgotten that," Liz exclaimed. "And she could do the lead singer of that boy band too, remember? The one that Emily insisted she was going to marry? She had him down to a tee, and it made you furious."

Emily stuck out her tongue at Liz, saying with a giggle, "Well, you were going to marry Jon Bon Jovi if I remember correctly. How's that going?"

"He doesn't know what he's missing," Liz said with a grin.

Chrissy snorted with laughter. "I can't believe we were the generation of permed hair and Walkmans. I remember spending an entire year trying to look like Blossom. I had the hat, the vests, everything. My kids can't even imagine that far back, but in some ways it doesn't seem all that long ago, does it?"

They all chuckled at the memory.

"Wow, we were all so different back then, weren't we?" Chrissy said.

"Oh, I don't know," said Emily. "Liz is pretty much the same. You even look the same, and for that I am jealous," she said with a playful swat.

Liz sighed. "Nope, I'm definitely older and wiser. Well, older anyway. All that black and white clarity has faded to shades of gray. I thought I knew it all then. Now I feel like I don't know anything for certain."

Chrissy's brow furrowed. "Yikes Liz, for real? What's going on?"

As they ate their entrees, Liz updated Chrissy on everything that had happened over the last couple of months. She shared photos of Lauren and Noemi and told her about the encounter with her mother.

Then she admitted to the others that she had continued to see Xander. Finally, she told them about his proposal and how it had ended.

"Oh wow. So you said no, I'm assuming?" Emily asked.

"Yes. I mean, yes, I said no. Well, I kind of said no. Of course it's a no, after what he said about Lauren and Naomi, it would have to be."

Emily frowned. "No offense Liz, but I don't think much of him, he sounds like a first class asshole."

"He is a *total* asshole. I'm in full agreement there!" Liz said, draining her wine. "Who's up for Irish coffees for desert?"

After coffees had been ordered, Liz turned to Chrissy and said, "Emily told me what happened with Josh. I'm so sorry. She said that you were considering leaving Pasadena?"

Chrissy sighed heavily. "Yeah, it's been a tough couple of

months, but now we have a good path ahead of us. We'll make it work. We're a strong family, and Josh is a resilient kid. It scares me, though, that I had no idea. I suppose we never really know what's going on with our kids once they get to a certain age. All we can do is love them and listen to them. I think that's what I learned from what happened to poor Rachel."

They sat, staring at their coffees, thinking of their absent friend.

Liz broke the silence.

"Well, we can't change the past, and I know Rachel wouldn't want us to beat ourself up like this. I miss her too, but we all choose our path in life, so what would she want for us? If she could speak to us now, what would say? She'd tell us to be honest with ourselves and be brave enough to be who we want to be. Let's not pity her, or question what we should have done differently. Let's see her as our guardian angel, here to help us through these tough times, and come out stronger on the other side."

They smiled at each other, tears in their eyes.

Liz held her glass high and said, "To Rachel"

"To Rachel" echoed the others, and they clinked their glasses as the stars and the fairy-lights flickered overhead.

29

"OK, it should be just here on the left," Chrissy said, squinting at the GPS. "Here we are. Yikes, Emily! This is super fancy!"

Chrissy signaled and swung the car into the drive-through valet parking at the front of the building.

"Oh God, I'm so nervous," said Emily, staring up at the sleek building with its angular gray metal and glass. It was modern and minimalist and screamed opulence, a reflection of its tenants; Apex was one of the most successful venture capital firms outside of the Bay Area.

Liz leaned forward from the backseat of the car and put her hand on Emily's shoulder.

"You got this. You look amazing, you bloody *are* amazing, and they'll be lucky to have you. Go get 'em girl," she said with a warm, encouraging smile to her precious friend.

"OK," Emily said, looking at her watch and trying to control her jitters. "It's 10.45am, and they said to be here at 11am, so I'm good. Kolleen said that we should be done by

3pm, so shall I meet you here just after 3?"

Chrissy put a hand on Emily's knee and said, "Don't worry, we'll be here. And if you're running late just call me OK? We're totally flexible, aren't we Liz," and the two smiled at each other, and then back at Emily.

A man's head appeared in Chrissy's window. "Hi ma'am, do you need valet?"

"No, we're just dropping off. Thanks though," she said, smiling and turning to Emily, shooing her out of the car. "Now go and have an amazing time. We can't wait to hear all about it."

Emily jumped out of the car, smoothed her charcoal gray pantsuit and nervously touched her perfectly styled hair. She looked both elegant and apprehensive, and her friends loved her all the more for it. Liz slipped out of the backseat and into the vacated passenger seat.

They watched as Emily walk in through the automatic glass doors, then they pulled away, rejoining the busy Santa Monica traffic.

"OK," said Chrissy. "We have four hours to kill. You wanna grab an early lunch somewhere?"

"Sounds good to me," replied Liz, stretching out her long legs. "Although now I wish you had a convertible so I could stand up and wave my hands in the air as we drive down all these palm-tree lined roads, I'm digging the movie vibe right now," she grinned at Chrissy, pursing her lips and looking over the top of her sunglasses.

"You're such a goofball," said Chrissy, laughing at her. "So. Back to food. There's a place close by called Lunetta, it does all day breakfasts but they also have burgers and salads, so a good range of options."

"Sounds great," said Liz, beaming.

They opted for a table indoors, the A/C offering a cool respite from the California sun that was already baking the beaches and sidewalks outside.

As they settled themselves at the table, the server, a skinny tan girl in her twenties with a sun-bleached messy pixie cut and arm tattoos, sidled up and asked them if they would like to order drinks.

"They do a delicious watermelon mimosa if you want to try?" Chrissy asked Liz. "It's so refreshing."

"Sure, why not? When in Rome, eh?" Liz said, grinning at the server.

"No problem," said the server with disinterest. Liz watched her as she walked away.

"Do you ever feel old, Chrissy?"

"All the bloody time! Why?"

"It's stuff like that. That girl. She's probably only 20 years younger than me, but it's like she doesn't even *see* me. Like I'm an old lady or something, or a different species she couldn't possibly have anything in common with."

"I know. I remember my mum saying that it's only the outer shell that gets older, while you stay the same on the inside. And yet it's the shell that everyone sees and judges you by. She said she couldn't wait until we all turn into astral beings, so women could stop worrying about wrinkles and cellulite."

"Your mum is the best," said Liz, laughing. "How is she?"

"Fine, as far as I'm aware. I haven't spoken to her since I was in England in April. She seemed pretty happy on her narrow boat. She told me she was considering getting a cat until I pointed out that it might fall overboard and drown. Apparently she hadn't thought of that." Chrissy raised an eyebrow and shook her head.

"Didn't you have a cat once?"

"Yeah. Bathsheba. She was cute. She ran away, though. Mum said that maybe she felt she 'belonged somewhere else,' and she had gone to find that place. I think it's more likely that she found someone who would remember to feed her regularly," she said with a look of amused resignation. "Anyway, does your mum know you split up with Xander?"

"Oh bloody hell, I don't want to talk about that woman," said Liz, looking thunderous.

The moment was saved by the arrival of the drinks, and having glanced over the menu they ordered a light lunch, avocado on toast for Chrissy and lox on a bagel for Liz.

"So, what did she say when you told her?" Chrissy asked.

"Told who, what?" Liz looked confused.

"When you told your mum about you and Xander splitting up."

"Oh, I haven't told her,"

"Really? How come?"

"Well, I wasn't sure that it was over until last Thursday, and we flew out here on Saturday so there wasn't much time to share the 'good news' that my ex-lover, almost-fiancé, was an arrogant, cheating bastard"

"Are you sure, though?" Chrissy asked with a weighted expression.

"What do you mean?" Liz asked, a knot in her stomach.

"Are you sure it's over with Xander?"

There was an awkward silence.

"I'm only asking because everyone has their faults. Are you sure this is a game changer?"

"Could *you* marry someone like that?" Liz asked with venom, her jaw tightening.

"This isn't about me though, Liz. I'm not suggesting that what he did was OK, I'm just asking the question. Are you sure, deep down positive, that you won't be back in his apartment again when you get back to London?"

Liz realized, with horror, that she couldn't decisively answer that question. How could she still have doubts about this after what he had said about Lauren and Naomi? Did she still love him? Or worse, at some level, did she *condone* what he had said.

"Holy shit, Chrissy. Maybe I'm my mother's child after all."

Liz looked distraught, and Chrissy reached across the table to squeeze her hand.

"Liz, you are one of the most ethical, loyal people I have ever met. You are incredible and you should never question that. It's an honor to have you as a friend."

Liz looked up, tears in her eyes, questioning and pleading and more vulnerable than Chrissy had ever seen her. It made Chrissy's heart break.

"I love you Liz, I really do," she said, holding tightly to her dear friend's hand.

Liz wiped her eyes and shook off the weight of the moment.

"Well, that was embarrassing. I think I'll have a large glass of Chardonnay."

As they tucked into their fresh, delicious food, they chatted about the last couple of days and how lovely it was to be back together.

"So, you're definitely moving away from Pasadena?" Liz asked. "You seem to love it so much."

"Yes, I honestly do. But we need a fresh start, and Ferndale is a wonderful little town, safe and friendly, with a close-knit community." Chrissy smiled.

"Is this so you can keep a closer eye on Josh?"

Chrissy's smile faded.

"Partly. I mean, I'm not worried that he'd do anything like that again, but I am hoping that being in a small town will be better for him." Chrissy looked uncomfortable.

"Did you talk to him about why he did it?"

"No. He doesn't want to discuss it. He admits he made a mistake, and says that he wouldn't do it again, but that's all he'll say. He's still pretty ashamed of the whole thing."

"Do you think he was taking drugs himself?"

Chrissy looked troubled.

"I don't think so, but I can't be certain. I mean, if he was selling them, then possibly," she grimaced.

"I can't believe how the mothers at the school treated you. That was unforgivable." Liz looked thunderous.

"I know. But looking back on it, I'm not all that surprised. Scott was right, they're just snobs. It was all about appearance with them. I should have known better to think they were truly my friends."

"And you're hoping that the parents in Ferndale will be nicer?"

"Oh, I'm sure they will! They're all farmers and teachers and vets, so a down-to-earth bunch of folk. No airs and graces like these Pasadena moms."

"But I'm sure there are some down-to-earth people in Pasadena too, no?"

Chrissy's face fell.

"Well, I'm sure there must be. But they don't send their children to that school, that's for damn sure! Anyway," she said, waving to the server and signaling for the check, "do you want to take a stroll down the promenade before we pick up Emily? It's fantastic for people-watching." She said, grinning at Liz.

"Alright, let's go" Liz smiled back at her.

Dodging bicycles and tiny dogs on leashes, they walked through the 3rd street promenade. They stopped to listen to the musicians playing old Sinatra songs. They commented on the immaculate topiary and the cooling fountains. Then they watched a couple of elegant ladies drinking champagne on the outdoor patio areas of a chic restaurant, whilst a homeless guy slept on a bench opposite them.

People lounged in chairs under cheerful, primary-colored

umbrellas, looking at their phones or reading books. The place had a relaxed yet humming atmosphere.

"How come there are so many people around on a Monday? Doesn't anybody work in LA?" Liz asked, bemused.

Chrissy laughed and bumped her friend's arm.

"This is La La Land. People work 'differently' here," she said with a sideways grin.

Soon it was time to head back to the elegant Apex offices. As they pulled up in front of the building, they spied a radiant looking Emily, and next to her a tall, tan, blonde man in his mid-thirties.

"Ooh, Yum! Who's the hot surfer dude?" Liz asked, raising one eyebrow and looking him up and down.

"Liz!" said Chrissy. "You're right though, he is cute."

They both walked up to the car, and Emily beckoned to them.

"Hi you guys!" she said, beaming. "I wanted you to meet Brody. Brody, this is Liz and Chrissy," she said, gesturing to each of them. "And this is Brody. He's the founder of Apex."

Brody smiled a wide white smile and held out his toned arm to shake their hands.

"It's a pleasure to meet both of you. Emily has told me all about you. She's lucky to have such fantastic friends." He spoke in a casually confident tone, his California accent soft and lilting as he shook each of their hands in turn. He looked at each of them with his clear blue eyes, his gaze so deep that it made each of them blush.

"Brody is the founder of the company. He went to MIT and then worked for Accenture in San Francisco before coming back here to start a VC firm. He's my new boss!"

Brody smiled down at Emily and winked at her conspiratorially.

"I'm a Santa Monica boy, born and bred. I wouldn't want

to live anywhere else for long, I love it here too much."

"Well, it's a pleasure to meet you, Brody. I should move the car now though, as this is a valet parking lane." Chrissy said, smiling, her eyes shining.

"Oh yeah, of course. I hope I'll have the pleasure again soon? You need to come back and visit Chrissy, as you're only in Pasadena. And Liz, safe flight on Saturday, and take care of my girl here, OK?" he smiled at each of them, and then at Emily, who looked transcendent.

"Keep in touch, OK? And call me if you have questions, or need anything at all," he said to Emily, and she nodded, beaming.

They took their places in the car, and as they pulled away, Emily waved goodbye to Brody before collapsing with a dramatic, happy sigh.

"So, Brody, eh?" Liz asked with a raised eyebrow.

"I know! He's amazing, isn't he? He's so intelligent, but humble with it, and he has a pin-sharp business sense. He's been so insanely successful, but he's still such a nice guy. He told me he goes surfing every morning before coming to work to 'remind him what's really important'. Wow, it's going to be crazy to work for him."

"Mm-hmm," said Chrissy with a sideways glance at Liz. "Well, do you want to go and look at a couple of these rental apartments now before we grab some dinner?"

"Oh God, no!" said Emily, beaming. "I'm way too hyped up for that. All I want to do is drink a cocktail and tell you guys everything that happened."

"Now you're talking!" Liz said from the backseat. "Let's get cocktails!"

Chrissy swung the car around.

"OK," she said, "Let's drop our stuff at the hotel and then I know just the place we can go."

30

Sunset
Monday, July 1st - Santa Monica

"I'm going to have a 'London Calling'. It sounds delicious, and its too ironic not to get it," Liz said as they perused the cocktail menu while perching on stools at the rooftop bar.

ONYX had a reputation for delicious cocktails and stunning views of the ocean, and Chrissy had been waiting for an excuse to check it out for a while now.

Emily sipped her 'Berry Mojito' and sighed with contentment as she looked towards the big wheel turning on the Santa Monica pier and the glittering Pacific Ocean beyond it. It had been an amazing day.

"So, so? Tell us all about it!" said Chrissy, stirring her 'Purple Haze.'

"Let's sit over on those couches. That way I can see you better," Emily said, jumping off her stool and selecting a suitable spot to sit.

"OK," she began, "So I waited in reception for about ten minutes for Kolleen. The place is amazing, but it's very young and hip and I felt a bit uncomfortable at first. Kolleen

195

was lovely though, and she put me at ease. We went into this huge meeting room with glass walls. It was like being a fish in a tank! The other partners came in and introduced themselves. They were all very young and tanned and athletic, you know what I mean? I felt kinda awkward and out of place. But then Kolleen came back with Brody and he was so warm and welcoming. He offered me a coffee, and I said yes. We chatted a bit about what I'd been doing with you guys this week, and I felt much more relaxed. Once everyone had arrived, they showed me a presentation about the goals of the firm, and their strategy for funding startups. They explained that ordinarily a new business venture would have to present their ideas to the partners, and they would decide whether or not to fund it. This venture is different though because in this case they know they want to invest in the business, they just need to find the expertise to get it right."

"And that's where you come in?" asked Liz, fascinated by this area of business she had not been exposed to before.

"Exactly! They asked me to talk them through how I had grown my business and how I source product. Then they asked how I would scale it into a sizable business, for example how I would go about setting up manufacturing and distribution channels. I was surprised because I knew the answers to all their questions. I must have been planning this in my head for a long time without even realizing it. Before I knew it, I was up at the whiteboard drawing out flowcharts and talking about quality control."

Liz and Chrissy both laughed with pride.

"What?" said Emily, confused.

"Well, you were always totally kick-ass at this type of thing. Remember, in business studies class? You *killed* at stuff like this," said Chrissy with a grin.

"Yeah, I suppose I did. And I studied manufacturing processes as part of my corporate law degree. It's been so long since I've done anything like this that I'd forgotten."

"You guys want to order some nibbles?" Chrissy asked, standing up. "This cocktail is going straight to my head."

The appetizers arrived, and as they tucked into the hummus and pita bread, Emily continued.

"Then we went to grab lunch at this little Italian place called Heroic Deli. They do the *best* sandwiches. Brody suggested the OMG, and it was delicious. It was huge, stuffed full of loads of different Italian meats and mayo and mustard and truffles. Mmm, it's making my mouth water thinking about it," she said, leaning forward to grab another piece of pita. "It was so nice to just hang out with Brody and Kolleen and a couple of the junior associates that will be helping me with the setup. I kind of already feel at home with them, even though we're so different."

"Have you tied down salary yet?" asked Liz, ever the pragmatist.

Emily blushed. "Well yes, we did talk about that."

"And? Are they offering you enough?"

"Actually, the package is way better than I thought it would be. The base is substantially higher than I'd expected, and I'll also get medical and dental and a bunch of other benefits. When I first researched the cost of living here, I had assumed that I wouldn't get benefits, so we're going to be pretty well off."

"Wow, that's great! How much are they offering? Oh sorry, you don't have to answer that, I'm so used to knowing all this stuff because of my job." Liz looked abashed.

"No, it's fine. I'm happy to tell you," replied Emily, and talked them through the package they had offered her.

"Holy shit girl! That's amazing!" said Liz, taken aback.

"I know, that's what I thought. But they seem to think it's my market worth." Emily said, looking a little embarrassed.

"Well, this calls for a celebration. Another round for the

Musketeers," said Liz.

The friends both laughed at the old reference, but Chrissy cut in.

"How about we move this party to the restaurant, that way we can settle in and enjoy the sunset?"

They agreed, and before long they were walking along the famous Santa Monica pier. They headed to the very end along the squeaky wooden planks and enjoyed a moment of reflection as they watched the surfers ride the waves in the last light of the day.

On their way back to the restaurant, Emily insisted on walking along the beach to the edge of the water.

"It was sensible of you to bring a change of clothes," said Liz as she watched Emily slip off her flip-flops and dig her toes into the hot sand.

"This is Emily we're talking about," Chrissy said. "Of *course* she planned ahead."

They laughed and, flip-flops in hand, they headed towards the surf.

They toyed with the waves, squealing with glee as the white foam chased them across the sand. Laughing and happy, they played like children as the sun turned orange, then red, before sinking below the horizon.

Sated and hungry, they headed back up the beach towards the restaurant. Emily turned to Chrissy and with wide, soulful eyes said,

"When you sent me your friend request on Facebook, I pictured your life in California, and it looked like this. It's so weird to think that this could be *my* life now as well. I never would have believed..." her voice trailed off.

"Come on ladies, I'm dying for a drink," shouted Liz, who was striding ahead with purpose.

They settled themselves at a table on the patio overlooking the ocean and ordered drinks and appetizers for the table.

"The food here looks delicious," Emily said with enthusiasm, perusing the menu. "Brody said he wants to take me to Cha Cha Chicken tomorrow for an early dinner before we leave. He says it's a Caribbean restaurant and that they have the best jerk chicken, and live salsa music so you can dance if you want to."

The others gave each other weighted looks.

"So, is this just a crush, or is it true love? You and Brody, I mean?" asked Liz, raising an eyebrow in Emily's direction.

"Oh stop. He's just a really great guy, and my boss, remember?"

"Mm-hmm, whatever you say" Liz replied, drinking her margarita primly.

Emily looked uncomfortable, so Chrissy changed the subject.

"What's your impression of Santa Monica, Emily? Can you see yourself living here?"

Emily turned gratefully to Chrissy and said, "I've been thinking about it, and I'm not sure that Santa Monica is for me. In fact, I've fallen in love with Pasadena, so I'd rather live there. Santa Monica smells like sunscreen and fumes, and everyone is so young and gorgeous, whereas Pasadena is older and more established, and smells of jasmine and freshly cut grass. It feels more like home."

"It's always smells with you, isn't it?" said Liz in a sardonic tone.

"Well, yeah - that's going to be my job after all. You gotta have a good nose when you're sourcing fresh ingredients for products."

Liz shrugged.

"Anyway," continued Emily, "I asked Brody if I would need to be in the office every day, and he said I'd only need to come into work once a week if we wanted to live further out. Would it be weird if we lived in Pasadena?" she asked

Chrissy. "That would make us neighbors, but is that too close for comfort for you?"

"Not at all! It would be amazing," said Chrissy, her heart filling with joy at the thought of having her friend so close. Then with a stab she remembered, and the smile vanished. "But we won't be in Pasadena. We'll be in Ferndale"

"Oh gosh, yes. I forgot," said Emily, her face falling. "But we could come and visit you?"

"Of course, you would always be welcome."

The entrees arrived, and they ate fresh seafood with truffle fries, and drank Chardonnay.

Liz raised her glass in a toast. "To Chrissy, for being the most amazing host. Thank you so much for making all this happen, Chrissy."

They drank, and Chrissy said, "Well, actually, I didn't make this happen. Emily made this happen with her insanely good business acumen."

They laughed, then Emily said in a serious tone. "My life is changing beyond all recognition. It's like a dream, and I'm worried that at any moment I'm going to wake up. But the catalyst for all of this is Rachel. None of this would have happened if she hadn't brought us back together."

Once again they sensed the presence of Rachel, and it stilled the mood.

"Sorry to be insensitive, but do you guys want dessert?" Chrissy asked hopefully.

They shared a cheesecake and a warm chocolate truffle cake between them, and the groans of delight made them all laugh.

As they walked back to the car, Liz stopped dead.

"Shit! I've finally worked out who Brody reminds me of!"

"What? Who?" Chrissy asked.

"Emily, remember that guy you dated in the last year of school? I think his name was Ben. *That's* who Brody reminds me of."

Emily blushed a deep scarlet.

"Oh my god, yes!" Chrissy said with amused recollection lighting up her eyes. "He was just like that, all charming and blonde and ruffled and gorgeous. God, Emily, you had it *bad* for that Ben guy, didn't you?"

Emily looked trapped and defensive. "Brody is nothing like Ben," she said in an agitated tone. "The only thing they have in common is that they both have blonde hair. Can you guys please drop the whole Brody thing, it's not funny anymore, and actually it's getting a little offensive."

She stormed down the road as Liz and Chrissy looked at each other and grinned like naughty schoolgirls.

Chrissy swatted Liz and said, "Don't laugh, OK? Because if you laugh I will too, and then it'll be a super awkward ride back to the hotel."

"We're sorry, Emily," Liz shouted after her. "Mea culpa. Please forgive us. We won't do it again," she said, winking at Chrissy. Then more quietly she said, "Wow, she's super sensitive about this isn't she, we're only joking after all."

Chrissy shrugged and linked arms with her old friend as they waited for the Uber.

31

Mounting Costs
Tuesday, July 2nd - Santa Monica

After dropping Emily to the Apex offices for her second and final day, Chrissy and Liz drove over to Santa Monica Place, a sleek, luxurious, open-air mall with high-end stores and a myriad of dining options.

As they rode the elevator down to the ground level Chrissy's phone buzzed, signaling an incoming text. She glanced down, and her brow furrowed.

"Sorry Liz, it's Bonnie. She wants to talk to me about the house in Ferndale."

"No problem at all. This place is amazing. I'm happy to just wander around and window shop. Shall I meet you back here in twenty minutes?"

"Sure."

As Liz walked away, Chrissy took a seat on a wicker chair next to a fountain and called Bonnie.

"Hi, sweetheart. Thanks for calling, I wanted to let you know that Walter and I spoke to Frank about the Rectory, and he had some interesting insights."

"Great! Sorry, who's Frank?"

"Oh, of course, I forget you haven't met everyone in town quite yet. Frank is our local contractor, and he's very knowledgeable about old houses. Walter saw him at the gas station this morning and they got to talking. Walter mentioned that you guys were considering making an offer on the Rectory, and Frank told him that Dorothy's family asked him to take a look at the place and see how much work needed to be done before they could put it on the market. Well, of course Walter knew just what to do, so he invited Frank over for lunch so we could get the inside scoop."

Chrissy chuckled. "And? What did Frank have to say about it?"

"He told us he'd poked around to see what was what, and then he'd given them some estimates."

"Did they already do the work?" Chrissy asked.

"Well, no. Frank said they've decided to sell the house 'as is'"

"Hmm. Did he tell you what the estimates were?"

"Hang on, I made notes, let me grab my notepad."

There were muffled noises before Bonnie continued.

"Ok, here we go. Frank said that the costs of the project will depend on how much of the original home you want to preserve. To give a more accurate estimate, he'd need to know if you plan to update and modernize it, or restore it to its former glory. He said the roof will need to be replaced either way, and if you want to keep the original shingle style, it'll cost upwards of $35,000. The roof will be the biggest expense. Also, you'll need to shop around to get home insurance, because a lot of companies won't cover shingle."

"Oh. Ok."

"He said that two of the fireplaces need to be relined, that'll cost about $12,000 each. The boiler system is questionable, and if you want any kind of water pressure, then you'll need new plumbing. He estimated about $15,000 for that. Also, the house has the original knob and tube wiring, so that'll all need to be pulled out and brought up to code. He said it would be best to do the plumbing and electrical work while the roof is off, that way you can minimize damage to the interior."

"Wow," said Chrissy, feeling a knot in her stomach. "That sounds like a lot of work. Do you think it's too much for us to manage? What did Scott say?"

"Scott and the kids are still away camping, so he wasn't around to hear it. They'll be back later today though, so we can update him then. It is a lot of work, but Frank said it's actually a blessing the old place hasn't been fiddled with too much. He said that the foundations are strong, and if you committed to it, you can restore it properly, without cutting any corners. He's a sucker for these old places though, and living in an old home isn't for everyone. I think you'd have to love the quirkiness of it all, the warped and drafty window panes, the crooked floors, the fact that your air conditioning comes from opening the windows and letting the breeze blow through. I'm not sure, Chrissy. Is this really what you want? I know it sounds romantic to live in a restored Victorian rectory, but won't you miss your creature comforts?"

Chrissy smiled. "Oh, I don't know. I think it sounds fun, and it's all part of the adventure. Just imagine when it's complete, it'll be like living in a classic novel, with the beautiful tiled floors and the ornate fireplaces. I'm so excited!"

"Ok, dear. Whatever you think best," said Bonnie, sounding reticent.

"Bonnie? Can you take a photograph of the cost estimates and text it to me? I'll call Scott and talk to him about it, and then hopefully we can make an offer."

As Chrissy examined the estimates and timelines, Liz came

striding towards her, carrying a Bloomingdale's bag.

"Everything ok?" she asked.

"Yes. Oh Liz, I'm so excited! Bonnie and Walter spoke with a contractor about the old rectory house we want to buy in Ferndale. He said there's a lot of work to do, but the foundations are sound and the house will look amazing when it's finished."

"Yikes," said Liz, looking uneasy. "What does he mean by 'a lot of work'? I've heard these old places can be money pits if you're not careful."

Chrissy twitched her nose. "Um. Well, we'll need new wiring and new plumbing, and a new roof."

"Holy shit. Not much then, eh? And how long will all that take?"

Chrissy's nose twitched again. "Around three months initially, for the big stuff. The contractor said for a project this size he'd normally budget about $250,000 over a three-year period. Give or take twenty percent. That includes a new kitchen and new bathrooms, and landscaping for the garden."

Liz raised one eyebrow and looked at Chrissy.

"But it's all part of the adventure, Liz! We're rediscovering ourselves. Reinventing who we are."

"Yeah, and you'll be doing it in a cold, damp, death trap by the sounds of it."

Chrissy play-swatted Liz. "You have no imagination. Think how romantic it will be."

"Personally, I find electricity and running water *very* romantic."

Chrissy couldn't help but laugh. Liz was the best, and she loved having her back in her life.

"What did Scott say about it?" asked Liz.

"He wasn't there, so he doesn't know yet. In fact, I want to give him a call right now if that's ok? I'll update him on these estimates, and then maybe we can make an offer on the house."

"But don't you need to sell yours first?"

"No, we can make a pre-emptive offer, contingent on us selling ours."

Liz raised an eyebrow again and shrugged.

As they walked through the mall in search of a lunch spot, Chrissy dialed Scott's number.

"Hi babe. What's up?" he answered.

"Hi there. Did you guys have fun? Can you talk for a minute? I spoke to your mom about the Rectory, and its great news!"

There was silence for a second before Scott said, "What did she say?"

"Well, your dad ran into Frank at the gas station this morning and he asked him over for lunch. You know Frank? The contractor?"

"Yeah,"

"Well, the family of the old lady who passed away asked him to take a look at the Rectory and pull together some estimates for the work that needs to be done. There's quite a bit that needs updating, but he says that the foundation is strong and it'll be amazing once it's done."

"How much?"

"Time or money?"

"Both."

Chrissy swallowed. "Bonnie wrote it all down and texted it to me. Maybe we could talk it through later? Like I said, there's quite a lot of work needed, but it'll be totally worth it. I was thinking that once we'd looked through it all, maybe we could put in an offer? On a contingency basis, of course."

"Wow, Chrissy, now slow down there. We haven't even put our house on the market yet."

"Yes, I know, but we shouldn't wait too long. We don't

want to lose it."

Another silence.

Chrissy chewed her lip.

Finally, Scott spoke. "Look, Chrissy. I understand you're having a hard time right now, but I feel like we're moving too fast on this. We have a good life here in Pasadena, and I'm not sure I'm ready to walk away from it all."

"But we agreed," said Chrissy, her jaw clenching.

"No, we didn't. You decided. That's a very different thing. I'm not saying that we shouldn't move, I just think we need to take a breath and make decisions with a clear head."

"Yes, I know. And that's why I'm getting estimates. So that we understand what we're walking into before we commit ourselves." Chrissy's voice had a steely edge to it now. She was sick of Scott acting so imperiously.

"Now, let's just be clear, Chrissy." Scott was angry now. "You are not 'getting estimates'. It was a coincidence that Dad ran into Frank. And for your information, Frank is a lovely guy, but he's more of a handyman than a contractor. Mom and Dad asked him to replace their decking a couple of years ago and it took him almost four months, and when it was finished it still leaned to the left. God knows how long this work could take, and how much it will actually cost. We'd need to get a specialist to come out from San Francisco to look at it. I don't know Chrissy, it scares me to think about what we could be getting ourselves in to."

There was a pause before Scott said in a low tone, "Chrissy, I don't think you understand what you're asking of me here. To give up my career and my home. And what you're asking of the kids as well. I know you're miserable, but I'm worried this is all too much."

Chrissy felt like crying.

"I need this, Scott. I need a fresh start. Please," she said, her voice breaking.

Scott sighed, raggedly. "OK, baby, I hear you. But let me find someone who specializes in restoring old houses to give us a proper quote before we talk about making an offer, agreed?"

"Ok, that sounds fair," said Chrissy, her voice shaking.

Scott rang off.

Chrissy and Liz found a little French bistro and ordered lunch. Liz was subdued as she sipped her sparking water.

"You OK?" Asked Chrissy.

"Yeah" replied Liz.

"What's up? It's not like you to be so quiet."

Liz bit her lip, and said, "I've been thinking about you and Scott and this old house."

"Oh?"

"Why are you so obsessed with moving, Chrissy? I get that the school treated you like shit, but why do you have to move to the middle of nowhere?"

"I don't know. I just feel like a new place would bring us new fortunes, you know?"

Liz looked at her knowingly. "You sound like your mum."

Chrissy flashed with indignation. "It's hardly the same thing, Liz. And I'll thank you to stop passing judgement on me. Your life isn't so perfect either."

Liz smiled, "You're right there."

An uncharacteristic shadow of solemnity fell over Liz.

"But Chrissy, just be careful how hard you push Scott. He's a good man, but even good men have their limits. He loves you desperately, but everyone has their breaking point. You may get what you want in the short term, but consider the long-term damage you could be doing to your relationship. Is that really a price you are willing to pay?"

Chrissy wanted to argue, to tell Liz that she was mistaken, but somewhere deep within her she saw the truth of it.

She could see no other way, though. She needed this. She needed to escape.

32

Brody
Tuesday, July 2nd - Santa Monica

In the heat of the evening, Emily basked in the warm, vibrant atmosphere of the Caribbean restaurant. Her mouth watered as she breathed in the spicy fragrances drifting from the kitchen towards the patio area.

She sat at a simple wooden table, watching Brody as he ordered their beers. He was leaning against the brightly colored bamboo bar, chatting with the barmaid, who was giggling and fluttering around him.

"Like a moth to a flame," thought Emily, amused.

Brody turned and smiled his stunning white smile at Emily. He carried the beer bottles back to the table, and as they clinked them together, he offered a toast.

"To new friends, and exciting opportunities."

Emily beamed and drank the cool, refreshing beer.

Brody smiled, "I hope you don't mind, but I ordered us a selection of plates."

"Not at all. This place is amazing! The colors and the decor. You could really believe you were in the Caribbean."

Brody laughed. "I'm glad you like it. It's one of my favorite places to come and unwind. Actually, I spent some time in the Caribbean when I was younger, so it brings back a lot of happy memories."

"You did? Why were you there?"

"I went after high school to spread my wings a bit. I worked for a company that chartered yachts and sailboats. I would take families and corporate parties out and teach them to sail. Sometimes we would move private boats from one island to another, clean them up and have them ready for the owners when they arrived. Often we just sailed them over to the docks for maintenance and repair."

"Wow, that sounds amazing!" Emily said, tucking into the delicious chicken wings that had been delivered. They were hotter than she was used to, but she was enjoying the unusual heat and spice.

Brody continued. "The Caribbean is gorgeous. One time I had an overnight delivery from Jamaica to the Caymans. She was an amazing boat, a 28ft 1930s Hillyard, beautifully restored and a joy to sail. Her wooden deck was polished to a shine, and she had crisp white sails. I have to admit that I was in love with her before we even left Montego Bay. It was just me, this beautiful boat, and the ocean. I watched the sunset as a pod of dolphins skidded and jumped by the bow. They stayed with us until the sky darkened, and the first stars appeared." He swigged his beer and smiled, staring into the distance.

"She handled so smoothly, and she was so responsive, I barely needed to touch the tiller. Her name was 'Speranza'. It means 'hope' in Spanish. Her owner was a famous poet, and she'd chosen the name in honor of Oscar Wilde's mother. She was a poet in her own right, you know, and wrote under the pen name 'Speranza'."

His eyes were glistening now. "I sailed for hours under the

most incredible night sky I've ever seen. I could see the Milky Way and a thousand other stars. It was so quiet, and the expanse above me so huge, I felt like a tiny speck against all that magnificence. As we came into the bay, the bioluminescence made the water around us glow. As the bow cut through the waves, they shimmered with a radiant light. I sat next to 'Speranza' and watched the first pink light of the sunrise. It was glorious. That ship was my first true love. In fact, I've never felt like that about anyone or anything since. I think that's why I go surfing at dawn, I'm trying to recapture the beauty of that morning."

There was a silence between them, and Emily could see the raw emotion in Brody's eyes. His deep blue eyes, as deep as the ocean itself.

Then he shook himself and smiled. And the spell was broken.

"Wow, I'm so sorry," he said, looking bashful, "I've never told anyone about that before."

"No need to apologize. It sounds magical. You've given me wanderlust, though. Now I want to go to the Caribbean, too," said Emily, dreamily.

To lighten the mood, she asked, "So how did you go from sailing boats around paradise islands, to running a venture capital business?"

Brody chuckled. "Well, one of the charter groups was on the island to attend a conference on AI and emerging technology. I got talking to a guy about a couple of algorithms I'd designed in high school, and it turned out he was a professor at MIT. He told me that if I applied to their computer science program, he'd sponsor me. I did, and the rest is history."

"Is that where you came up with the idea for the health platform?"

"Yeah. I always believed that consumers want to make

informed decisions when they were buying products. Like which support fair trade practices, and which contain harmful chemicals, etc. So I created algorithms that pulled data from all over the web to rate the safety and environmental impact of beauty products. As you know, the platform has become incredibly successful, but now we want to produce our own line of products that meet the highest standards of purity and best practice. And that's where you come in, Emily," he said, winking at her. Emily's cheeks burned.

"But surely there are people out there who are more qualified than me? Not wishing to do myself out of a job, but why me?" Emily said, looking bemused.

"Yeah, I've never been one to put much stock in qualifications over personality in this game. For lawyers, yes. For doctors, totally. But I've met enough overqualified MBA-toting assholes to make me believe it's more about the person and their approach than about what's on the paper. Kolleen was blown away when she first spoke to you, and she insisted we meet with you. I'm glad she did," he said with a dazzling smile.

"Well, I'm glad you feel that way, but I am fully aware you are taking a big risk by offering this position to me. To be honest, I'm a bit of a fish out of water in the office. Everyone else is so, well, young and gorgeous, and you all seem to have such perfect lives. I feel so, ordinary." Emily's eyes dropped.

Brody leaned forward, taking her hand in his. Emily looked up, a bolt of electricity running through her.

"Believe me, Emily, you are *anything* but ordinary. You are incredible, and I am going to make it my purpose to ensure that you see that as clearly as I do. And ignore all the skinny, tan, California bullshit that folks around here project. Things are never as rosy as they may seem. I won't go into it, but my childhood was pretty grim. How do you think I ended up on my own in the Caribbean at seventeen?"

"Oh. I'm so sorry, I never would have thought.." her voice trailed off.

Brody released her hand. "God no. It's my fault. I don't know why I said that. I really am spilling my soul to you, aren't I? I can't help it, though."

He looked at her, a hunger in his eyes that made her both excited and scared.

Emily stood abruptly. "It's late. I should call Chrissy. She's waiting for me, and she has to drive us back to Pasadena tonight. Dinner is on me to say thank you for such an amazing day. Could you ask them for the check? I just need to use the ladies' room first."

Brody stood and reached out his hand to stop her. "Emily, I'm so sorry. I never meant to make you uncomfortable. Please, dinner is my treat to welcome you to the team."

Emily softened. "Thank you. And I'm sorry for being uptight. This is all very new to me."

As they stood outside the restaurant waiting for the others to arrive, the atmosphere was light-hearted again.

Emily asked Brody about surfing, and he demonstrated how to 'catch a wave' by balancing on the curb. They both laughed as he pretended to 'wipe out', and then he offered to teach Emily some of the basic techniques.

A whisper of wariness made her hesitate for a moment, but with a grin, she agreed to be a willing student.

Enthusiastically, he adjusted her hips and her shoulders, and as he chatted about the correct form, she could feel his strong, taut body behind her.

As his hands ran down her arms, they both fell silent, the heat rising between them.

In that moment she wanted to turn towards him, feel his arms around her, pulling her into him.

Just then, Chrissy's car arrived and, blushing and flustered,

Emily said her brief goodbyes.

As Chrissy pulled away from the curb, Emily sat back, exhaling. It had been an intense day, and she was drained.

"Everything OK? Did you have a good time?" Chrissy asked.

"Yeah. I'm just wiped out. Sorry, can I give you the rundown tomorrow?"

"Sure," replied Chrissy. "Chill out and we should be back in about an hour."

They drove home through downtown LA, the lights of the skyscrapers twinkling above them against the night sky. Chrissy and Liz were engaged in a passionate debate about the current political situation in both the US and the UK. Emily listened halfheartedly, looking out of the window as the buildings whooshed past.

She smiled and shivered with excitement, thinking about her new job. Not long now until this dream would be a reality. She felt like a small child waiting for Christmas morning.

Her mind drifted back to the ocean, the warmth of the sun and the smell of salt in the air. She remembered all the delicious food and the wonderful company of the last couple of days, laughing with her friends and sharing memories. As she reminisced, her heart swelled with contentment, and she closed her eyes to savor the moment.

Then she thought of him, his deep blue eyes shining as he looked at her.

She pictured him surfing in the early morning light, his taut muscles moving as one with the surfboard and the waves, the water glistening on his skin. How beautiful he must be, all alone against the sunrise. She thought of him standing behind her, so close she could smell his cologne. A tingle ran through her as she imagined his lips on hers, his skin on her skin.

She stopped, shocked. What was she thinking? Maybe the others had been right? No, it was ridiculous. She respected him as a businessman and her new boss, that was all.

She breathed a heavy, tight breath, and made a pact with herself not to think about him again.

33

Loss
Wednesday, July 3rd - Pasadena

Liz stood under the shower and let the steaming water envelop her. She smiled to herself as she rubbed shampoo through her hair and thought about the beautiful forest they had hiked through that day.

In her mind she was back there again, the sunlight glinting through the leaves above her, backlighting the different shades of green. She could hear the cool stream rippling and rushing as she jumped from rock to rock across it, and smell the rich earth beneath her feet.

Chrissy had driven up the Angeles Crest Highway, and they had walked deep into the Angeles Forest under a heavy canopy of trees. Just as they were adjusting to the cool damp earthiness of the forest, they turned upwards, scaling the side of the mountain until they broke out into the clear, bright heat of the day.

The views had been breathtaking. The majestic San Gabriel Mountains lay before them, huge undulating ripples of green and pink and tan, with paler and paler ranges beyond them as far as the eye could see. A visual echo stretching into the distance.

They stood in the enveloping silence, only the faint sounds of a wheeling bird of prey above them, and the distant rush of the river far below to break the stillness.

They had stood for the longest time, breathing in the peace and admiring the incredible vista. The sense of calm was so rich and sweet, it brought a lump to Liz's throat. Against these mountains, she felt both insignificant and free. Both exhilarated and humbled. She'd wanted to stand in that stillness forever.

She sighed and stepped out of the shower, wrapping her long hair in a towel. She'd been craving some exercise after all the delicious food they had been eating, and she felt so much better after that strenuous hike. Now she was energized, and ready for a night out on the town.

"You ready for a glass of wine?" Chrissy shouted up the stairs.

"You bet I am! White would be great if you have it?" she replied.

They were all in various states of preparation as they listened to 80s music and danced around, drinking their wine.

"It's like being back at school, getting ready on a Friday night to go out to the pub," Chrissy said with a wide smile.

"Except we're not all filled with angst about how we look, or whether or not a certain boy will talk to us," Emily replied with a wry smile. "God, I don't miss those days at all!"

They all laughed, and as Liz reached for her wineglass, she heard her phone buzz. She grabbed it and looked at the message. It was from Lauren.

Hi Liz. I'm sorry to disturb you. Can you call me?

* * *

Liz felt a stab of alarm. It was 5.30pm here so that would make it 1.30am in London.

Sure. Hang on.

She walked into the bedroom and called Lauren. Lauren answered, her voice shaking.

"I'm sorry to call you when you're on holiday, Liz. I just had to hear your voice."

"What's the matter? What's happened?" said Liz, going cold.

"I have some bad news. It's Bibi."

The ground dropped beneath her, and she sat down heavily on the edge of the bed.

"Oh Liz. She's. Well, she passed away," Lauren whispered.

Liz felt a stab as real as if a blade had entered her chest. Tears came and wouldn't stop.

"What happened?" she asked in a quiet, trembling voice.

"Heart attack. It was fast. She wasn't in any pain."

"When?"

"Monday night. Late."

"Oh God, Lauren. I'm so sorry," Liz said, shaking.

"It's ok. I mean, it's not ok, but, thank you. I'm sorry I didn't tell you earlier. I've been in kind of a daze."

"Can I do anything?" said Liz, feeling helpless.

There was a silence, then Lauren broke down into heavy, wretched sobs.

"That's not the only thing. Oh Christ, I don't know what to do. I didn't know who else to call."

Liz felt as if she was falling through blackness.

"What Lauren? What else?"

"The landlord came over earlier today. I assumed that he'd come to offer his condolences, so I was completely unprepared for what he was going to say. He told me he's selling the house. A developer wants to buy the entire block and rip it down to build a fancy new apartment complex, and they've made him an offer. He said that up until now he'd felt some obligation to say no because Bibi has been living here so long, but now that she's gone he's agreed to the sale. He wants us out, Liz. I'm so scared. I don't know what to do." Lauren broke down again, desperate sobs that cut at Liz's heart.

Liz couldn't think straight. Her head was pounding.

"OK, Lauren. Don't worry. We'll sort it out OK? I'll help you, I promise."

"Thank you. I'm going to go to the Citizens Advice Bureau tomorrow to see if I can get some sort of housing allowance, but I think I'm going to have to quit college and get a job so I can pay rent. Oh God, Liz, I don't want to end up in temporary accommodation, or worse still, homeless. I'm really scared. I don't know what I'm going to do."

"It's OK. I'll be back on Sunday and we'll work it out, don't worry, it'll be OK, you hear me?"

"Thank you. It's so nice to hear your voice," Lauren said, sounding so small and vulnerable it made Liz's heart break even more.

Liz sat in shock. Soon the door creaked open and Chrissy came in, followed by Emily.

"What's happened?" Chrissy asked in a sober, hushed tone.

Liz sobbed and told them what Lauren had said.

They sat on either side of her and held her tight as she cried. Harrowing sobs erupting from deep within her soul. She hadn't realized until that moment just how much she had loved Bibi.

Chrissy wrapped her in a warm blanket and walked her to the Lazy Boy in the living room. Then she handed her a cup of tea, milk and two sugars, the tried and tested British remedy for any nasty shock.

They all sat in a glum silence, but Liz was comforted by the presence of her two watchful sentries.

Eventually she looked at them, her eyes filled with sorrow and frustration.

"I do not know what I can do to help her? I suppose I could give her a loan to cover part of her rent, or help her find some low-cost housing? Doesn't the government have an obligation to help people out in these sorts of circumstances?"

"Don't worry, Liz, I'm sure it'll be fine. Just give yourself some time to get over the shock before you try to find any solutions," said Chrissy, putting her arm around her.

The evening plans were scrapped, and instead they sat in the front yard in the fading evening light, watching the mountains turn to a burnt orange once again.

They drank G&Ts, with limes picked straight off Chrissy's trees, and talked about people they had lost, and opportunities they had missed. The atmosphere was cathartic and soothing, with a touch of melancholy.

Emily touched the bobbing heads of the white and purple agapanthus next to her.

"I remember when I was younger," she said, "I used to love reading books about women who changed the world. Brave women like Amelia Earhart and Helen Keller and Joan of Arc. I imagined I would be one of them, that I would have an impact on the world, make a difference. I think that's why I studied law. Maybe I fancied myself as the next Ruth Bader Ginsburg," she said, with a snort of derision.

"Then I met Ed, and we talked about having a family. Before I knew it, we were planning a wedding, and then looking for the perfect family home. He fell in love with our little cottage the minute he saw it. It's the home he'd always pictured, you know what I mean? With the white picket fence and roses round the door, and a rosy faced wife there to greet him. I was happy too. I felt settled and secure, and I loved how I could walk across the fields and over the stream and listen to the sheep bleating in the distance."

She took a sip of her drink.

"We started trying for a baby in the Spring when the lambs were gamboling about on their little spindly legs. We were both so excited, and I started to redecorate the room that would become the nursery. But nothing. It was months, and then a year, and two years. We went to the doctor, who referred us to a fertility specialist. They said there was nothing wrong, and that we were bound to fall pregnant, eventually. Our friends were all having babies, and I cried every time someone told me they were pregnant. Four years later, and still nothing. My friends were having their second babies now, and I felt hopeless and broken. I remember one of Ed's colleagues putting her hand on my arm and saying in a comforting tone that 'maybe it wasn't God's plan for us to have a child'. I felt like slapping her. Sanctimonious bitch. It definitely put a strain on our marriage, and in the end we did IVF. It worked first time, and we had Philip. He was premature, but not dangerously so. Ed joked it was because he'd already waited so long to make an appearance, he wasn't willing to wait any longer." Emily chuckled to herself at the memory.

"Did you have IVF for the other two as well?" Chrissy asked.

"No, it was so strange. It was as if Philip had kicked the cogs into action, and everything started working as it should. We had assumed we would only ever have one baby, but then I fell pregnant with Sophie. It was a wonderful surprise. And I have to admit that Harry was a bit of a surprise as well." Emily flushed. "It was a long six years of waiting, but I'm so glad I was able to be a mother." Emily smiled as she thought of her babies.

Liz sat forward in her chair. "So, were you working during this time?"

"I did some office management work for Ed's company, but I never had a career. Maybe if I'd known how long it would take me to get pregnant, I would have done things differently. That's why I want this job so much. I love my babies, but I want a career as well."

"Is Ed supportive of the new job?" asked Liz.

Emily looked at the ground.

"Officially, yes. But I'm not sure he realizes what it's going to be like. He says he's excited about being a stay at home dad, he loves cooking and he says he'll enjoy the free time and the chance to take up a hobby. I don't think he understands what it's like to manage the logistics of three young kids. Of course my mum is horrified by the whole thing. She thinks I'm being selfish and irresponsible by putting everyone in this position."

"Mums are the worst," said Liz with venom.

"Thanks a lot!" said Chrissy and Emily, both laughing.

"Oh yeah. Sorry. I didn't mean *you* guys, obviously," said Liz with a sheepish grin.

They spent the rest of the evening putting the world to rights. Reminiscing and laughing and drinking. They drank all the gin, and then all the rum, and then all the tequila. Finally, they crawled into bed in the early hours of the morning, extremely inebriated, but happy and content.

The final noise in the house was Liz yelling drunkenly from her bed, "Good night John Boy, good night Mary Ellen! Don't puke on the floor!"

And then all was quiet.

34

Diablo Winds
Thursday, July 4th - Pasadena

The Santa Ana winds had arrived, and the hot dry air that blew across the valley made everyone scratchy, discontented, and itching for a fight. They weren't called the Diablo Winds for nothing.

Chrissy and Emily crawled out of their beds at 10am, and were in the kitchen nursing evil hangovers.

"I can't decide if I want to throw up now, or after I've had breakfast," Chrissy said groaning, and holding her head.

"Don't. Speak." said Emily in a hushed tone, sitting slowly and cautiously on one of the kitchen chairs.

"You want coffee?"

"I don't know."

"You want Alka Seltzer?"

"Yes. Definitely, yes."

They sat opposite each other in silence, riding the waves of nausea.

Chrissy groaned and said, "We were supposed to go to the 4th July Parade in Sierra Madre today, but its started already."

Emily snorted. "I don't even think Liz is awake yet. Oh no, hang on, I hear the shower," she said, looking upwards.

"I've got fresh fruit and granola, if you want some?" asked Chrissy unenthusiastically.

Emily grimaced and shook her head.

"Hang on, I've got a better idea."

After some digging around at the back of cupboards and a trip to the outside fridge, she had pulled together the core ingredients for a 'good old-fashioned fry up'.

The smell of frying bacon brought Liz to the top of the stairs.

"Oh fuck, that smells *so good*!" she shouted.

Emily shut her eyes, her jaw tightening. "Liz, please don't swear," she said through gritted teeth.

After consuming piles of bacon, sausage, baked beans and toast, they sat, enjoying the stabilizing feeling of a full stomach.

"Yup, grease is fucking amazing," said Liz, pushing her empty plate away and drinking the last of her orange juice.

Emily turned on her, eyes flashing. "Must you constantly use that language? It's trashy and unnecessary, and very unbecoming for a grown woman."

Liz raised her eyes, centering her body towards Emily. "Oh, *'unbecoming'* is it? Well, I wouldn't want to offend her fucking Royal Highness over here! Wind your neck in, Emily, it's not my fault you're so hungover," she said as she slammed her glass down.

Emily stood and stared at Liz, her eyes hard. "I know it had the desired effect of shocking everyone when we were teenagers. I also know you were only doing it to get a rise out of your mother. But you can drop the 'rebel without a cause' act now, Liz, you're forty for God's sake. Grow up."

Liz pushed her chair back with a piercing screech that made everyone's hair stand on end. "Fuck you, Emily. Don't you dare patronize me, and if we're going to point fingers at people for acting a part then you don't have to look too far, do you? People in glass houses, right? Don't take your frustrations out on me because I will tell it as I see it, and you might not like what I have to say."

Emily was breathing heavily, her eyes locked on Liz. She said cooly, "What are you saying, Liz? Is there something you'd like to get off your chest? You've never been shy about shooting your mouth off before, why so coy now?"

"Oh, whatever, Emily, don't play sweet and innocent with me. It doesn't fly. You're such a bullshitter. I saw the way you looked at Brody, with that same giddy, lustful expression you used to give Ben. You were a bloody nymphomaniac when you were dating him, screwing anywhere, anytime. I've seen you with Ed. I bet you *never* looked at him that way."

Emily went pale. "Well," she stuttered, looking both trapped and enraged, "It's different. I was a teenager when I was dating Ben. Ed and I have responsibilities, and a family. It's completely different. Anyway, what would you know, Liz, you've never had a decent relationship in your life!"

"So, you're telling me that when you first got together with Ed, you used to look at him that way? Did you ever feel that kind of passion with him?"

Emily stared at the ground.

"No, I thought not," said Liz, her eyes flashing. "Did you settle, Emily?" she spat. "Did you settle for a sensible, boring life, with a sensible, boring husband? You hoping for a do-over with Brody the surfer?"

Chrissy stood up, stepping between her two friends. "Liz, stop! Please!"

But Emily stepped forward, feeling the anger rushing through her, knowing that if Chrissy hadn't been in the way, she would have hit Liz.

"You bitch!" she hissed, her head exploding with pain.

"How *dare* you judge me when your life is so fucking pathetic? Despite all your swagger and your swearing and your attitude, you've never had the guts to actually *care* for another living thing. You're a coward! You're a sniveling coward who's terrified to risk being vulnerable in case you're rejected. You hide behind that sham of a relationship with your obnoxious rich boyfriend because he's as emotionally stunted as you are. You pretend to have life all figured out, when in fact you're just a scared little girl who's still trying to prove to herself and everyone around her that she's not her mother!"

Emily was panting, every muscle taut, ready for whatever would come next, and secretly hoping that Liz would lunge at her.

"What the hell, you guys? Get it under control!" Chrissy shouted, horrified to see her two best friends turning into rabid dogs.

"Oh, fuck off Chrissy," said Liz. "At least Emily has the guts to say what she's actually thinking."

"Thank you Liz, you old cow," said Emily, her face softening, the shadow of a smile passing across it.

Liz chuckled, smiling at her old adversary.

"Well, hello, and welcome back, bitch. It's good to see you break out of that fucking Martha Stewart plaster-cast you've been living in. For Christ's sake Chrissy, get out the way so I can hug this crazy woman."

Chrissy stepped aside, bemused, and watched her friends hug each other as if they hadn't seen each other in years.

"So, are we done here?" asked Chrissy. "You guys aren't going to scratch each other's eyes out after all?"

"Well, we're not making any promises," Liz said, as she and Emily grinned at each other conspiratorially.

"I have no idea what is going on, so I'm going to go and take a shower, OK?" said Chrissy, shaking her head and walking out the room, as the other two collapsed into laughter.

When Chrissy had gone, Liz turned to Emily and said.

"Joking aside, I'm really sorry. That was an awful thing to say to you. I know you would never do anything to hurt Ed and the kids. I'm hungover and hurting and it came out all wrong, but I have been worried about the effect Brody has on you. I wouldn't want anything to jeopardize your family. It was just my clumsy way of saying 'be careful.'"

Emily smiled.

"I know. If anyone else said something like that to me, I would never forgive them. But I trust you more than anyone in the world, Liz. You've always loved me and been straight with me, and I value that more than I can say. And you're right, Brody represents a lot of missed opportunities, but I'm not a teenager anymore, and I wouldn't risk everything I have on a whim."

They hugged each other tightly. Then Emily pulled away.

"I shouldn't have said what I said, either. I was lashing out because you'd hit a nerve. I didn't mean any of it, and it was beyond cruel to say it after you've just lost Bibi."

Liz smiled at her friend.

"We both spoke some truths, ugly as they were. All I can say is that I am so glad to have you back in my life."

They spent the rest of the afternoon lying around the pool, eating chips and dip, and floating around on the pool loungers.

"This is pure heaven," said Emily, sighing with contentment.

"Yup. I might move out here with you," said Liz with a grin.

"That would be amazing, but it's never going to happen. You're a London girl through and through," smiled Emily, looking at her friend with so much love.

"OK," said Liz, standing up with purpose. "I'm going to make us each a Bloody Mary."

"Oh God, *please* no," pleaded Emily, "my stomach can't handle any more alcohol."

"Nonsense," said Liz, sounding matronly, "Hair of the Dog and all that. Plus, it's 4th of July! I have to celebrate my American friend, and my soon-to-be American friend."

They all laughed, and Chrissy peeled herself off the lounger she was lying on. "Hang on. Let me show you where everything is so you don't destroy my kitchen," she said in a droll tone.

As they prepared the cocktails, Chrissy paused and looked at Liz with a weighted expression.

"When you guys were fighting earlier, did you mean everything you said?"

"Kinda, yes."

"And how did you feel when Emily said all that stuff about you?"

"I have to admit that it stung a bit. Which must mean it's at least partly true," said Liz with a shrug.

"But now you're not mad at her? I'd still be furious weeks later if someone said something like that to me."

Liz put down the knife she was using to cut the celery and looked at Chrissy.

"Chrissy, don't take this the wrong way, but Emily and I are like siblings. We always speak our minds, even if it's not always presented in the nicest way. But it doesn't mean we don't love each other. In fact, we love each other all the more because of it. I love you like a sister, but I would never speak to you like that because I'm not sure you could handle it."

Chrissy's jaw tightened as she frowned.

"So you would never tell me the truth?" she asked.

"I'm not saying that," replied Liz, "I'm saying that you'd need to hear it in a different way."

Chrissy shifted her weight and said, "OK then, tell me the truth."

"About what?"

"Tell me what you think of me," Chrissy said, dropping her gaze, her breathing growing shallow.

For a long time Liz looked at her with eyes full of love and concern. Then she said,

"OK then. I think you've spent your life searching for something, without ever really knowing what it is. I think it's made you miserable, and now it's making your family miserable as well. I think you're trying to construct a perfect life where you can play the perfect part, but it's not real. I think you're angry with your mum for not looking after you well enough. For not being a 'proper mother' whatever the fuck that is. I think you want to do better, to give your kids a better childhood, to be a better mother to them. But what you've missed is that you have nothing to prove, you're already an amazing mother, and an amazing person in your own right. You keep running and searching, when everything you need is right in front of you."

The tears welled up in Chrissy's eyes.

Liz put her hand on Chrissy's.

"Do you really want to leave Pasadena? Or are you just running again? Building more castles in the air, when you have everything you need and love right here?"

Just then Emily walked through the door, and the moment was broken. She sensed the intrusion and said in an apologetic tone.

"Sorry, I just needed to get some water. I'm still painfully dehydrated."

"No problem," said Chrissy, wiping her eyes. "Yeah, we should all drink a couple of glasses before we start on the booze again."

They smiled and clinked a toast to hangovers.

"May they always be behind us, eh?" Liz said with a wink.

35

Freedom
Thursday, July 4th - Pasadena

That evening, as the sun dropped in the sky, the friends walked down the hill to the Rose Bowl stadium to watch the incredible annual fireworks display. The air was balmy, and the girls were joyous, the tension of the morning now forgotten.

Chrissy and Emily walked arm in arm, and as they past the multi-million dollar homes, Emily admired the delicate roses in the gardens and the trees that lined the avenue on both sides.

Chrissy smiled and said, "These are jacarandas. In May they bloom with the most incredible lilac-colored flowers, little glorious trumpets ushering in the heat of the summer. This avenue becomes a haze of purple, a canopy of color that would take your breath away."

"Oh, that sounds stunning," breathed Emily in reverent wonder.

"It's one of my favorite times of the year," replied Chrissy. "Another is early Spring, when the orange trees are in blossom and their sweet smell is everywhere. I get up early in the morning and sit in the garden just so I can breathe it in. It's intoxicating."

"That sounds like heaven," Emily murmured. "The last week has been magical. I can't believe that in forty-eight hours we'll be flying back to England. I worry that I'll wake up and discover it was all just a dream."

Chrissy squeezed her friend's arm. "You're going to be living in this dream before you know it."

Emily's eyes shone with both excitement and trepidation. Was she doing the right thing? Could this really be their new life, or was it all too good to be true? She felt her mother's reproachful gaze upon her, and guilt and doubt seeped into the corners of her mind.

*****

The atmosphere was jubilant as they arrived at the gates of the stadium. People jostled and laughed and shouted to each other in excitement. It reminded the friends of outdoor concerts they had gone to in their college days.

Chrissy led the way. "I suggest we grab a beer and a hotdog and then find some seats."

The others agreed with enthusiasm, and before long they were sitting in the stands with beers and hotdogs in hand. Thousands of people packed into the stadium, many dressed in red, white and blue, all in high spirits. A lady excused herself as she squeezed along the row in front of them. She was wearing an elaborate Uncle Sam headdress and had a red, white and blue sparkling boa draped around her neck.

Before long, the crowd had started a 'wave' that rippled through the stands. Everyone joined in the fun, enjoying the camaraderie it created.

As the last of the daylight faded, they watched the stunt

bikes perform perilous tricks, while the audience gasped and hooted and clapped. Then the mood turned somber as photographs of fallen military personnel were projected onto a big screen.

Liz sipped her beer as she listened to a cappella group singing songs from the new live action Disney movie 'The Lion King'. She watched a family a couple of rows away, the grandmother singing along with her granddaughter. They laughed and hugged each other, animated and jubilant, the love in their eyes so clear to see. Liz smiled and thought of Naomi and Bibi.

A sharp stab of loss reminded her she would never again see Bibi's smile, or hear her laughter. She would never again see the twinkle in those misty blue eyes.

*****

The lights dimmed, and an expectant hush fell across the audience.

A voice boomed from the loudspeaker.

"Welcome to the Rose Bowl Stadium. We are glad that you are here with us tonight to celebrate our country's journey to freedom, one that began over two hundred years ago. Our pyrotechnics team has given us the word that they are ready to start the show, so let's count them down, shall we?"

The atmosphere became electric as the crowd joined the presenter in the countdown.

10, 9, 8, 7... Chrissy beamed at Liz, whose eyes were full of tears.

6, 5, 4, 3... she looked at Emily, who shone with happiness.

2, 1...

The night sky lit up with red and white brilliance.

Explosions of color filled the air until the darkness was obliterated by the breathtaking colors. It was almost overwhelming, and Chrissy reveled in the intensity.

The loudspeaker played "America" from West Side Story, and she sang along with those scrappy, hopeful teenagers, trying to find their place in the world.

The tears came as she remembered Liz's words. Was she really as lost as Liz had implied?

She remembered the day she had arrived in California, a young immigrant herself, full of hopes and dreams. She had been searching for somewhere to belong, somewhere to truly call home. Had she found what she was looking for? Partly, yes. She had found Scott, and now they were a family, and she loved them all to distraction.

But Liz had been right. Under the surface she was still restless, ill-at-ease, like something was missing.

Her mind flashed back to the sinister wood of her nightmares, and for a moment she was back there, running and stumbling in the darkness.

She inhaled a jagged breath and shook it off. "Ferndale is the answer, though," she said to herself. "That's what I've been searching for all this time, and we're almost there."

With a newfound sense of reassurance, she took a deep, calming breath and lifted her eyes to the night sky to watch the symphony of color above her.

*****

Emily listened to the loudspeaker project, 'The Declaration of Independence,' and something stirred deep inside her. She heard the words "tonight we celebrate our freedom," and she listened as the voice described the struggles of a new nation trying to break away and become something new.

A lump grew in her throat, and she grabbed Chrissy's hand, squeezing it hard. She had never felt any real patriotism towards her own country before, but now she understood what it meant to fight for freedom. To fight to be recognized. She understood the anger and frustration, the need to be free to follow your dreams, to forge your own path and reach for something more.

At that moment a shift happened within her, followed by a wave of certainty and exhilaration. All her worries fell away, leaving only the stark, raw truth. She wanted this so badly it hurt. And she knew she could do it. She was strong enough, clever enough, brave enough. In that moment she knew she was making the right decision. She had found where she belonged.

*****

"All men are created equal." Liz heard the words, and her jaw tightened.

"But we are not treated as equals," she argued to herself. "We are not judged equally, we don't have the same opportunities. The game is rigged from the start. Lauren and I were born not far from each other, but we grew up in different worlds. I had all the opportunities and privileges afforded a wealthy child, where Lauren had none. Bibi was an incredible woman, but she had to push, and strive, and fight all her life. She was honest and hardworking and she did the best she could, but she was swimming against hidden currents that constantly dragged her back. Insidious, destructive currents, that only affect the most vulnerable amongst us.

And now Lauren is taking up that mantle, struggling against poverty and prejudice as she tries to build a life for herself and Naomi. All her life she's had to fight for the very things I've taken for granted. Lauren and Naomi are good people, they deserve so much better than this."

In that moment Liz ached to hold them close, to apologize

for a system that inherently rewards some, while punishing others, and for her own convenient blindness to it.

She wanted to promise them that in all her actions from now on she would fight for them, as if they were her own flesh and blood. They felt like her family just as much as her mother and father and brother ever had, and she owed it to Bibi.

*****

As the fireworks died down and the stadium cleared, the friends were quiet, lost in their own thoughts.

They walked home in contemplative silence, comfortable enough in each other's company not to have to make small talk.

At home they sat under the stars in the warm night air, breathing in the scent of jasmine as Chrissy poured champagne into tall crystal flutes.

"Happy 4th July" they toasted, clinking their glasses together.

After a moment Chrissy said, "Do you remember the pact we made the night of Rachel's memorial?"

"Wow, it seems like a lifetime ago now, doesn't it?" Emily shook her head.

Liz sighed. "I realize now how naïve I was back then. I thought I had it all worked out. So much has changed in just a couple of months, hasn't it?"

Chrissy smiled. "Who could have known what life had in store for us? It's as if we came back together just in time. I'm not sure I would have been able to cope with everything that has happened if it wasn't for you guys."

They smiled at each other, and the contentment settled between them. They knew in that moment they would never lose each other again.

That night, as they lay in bed, they each thought of the fireworks of the day. The arguments and insults, the truth laid bare, and the magnificence of the light show at the stadium. They cherished the memories of the last couple of days, and, as they drifted off to sleep, they each laid plans for the future.

36

Homeless
Monday, July 8th - London

"Do you want another cup of tea?" Liz asked in a whisper.

"Yes, please," replied Lauren, wiping her eyes.

Liz refilled the kettle and stood over it in silence until it boiled.

She poured the scalding water into the mugs and watched the brown color seep from the tea bags, swirling around, growing darker as it released its earthy, comforting aroma.

After disposing of the tea bags, she took the milk from the fridge and added it to each mug. She placed a mug in front of Lauren and, holding her mug close to her, she sat opposite her.

Lauren looked weary and deflated, the sorrow hanging from her like a shroud. Her face looked pinched and her eyes had dark shadows under them. She stared at her tea.

"I think Bibi would be happy with the arrangements," she said. "The ladies from the church choir are going to sing some of her favorite hymns and do some readings. I'm writing a eulogy."

She sat, staring at her mug, as Liz watched her, not knowing what to do or say to ease her burden.

"It's so quiet without her." Lauren said, the tears rolling down her cheeks.

Liz fought the lump in her throat.

"I know. She was an amazing person. I'm glad I got the chance to meet her," said Liz, her voice breaking.

Lauren met her gaze with warmth and love in her eyes.

"She loved you, Liz, you know that? She saw the fighter in you, but she also saw your softer side. There was always a special sparkle in her eyes when she talked about you."

Liz looked down as she bit back the tears.

"She made me who I am," continued Lauren in a distant tone. "I was ten when I came to live with her. A scruffy, sassy little urchin. I respected no one, and trusted even less. She moulded me. Never gave up on me. She always held me to a higher standard. We never had much money, she'd come to London with nothing to her name, and she'd worked and saved until she could open her own fish and chip shop. Everyone loved and respected her, and feared her a bit too because she was a fierce Glaswegian who wouldn't take no shit from no one." Lauren chuckled at the memory.

"Sometimes I got teased at school because my clothes were secondhand. She would say, 'it doesn't matter what you're wearing, it matters who you are. You're clean and respectful and that's what counts.' I remember she would always correct my grammar, which drove me mad. When I got something right in my homework, I'd say I felt 'dead clever.' She'd tut and say 'you mean you feel *very* clever, or *extremely* clever. You're not dead yet, young lass.'"

Lauren laughed, her eyes glistening with love and heartache.

"On Sundays after church, we would sit and do the crossword together. In the evenings she would read to me while I drew or painted. For a couple of years we didn't even have a TV, and Bibi said it was a blessed relief not to have that thing constantly on, sucking my attention away from more important things. She was strict, but fun as well. She would tell amazing stories and play games with me. I remember how she would chase me around the living room and jump out from behind the sofa to grab me. I would scream with glee while she pretended to 'eat me all up.'"

She smiled a sweet, melancholy smile, and then her face dropped.

"My Mum used to play the same games with me. She must have remembered them from when Bibi played them with her. My Mum was an amazing storyteller, too. We would make tents in the living room and pretend we were in the savannah watching the wild animals walk past. She would pretend to be a fierce lion stalking me through the tall grass, and I had to get away before she caught me."

Lauren stood and took her mug to the sink.

She stared out the window at the tiny backyard as she washed and rinsed it, placing it on the drying board and folding the tea towel over the sink. She went through the motions out of habit, finding some peace in the normality of it all.

Liz cleared her throat.

"Lauren, how come you ended up living with Bibi? What happened to your mum?"

As soon as the words left her mouth, she wished she could take them back. What an inappropriate time to ask such an intrusive question. "God, I'm sorry, Lauren. You don't have to talk about it if you don't want, I shouldn't have asked," she said, ashamed.

"No, it's fine, we're friends. I'm happy to talk about it," replied Lauren, turning and smiling at Liz.

"My mum was a wild child, despite everything Bibi did to

try and keep her safe. She got pregnant with me just after her fifteenth birthday, and even though Bibi said she would help with the baby, my mum ran away with her no-good boyfriend. He used to beat her up, so after about a year they split up. Mum worked jobs here and there, trying to make ends meet. It was tough with a baby in tow, though. At one point, she was working behind the bar at a pub. She would leave me in a playpen in the back room, but I would scream and cry, and in the end the owner fired her because I was too loud and annoying. We moved around a lot when I was little. Mum tried to make enough money to get by, but often there was no food in the house. I remember this one time after we'd been kicked out of our flat for non-payment of rent, we ended up sleeping in a friend's car for a couple of nights. It was so cold that my teeth were chattering, and I was worried I'd chip them. Then we stayed in a bed-and-breakfast for a couple of weeks. In the morning before school I'd put a tin of baked beans on the radiator so that by the evening they'd be warm enough to eat with a slice of bread. Mum did her best, but it was a hard life, and in the end she got involved in drugs. It changed her. It was like all the life seeped out of her, leaving just a shell."

Lauren swallowed hard, and Liz saw the pain in her eyes. She reached out, but Lauren waved her away. She needed to tell this story. It was time.

"By the time I was nine, it was getting bad. On the days when we had some money to put into the electrical meter, which wasn't often, I'd heat up some pot noodles and try to feed them to her. But she wouldn't eat. She'd just stare ahead, like she didn't even see me anymore."

Lauren dropped her head, looking small and fragile as the memories cast dark shadows over her face. She continued in a low, quiet tone.

"Then men started coming to the flat. They treated her

badly. I would hide under my bed when they were around. They started dealing from our flat, and that's when the police showed up. Social Services took me away and brought me to Bibi. I don't know that Mum even realized I was gone."

"Oh God, I'm so sorry," said Liz, the tears running down her face.

"No, in fact, it was the best thing that could have happened. My Mum did a rehab program in prison and she got cleaned up. When she got out Bibi and her talked about it, and decided it would be best for me to stay here with Bibi. Last I heard, my mum had moved to Spain with her new boyfriend. I hope she's OK. I don't blame her or anything, I genuinely believe she did the best she could."

Liz looked at Lauren with a deeper understanding and respect. She had never imagined that Lauren, so sensible and caring and devoted to little Naomi, could have experienced such trauma and hardship in her own young life. She also had a deeper respect for Bibi, and the troubles she had faced.

"You were lucky to have Bibi, that's for sure," said Liz.

Lauren sat down again and put her head in her hands.

"Poor old Bibi, she did everything she could to protect me from making the same mistakes my mum made. I was on track for an amazing career; doing a business degree with an internship at Goldman Sachs for Christ's sake, with bright prospects if I excelled in the job. I promised her that when I got a salaried position, I would buy her a house with a garden where she could retire, and she'd never have to worry about money again. Of course she never wanted nothing from me, but I so badly wanted to pay her back for everything."

Lauren looked at Liz with haunted eyes.

"I remember the day I told her I was pregnant. She tried to hide it, but I saw the hurt and disappointment in her eyes, and it made me so ashamed. Unmarried and pregnant at eighteen, with no job, no qualifications to speak of, she must have thought, *'Here we go again'*. But of course she was supportive, and she loved Naomi more than anything. She was so proud of me when I started my nursing degree, and I felt like I was finally back on track to making something of myself. But now..."

Her voice trailed off, and she looked at Liz with desperation.

"Liz, I'm worried that I'm just another a fuckup like my mum. Maybe Bibi and I were kidding ourselves all along. Maybe I'm just trash after all. We're going to lose this house. What if I end up homeless, or living paycheck to paycheck trying to keep the lights on and food in the fridge? Naomi deserves so much better than that. Bibi deserved better, too."

The tears welled in Lauren's eyes and she put her head on her folded arms and sobbed, her body convulsing with sorrow and fear.

Liz reached out a hand and placed it on Lauren's back, tears streaming from her own eyes. Then she said,

"Lauren, I have something I want to talk to you about. I've been thinking about it since you called me to tell me about Bibi. It's going to sound kinda crazy, but I want you to hear me out, OK?"

Lauren raised her head as Liz continued.

"I'm living in a short-term rental right now. I rented it when I moved out of Xander's place. I was planning on finding something more permanent once I got back from California." She shifted nervously. "Why don't we get a rental house together? You, me and Naomi? That way you can still go to school and finish your nursing degree."

Lauren looked shocked.

"But I can't go to school and work enough to pay half the rent on a house. How would that even work?"

"Well, I'm going to be a partner in my new firm pretty

soon, so I'll be earning enough to cover the rent. If you want to work a couple of nights a week to contribute, then I'll look after Naomi while you're gone, but there's no obligation at all. It doesn't have to be a permanent arrangement, just until you qualify and find a job. You can't give up on your career now, you're so close."

Lauren stared at Liz, confused.

"But why would you do that? We're not your responsibility. We're not even your family."

Liz looked down, her cheeks burning.

"I know. But I care about both of you so much that you feel like my family. I always thought I was so strong, that I didn't need anyone, but now I know that's not true. I need the two of you in my life. You make me a better person." She said, the tears running down her cheeks.

Lauren took a moment to process what Liz had suggested, and then she looked at Liz with relief and gratitude. She stood and hugged her tightly, blinking back the tears.

"If you're really willing to do this, Liz, I think it could be amazing. Naomi already adores you and calls you Auntie Liz, and I've seen how protective and loving you are with her. I would trust you with her life. It won't be for long, I promise, and I'll pay you back, agreed? I can't believe this. I can't thank you enough."

They smiled at each other and then hugged and cried.

They made yet another cup of tea and started making tentative plans.

Lauren looked at Liz and said,

"People are going to question what kind of relationship we have and why we're living together, you know that, right? There's going to be a lot of assumptions and judgements and people can be pretty cruel, you know? Can you handle that?"

Liz snorted and shrugged, "Fuck 'em. They can think what they like. I'm done caring about other people's misguided opinions. Let them have their theories, it makes no difference to me."

They laughed and clinked their mugs together in celebration.

37

Chrissy stood in the kitchen, smiling awkwardly at the prospective buyers.

She straightened the collar of her blouse and adjusted her pencil skirt. It had been a while since she'd worn business attire and she felt like a newbie greeter at a restaurant, not sure what to say, or where to put herself. Occasionally she'd blurt out, "let me know if you have any questions, I'm happy to help," and the buyers would raise an eyebrow and smile at her as if to say, 'Wow, lady, you're trying *way* to hard.'

In contrast, Ryan was in his element.

He was in the living room schmoozing with a couple of other realtors and their buyers. He knew precisely how to play these open houses, and no doubt he would be juggling multiple offers within the week. Chrissy was in awe. She'd never been so impressed by him as she was right now. He was flying high, and in contrast, she felt intimidated and out of her depth.

Maybe he'd been right? Maybe it was because this sale was

too personal for her? This was her home, after all. Although she suspected he'd just said that to help her save face.

She had to admit that, when the chips were down, this was not the right career for her. She didn't have the necessary killer instinct to make it as a realtor.

Another young couple walked into the kitchen, and she stood to attention and engaged her widest smile. As they passed, she smirked to herself, thinking how ridiculous she must look. Like an overly eager animatronic doll. She was tempted to break out into a full 80s robot dance, and she pictured the horrified expression on Ryan's face if she did. What did he know anyway, he wasn't even born in the 80s!

She stifled a giggle and the lady examining the soft-close drawers looked at her with disdain. For a moment Chrissy wanted to stick her tongue out and say, "This is *my* house, you pompous old cow. My husband and I bought it when the market was soft, and now we're going to make a killing, so who's the fool now, eh?" but she rose above it, and went to check in with Ryan in the living room.

He was holding court, looking like a model from a Hugo Boss commercial.

"How's everything going?" she asked.

"Great!" he replied. "We've got a lot of interest, and I reckon we'll get above asking price." He looked at her, and his expression changed. "You OK? This whole thing must be kinda weird for you, no?"

"Yeah, it's strange to see the house dressed to sell. But everything looks amazing. You did a really fantastic job," Chrissy replied, grateful for all Ryan's hard work.

They'd fostered a good relationship over the last six months. Chrissy's old 'Mom friends' had thought it was strange that she reported to someone twenty years her junior, but Chrissy had no hang-ups about things like that, and she and Ryan got on well. She realized now it was probably because she'd seen him as more of a son than a boss, and he'd never viewed her as any kind of serious competition.

Yup, this was definitely the wrong line of work for her.

She'd just have to find something else to do with herself when they moved to Ferndale.

She looked around the living room, transformed as it was into a showroom for luxurious living. The high vaulted ceilings still gave the air of space and freedom she had always loved, but her paintings were gone from the walls now, replaced with nondescript artwork, the kind that would hang on the walls of an exclusive hotel.

When she first started working for the firm, Ryan explained the importance of 'creating a blank space,' for the buyers. "They need to imagine themselves living in the house. To see their dream life laid out before them. It's too distracting to be aware of an actual family still live in the home, a family that isn't them."

So, under Ryan's instruction, Chrissy had packed their belongings into boxes and put them into storage.

She'd carefully erased any evidence that they lived there. No more family photographs, no shoes scattered in the doorway. Nothing to show that her babies learned to crawl in this very living room, or that there had been a baby gate blocking the staircase while they were toddlers. So many memories, all packed away.

She looked at the wall where her favorite painting used to hang. A huge oil canvas she'd bought at an art show is Sierra Madre, a couple of years back. The painting depicted an ancient adobe house with bright pink bougainvillea climbing against it, while a scruffy cat sunned itself on a side wall. The colors had been so vibrant and the canvas so large that she wasn't sure if Scott would like it, so at first she had passed it by. But the painting haunted her as she walked around the other exhibits, calling her back with a siren song, until she had returned and bought it, not knowing where it would go, or whether it would even look right, but knowing she *had* to have it.

Full of angst, she had waited for Scott to come home. She'd propped the painting up against the couch for him to see, and was pacing back and forth as he came through the front door.

She'd already decided to agree with him when he chided her and told her was a terrible mistake and a waste of money. But to her surprise, he had loved it.

"You should trust yourself more," he had said. "You've got a good eye for this kind of stuff. You have an artist's soul, even if you won't admit it," he had said, his smile making her fizz all over.

Now that painting was boxed up and ready to be moved to a new house. A new life. And she cringed at the realization that it might stay in that box forever. After all, it would never look right on the walls of a Victorian gingerbread house.

Just then, her cell phone rang. It was Scott.

Chrissy answered, stepping outside the front door. "Hi baby, you OK?"

"Yeah. How's it going?"

"It's going really well. Ryan has everything under control."

There was a pause.

Chrissy cleared her throat and said, "How's work? Is the handover going OK?"

"Yeah. Bill's taking on most of my elective surgeries for the rest of July. He has some headroom, so he's happy to step in."

"Oh, that's great. Bill is a good guy. They'll be safe in his hands."

Chrissy shifted her weight. Her high heels were pinching.

Scott cleared his throat. "So, does Ryan think we might have an offer soon?"

"Yes," said Chrissy in a bright tone, "and he says we might even get over asking price, isn't that fantastic?"

There was a pause, then Scott said, "Yeah, that's great. Well done Chrissy. This will be your first sale, won't it? Your first commission check?"

"Um," Chrissy squirmed. "Well, Ryan and I discussed it, and he feels that because it's such a high ticket property, it would be best if he handled the sale. That way we can ensure we get the best possible price."

Silence. Chrissy bit her lip. She knew how it must have sounded.

"Fair enough," said Scott, sounding steely. "I'll see you later, then."

"Sure," said Chrissy, feeling deflated. "Love you," she said, as she heard the click of Scott hanging up.

She stood at the front of the house; the anger rising in her. *How did he expect her to manage a $1.6 million dollar sale right out of the gate? Didn't it make more sense to put it in the hands of an experienced realtor like Ryan? At least Ryan could get them the highest possible offer, and then they could get the hell out of this shit-hole forever.*

"Fuck," she said under her breath, kicking at the gravel.

"Excuse me," said a lady right behind her, trying to gain access to the open house.

"Oh gosh, I'm so sorry," said Chrissy, backing away, looking cowed.

The lady gave her a haughty look before sweeping in through the front door.

Chrissy sighed and looked at the sky. She couldn't wait for this day to be over.

"Hi, Mom," she heard from the bottom of the driveway, and her beautiful son appeared, carrying an enormous bouquet of sunflowers. God, she had forgotten she'd asked him to pick them up from the florist for the table arrangement in the dining room. Her heart bounced with joy.

"Hey baby, I'm so glad to see you!" she said, wrapping her

arms around both him and the bouquet.

"Watch out Mom, you'll crush the flowers," he said with a grin, and they headed into the house.

Once the flowers were in place, Josh turned to Chrissy and, with a furrowed brow, said, "Can we hang out outside, it's too weird in here with all of our stuff gone."

"Sure," said Chrissy. She was happy to be out of the house for the same reason.

"It's crazy. It's kinda like our house, but not. It's like someone else lives here already, with all their furniture where ours used to be." Josh said, as he sat on the wall in the backyard. "You know what it feels like?" he said, with big, earnest eyes, "it's like we're ghosts, haunting a home that used to be ours."

A stab of pain pierced Chrissy's heart. "You're right. That is how it feels, isn't it?"

They sat in comfortable silence for the longest time.

Finally, she said, "Are you looking forward to moving to Ferndale?"

There was a long pause, then Josh turned to her and met her gaze. "I know you want to go, Mom, and I recognize that I'm a big part of *why* you want to go. But if I'm honest, I'm not sure it's the right thing to do."

Chrissy held his gaze and frowned.

She wanted to disagree. She wanted to list out all the reasons why this was the best course of action. She wanted him to understand that there was no other reasonable alternative.

But she didn't.

She just looked at him and saw the pain in his eyes. She saw the love too, and she knew that if she put her foot down and insisted, he would agree to go. He would follow her anywhere. Just like his father. But at what cost?

"But Josh. You can't go back to that school..." her voice

trailed off.

"I know Mom. I know I can never go back there, and I'm fine with it. Actually, I'm happy. I didn't like who I was becoming at that school. I didn't feel like me anymore. I'd turned my back on my real friends and become this fast-talking, cruel prick. I should never have done what I did with the drugs. It was stupid and reckless and I could have killed someone. I'll always be ashamed of what I did, but it was part of the whole fucking thing. The lies, the pretense, the poisonous competition where no one cared about you, and no one had your back. You know what, Mom? You suffered too. The moms were as bad as the kids, sometimes worse! I'm glad that we're out of it. But Mom, that's not Pasadena. That's not home. We can still live here and be happy. I love this house, and I have good friends that I can be myself with. I can go to the local public High School with them, they're doing well and they're happy. I spoke to Jackie about everything, and she feels the same. She doesn't want to leave Pasadena, and I don't think Dad does either, although he won't talk to me about it. I don't want you to think that I'm trying to force you into anything, or make you feel like you're outnumbered. We all love you, and we'll move if you really want to. I'm just asking you to think about it one more time."

Josh reached out and took Chrissy's hand in his and squeezed.

His hand was so big, bigger than hers, even.

She looked up at him with tears in her eyes.

When had her baby become such a mature young man? Handsome and considerate. Gentle and wise. She had been too distracted to see the transformation. Too busy filling her time with unimportant things.

But here he was, holding her hand, showing her the way. He was guiding her, the way she had guided him when he was small. And she loved him for it.

"You're an amazing, Mom, and we all love you. Never question that," Josh whispered, and he held her tight as she sobbed.

38

Naomi
Saturday, July 13th - London

As Liz pressed the buzzer, a cold shudder ran through her body.

What was she even doing here? She should have known better than to be pulled back into these games again. Had she learned nothing from the last six months? But he had sounded so sure of himself, so calm and confident that it had made her nervous.

He had suggested that they 'talk everything over one last time', and something in his tone had raised the hairs on the back of her neck.

Now here she was again, outside Xander's apartment, asking to be granted access.

The buzzer responded and the downstairs door unlocked itself.

She took the elevator up to the penthouse, nervous and on edge as she had never been before.

Xander greeted her with his winning smile and ushered her into the apartment.

The scents of delicious home cooking encircled her. Delicate wafts of garlic and herbs, while soft jazz music emanated from the living room. He took her coat from her, and she felt exposed.

"I've cooked escargot if you want some? And I have a bottle of Chardonnay open to share while we talk." He handed her a glass, and she took it reflexively.

She hesitated and then sat while he busied himself at the stove.

"What do you want to talk about, Xander?" She asked, putting the wineglass down on the table.

He waved away her question nonchalantly.

"There's time for that later. Do you want escargot, or shall I just start on the steak?"

Liz stood, trying not to betray the tension in her body.

"Xander, I'm not staying. Just tell me what you meant by your text."

Xander turned and sipped his wine while he looked at her. He smiled. This was his turf, and she realized she had made a mistake by coming here. A rookie mistake, and she kicked herself. How could she still be so naïve?

"Liz, sit down. Let's talk."

Against all her instincts, she found herself sitting back down again.

Xander smiled and sat opposite her.

"Look Liz, I know this has been an incredibly hard couple of months, but I wanted to talk to you about everything that has happened, and maybe find some common ground? The news about Lauren came as an enormous shock to you, as it did to me, and I admit now that I didn't handle it well. I should've talked to you from the beginning, confided in you, but I was scared that I was going to lose everything that mattered to me."

He dropped his eyes as his brows furrowed.

"I'm glad that you've had a chance to get away from everything for a while. A chance to clear your head. I've been doing a lot of thinking while you were away, and I realize that I acted atrociously. I'm not proud of myself, but I'm hoping I can make amends."

There was a pause, and Liz, who had been staring at the table, lifted her gaze to Xander.

For a moment she fell into those dark eyes again, as rich as melted chocolate under those heavy, concerned eyebrows. For a second, she saw everything she had fallen in love with. This mischievous boy turned earnest and serious. She'd fought against this in the past, but the surrender had been so deliciously sweet, it had pulled her back again and again into its grasp.

Xander was talking softly to her. "I've thought about this for a long time, Liz. You obviously feel very strongly about this kid, and I think I have a way we can make it work. I'll file for custody, then we can get married and you can adopt her as your child."

Liz stared at him, not quite comprehending what he was saying.

He continued.

"I spoke with your mother while you were in Los Angeles. It seems that you hadn't been entirely straight with her about how you knew Lauren and Naomi. Of course I was honest and explained the connection, and I got the impression she was proud of you for taking up their cause. She did, of course, express some concerns about how involved you were getting with them. That's when I started to consider alternatives. Lauren is clearly an unfit mother, and I understand from my sources that she doesn't even have a secure living arrangement since her landlord gave her notice. I imagine it would be easy to prove in court that I can provide the child a better life than Lauren ever could, and then the three of us could live together as a family. She could even be a flower girl at our wedding, wouldn't that be sweet? What do you think? We don't have to tell anyone where she came from, we can just say we adopted her."

The emotions swirled inside Liz, making her feel almost nauseous with their intensity.

A maelstrom crashing one over another. Grief, anger, incredulity, shame. Until a single emotion rose, obliterating all the others.

Hatred. Bitter, malevolent hatred.

She stood and said through gritted teeth,

"This 'child' you're talking about, she has a name. Her name is Naomi, and you will never take her away from her mother. You talk about her like she is a possession, like she's a chess piece you can move across a board. How *dare* you play with her life like this to meet your own needs? She doesn't *belong* to you, and you can't use her as bait to win me back. You are sick, you know that? You are a sick bastard with no soul, and you will burn in hell if I have anything to do with it. Now let me go, I never want to see your sick fucking face again."

She reached for her bag and moved towards the door.

Xander pushed back his chair with such force it toppled over, crashing to the ground, making Liz jump in shock.

"Goddam it, Liz! What do you want from me? I'm promising you the fucking world here, and you're throwing it back in my face, again. I made one fucking mistake. One! And you are making me pay for it over and over. I was happy, and I thought you were, too. You told me you never wanted to get married, and you never wanted children. We were good, but then you had to go and fuck it all up. I swear that if you leave me for this little slut and her bastard child, I will rip you all apart if it's the last thing I do. I will take that fucking kid, and you will never see her again. You know what? I'm done with your shit, you are no better than that little gutter-slut and you deserve each other, you little whores."

Liz stared at him, her eyes cold.

"Oh Xander, now we see your true colors, don't we? And to think, I could have become your bride, all dressed in lace and ruffles. What a lie that would have been. You are a narcissistic piece of shit, and I rue the day I ever let you into my life. Naomi is the only good you have ever brought into this world, and Lauren is an incredible mother despite everything she's been through. I will never, I repeat, never allow you to harm either of them, and if you go after us then be ready for the full force of my anger. I swear, you've never seen me when I'm protecting my young, if you challenge me then you better run and never look back, because I will destroy you."

Xander snorted with derision.

"You women are all the same. You and your mother, you think you are from aristocracy, but you show your true colors, eventually."

Liz was taken aback. Was this a tactic? Was he trying to wrong-foot her again? What did he mean?

Xander saw the flicker of confusion pass across her face, and he sneered.

"Yes, you heard me. Your mother has no more class than you do, however much she pretends. When I shared my ideas about getting custody of Naomi, she gave me the same bullshit sob story you just did. You people don't understand what true nobility is. Sometimes there are casualties, but that's all part of the natural order. You're all trash, and I'm lucky to have escaped this quagmire of lower-class pretenders."

Liz took a deep breath, allowing her lungs to fill with clean, fresh air.

She felt a strange lightening sensation, like a heavy burden had been lifted.

She turned to Xander as confusion flickered across his face.

"Thank you. I needed this."

Xander's eyes scanned the room. He was uncomfortable with Liz's calm demeanor.

Liz flickered a smile.

"There was still an ember left, you see?" she explained. "An unanswered question of what might have been. But you have answered that tonight, and now I'm at peace. Goodbye Xander. Don't contact me again."

Liz picked up her purse and walked to the front door.

Xander didn't try to stop her this time, he didn't block her exit as he had done the last time she had left him. He just stood, watching her, deflated and unsure of himself.

As she closed the front door she saw for a moment the lines around his eyes, a deep pain of loneliness hiding behind that pride and derision. Then he turned his back on her.

She rode the elevator down to the ground floor for the last time. As the final glimmers of mourning passed, they were replaced with the growing relief of escape.

She no longer hated him, and she knew in her heart that he no longer posed any threat to her or her new family.

She smiled as she hailed a cab. She was ready to go home.

39

California Dreaming
Sunday, July 14th - Surrey

Emily watched as the four burly moving men loaded the last of the boxes into the truck. They pulled down the slatted door with a slam, waved goodbye, and drove off into the distance. She watched from the doorstep of her family home as all her worldly possessions disappeared around the corner.

With a deep sigh, she turned and walked through the front door of the beautiful country cottage; the roses bobbing around the doorframe.

The house was empty now, and her footsteps echoed as she walked into the kitchen. The cupboards and shelves were bare and washed down. The cozy kitchen, once the heart of their home, was now just an empty sanitized shell.

She walked through each room, replaying sweet memories from the past twenty years.

This house had held Emily through both heartbreak and joy. It had welcomed her babies as she placed them in their cribs, kept them warm on stormy nights and cool on muggy summer evenings. It had glowed with warmth and love on magical Christmas Eves, the ornaments on the tree sparkling in the crackling of the firelight. This had been their home, the only home the children had ever known, their oasis from the world outside. And now they were leaving.

Emily felt a weight upon her, the all-familiar creeping sense of self doubt. Was she doing the right thing? Was this just a selfish folly? Would this be the start of something amazing, or would she live to regret this moment?

She thought of California, and the life that awaited them. Closing her eyes, she pictured the palm trees, and the cerulean blue sky. She felt the heat of the sun, and the cool of the ocean, and her heart lightened. She imagined her children playing in the surf, their faces full of joy and contentment, and she breathed deeply, knowing that everything would be OK.

Her phone chimed, the screen showing a text from Liz.

How's it going? You almost done?

Smiling, she typed a response.

Yes! We've just finished. It's been totally insane and I'm gasping for a large glass of wine, but at least we're done.

Liz wrote back.

Great! Congrats! You got time for a chat later? I have some news.

Despite her exhaustion, Emily's interest was piqued.

Ooh, gossip! I have to be at my parents' house in an hour, but I have some time to talk now if you're free?

Her phone rang, and she beamed as she heard the droll voice

of her oldest and best friend.

"So, world traveler, how does it feel to be temporarily homeless?" Liz asked with rapturous glee.

"It's *amazing!*" Emily squealed. "I mean, it's totally terrifying and I'm pretty certain that I'm destroying everyone's lives, but at the same time it's fucking awesome, if you know what I mean?"

Liz laughed out loud to hear her friend sound so energized and vibrant. "Wow, that's my girl!" she said, bursting with pride.

"It's been a surreal week since I accepted the offer. Ed and I have had to make some tough decisions. Apex are paying for a fabulous rental apartment for us in Pasadena for the first month while we find somewhere to live, but the contract didn't cover relocation so we're having to pay for our flights and the shipping costs for anything we take with us. It's meant that we've needed to seriously consider what we take, and what we leave behind. Thankfully, the moving company had a last-minute cancellation, and they offered us the timeslot for half the usual price. It's been a crazy scramble to get everything packed up in just a few days, but it's saved us a fortune so it's been worth the effort."

"What are you leaving behind?" asked Liz.

"Well, we're leaving the beds. We could do with new ones anyway, so once we're settled in a new place we'll buy replacements. And we're leaving the kitchen table and chairs, and everything from the living room. Ed was heartbroken about the kitchen table because he loves it, and he knows the carpenter who made it. But it weighs a ton, and the mosaic tiles match the ones behind the Aga, so I've suggested we add it to the value of the house and see if the new owners want to buy it. I'm not sure it would look right in a house in Pasadena, anyway."

"How's Ed taking the whole thing?" asked Liz as she

poured herself another G&T.

"He's doing OK. I think he's excited about the move, but he's a real home buddy and he hates disruption, so it's been hard for him to watch the house being turned upside down. He's been hiding out at Brian's place. Those two have been inseparable ever since they were kids, and I think they're going to miss each other terribly. I've told him that there are *bound* to be other model railway enthusiasts in Pasadena that he can make friends with, but he seems so cut up and emotional that I'm trying to avoid the subject altogether so I don't upset him."

Emily jumped up onto the kitchen counter to rest her aching legs before continuing.

"Also, I've been surprised by how attached he is to everything. I'd say to him, 'do we really need these eight framed watercolors of birds? None of us even *like* birds' and he'd screw up his face and say that I was 'throwing away all our family memories.' So dramatic! In fact, as we've gone through this process, I've realized how much I hate clutter, and how much clutter we've accumulated over the years. It's been cathartic to throw stuff away, or put it in the pile to go to charity, you know?"

"You sound like one of those professional home organizers," snorted Liz with amusement.

"Yeah, well, it's felt a bit like that. It's freeing to get rid of all this stuff that's been piling up. Once all the clutter's gone, you can see the things you actually care about. I'm not joking Liz, I've got rid of literally thirty five different paintings that used to be on the walls in the hallway, in the living room, bloody everywhere, and I never liked any of them. Yes, it's going to be a fresh start for all of us, and I can't wait," she said with exhilaration.

"Are the kids excited?" asked Liz, enjoying hearing the enthusiasm in Emily's voice.

"Yes, but they're nervous about going to an American school. I've been researching online, and it looks like Sophie and Harry will be in the same elementary school together because of their ages. But Philip will be in middle school on his own, so that's a bit intimidating. Plus, we don't even know which school they'll be going to because it depends on where we find a house. I'm sure everything will be fine, though. Ed will be there to drop them off and pick them up every day, so I'm not too concerned."

"I'm sure it'll be great," said Liz, stretching out on her couch. "Have you seen photos of the rental apartment?"

"Oh my God, Liz. It's insane! You'll die when you see it. Hang on, I'm texting you the link."

There was a whooshing sound.

Liz opened the link.

"Holy shit, Emily. The penthouse? This is amazing," she said, scrolling through. "Four bedrooms and a wrap around balcony? Wow, the photos go on and on. It looks *huge*. I love the sleek modern kitchen and the bathrooms. A black and white color scheme? So elegant with all those clean lines, you'll never want to move out!"

"I know. I feel very spoiled. I told Brody we didn't need anything so fancy, just something clean and safe while we find somewhere more permanent. But he said we should arrive in style."

Liz raised an eyebrow. "And how is the gorgeous Brody?"

"Oh stop. He's fine. He's been very supportive."

"Mm-hmm."

"Oh! I completely forgot!" Emily said, keen to change the subject. "You said that you had some news? Come on - spill the gossip!" she said, wiggling with excitement.

Liz drew a deep breath.

"OK. You know Bibi passed away last month? Well, Lauren and I have made a decision. We're going to rent a house together so she can finish up her nursing degree and have someone around to help out with Naomi."

There was a stunned silence from the other end of the phone.

"Emily? You there?"

"Um, yes! Well, that's amazing, Liz. I'm a bit blown away, I must admit."

"I know. It's kinda uncharacteristic for me, isn't it? Especially as I am a, 'sniveling coward who's terrified of being vulnerable.' That was what you called me, wasn't it?"

There was an awkward silence, then Liz laughed and said, "I'm just messing with you girl. You were totally right, plus you were the only one with the guts to call me on it, and for that I am eternally grateful." A sincerity entered her voice as she said, "Actually, I wanted to thank you. What you said had more of an impact on me than you could have imagined. You helped me realize what an ass I was being. The last couple of weeks have been scary, but I am finally putting myself out there and allowing myself to truly care for Lauren and Naomi, and it feels *so good*!"

"Wow, Liz. I'm so happy for you. I can't believe I'm moving 5,000 miles away, otherwise I'd invite you guys over for lunch one weekend."

Liz smiled at the thought, and said, "Well, if I work my butt off and make some big commission checks, then hopefully we can come out to LA and visit you guys sometime soon."

"So, I'm assuming with this news that you and Xander are definitely over?"

Liz's jaw tightened. "Oh, Emily, you have no idea. I never want to see that bastard again."

"Yikes. What happened?"

Just then Emily's phone buzzed, and her mother's name appeared on the screen.

"Oh no, I'm so sorry Liz, I've got to go. My mum is making roast beef for dinner and she wants me to help with dessert."

"No problem. It's a story for another time anyway," smiled Liz. "Have a safe flight and FaceTime me once you guys are settled in, yes?"

"Of course! I'll miss you, Liz. I love you, you know?"

Liz smiled, her heart full. "I love you too, you crazy lady," and she said goodbye.

40

Ambition
Sunday, July 14th - Surrey

The family sat around the dining table tucking into a feast of roast beef, green beans with bacon, fluffy Yorkshire puddings and crispy roast potatoes covered in thick, rich gravy. For dessert there was ice cream and fresh strawberries, sweet as candy.

At the end of the meal, when everyone was itching to get up and leave, Emily said to her brood. "What do we say to Grandma Jennifer?"

"Thank you, Grandma," the kids said in sing-song voices.

As they all rolled through to the living room to lounge on the sofas and watch TV, Emily and her mother stayed behind in the kitchen to clear dishes and put everything back in order.

The tension, which had been almost undetectable over the dinner table, was now palpable. Emily and her mother had not made eye contact all evening.

Jennifer reached for her yellow dish gloves and snapped them on as she filled the sink with soapy water.

"Could you pass me the plates, please?" she asked in an acerbic tone.

Emily passed them.

Jennifer washed in silence. Emily took each rinsed dish, dried it, and put it away.

Emily was angry, but conflicted about how to handle it. She was sick of being made to feel guilty, like a small child in disgrace. She knew what her mother was thinking, but Jennifer would never speak her mind about something like this. It just wasn't her way. Emily was in half a mind to keep her head down until the flight next Monday, when she could wave sayonara to the whole bloody business, and get the hell out of Dodge. On the other hand, she couldn't stop the rising feeling of irritation. She was sick of her mother's guilt trips, the silent treatment and curt responses of "I'm fine" when clearly she was not. Before she had thought it through, she put down the tea towel, turned to her mother and said,

"Why don't you just say it, Mum? Just say what's on your mind."

Jennifer looked taken aback, and a shade defensive.

"What do you mean, sweetie?" she said in a bright, guarded tone.

"You've been quiet all day. I know you're not happy. We need to talk about this before I fly next week. I don't want to leave with this cloud hanging over us."

Jennifer sighed and said, "It's nothing. I'm just worried about you all, that's all."

Emily raised an eyebrow and waited for her mother to continue.

Jennifer busied herself with the pots and pans, uncomfortable to be pressed like this. She turned to Emily, flushed and frowning.

"What you want me to say, Emily?" She snapped off her gloves and placed them on the drying rack. "Do you want me to congratulate you, again? Well, congratulations. But I have to admit I'm worried, I'm worried this is a mistake. Your ambition has got ahead of you, and now your entire family is being pulled along in the wake. I've never understood your need to put yourself in front of everyone else. You've been like this since you were a child. I had hoped you'd finally settled down when Philip was born, but here we are again; Emily's needs come first. Emily needs to be in the spotlight. You had a perfect life in that beautiful little cottage, surrounded by your children. You wanted for nothing, and Ed has doted on you from the start. I worry we've spoilt you, Emily. You've always wanted more. You've never been satisfied."

She sighed and brushed her hair off her forehead. Her eyes flickered to Emily's, then dropped again.

"I know it's been hard with Ed being made redundant," she continued, "but he's a good man, and he would've found another job. I just don't understand how this hobby of making soap has turned into an all-consuming obsession. All it took was for some hotshot in California to show some interest, and you're off! Without a single thought for what Ed wants, or how it might make him feel. Don't you think it hurt his pride when they let him go? Don't you think that what he needed most was to hear that you still loved him? Still needed him? Still valued him as the provider? But no, all that was brushed aside in your determination to prove that you are number one. And now poor Ed," she said, looking towards the living room. "What's he going to do in California? Be a 'house husband'? How do you think that must make him feel? How degrading for him. But still he smiles and is supportive of your latest venture. Sometimes I worry he's too good for you, Emily."

They stood, staring at each other, Jennifer defiant, and Emily shocked to her core.

"Well?" said Jennifer in a triumphant tone. "You wanted me to speak my mind, and I have. Do you feel better now? No, I thought not."

She turned towards the living room, but Emily caught her arm. Jennifer flinched and looked alarmed. Emily dropped her hand, embarrassed.

In a quiet voice, almost inaudible, Emily said, "Is that honestly what you think, Mum?"

Jennifer straightened and said,

"Yes. I'm sorry to say it, but it is."

"You know, I'm doing this for all of us. It will be an incredible experience for the entire family to move to California."

"Yes, well, you keep telling yourself that if it makes you feel better. I'm afraid I've seen too many examples of women ruining their lives for so-called 'women's lib,' when actually they're just being selfish and doing whatever's best for themselves." With this, Jennifer swept out of the kitchen and into the living room, signaling that the conversation was over.

Emily stood in the kitchen, leaning against the countertop. She was winded. Shaken. And deeply ashamed. She stared into the distance as the tears rolled down her cheeks.

Once she'd regained her composure, she stuck her head around the living room door and said in what she hoped was a light and cheerful manner;

"Guys, I'm exhausted after the move today, so I'm going to head up to bed if that's OK? Goodnight everyone, see you tomorrow."

Ed's face registered concern, but after a quick warning glance from Emily, he knew to say nothing.

Emily lay in bed, listening to the family go through their various bedtime rituals. She could hear snippets of Ed and Harry's conversation, Harry singing a Disney song, while Ed talked to him earnestly about brushing his teeth. The tears rolled again.

Eventually, Ed crept into the guest room, pulling the door closed slowly so as not to wake her.

"It's OK, I'm not asleep," she said from beneath the covers.

"You OK, honey? I was worried about you," replied Ed, his voice heavy with concern.

"Yeah. Mum and I had a fight."

"Really?" said Ed, sounding incredulous. "I've never seen your Mum so much as raise her voice."

"Well, she didn't shout, but she most definitely told me what she thought of me," said Emily, and she retold the conversation between herself and her mother as Ed put on his favorite pajamas.

As he slipped between the sheets, she turned towards him.

"Is she's right, Ed? Am I'm being selfish?"

Ed stroked her hair and kissed her on the forehead.

"No, my beautiful lady, I think you're amazing, and I couldn't be more proud of you. This is exactly what we should be doing right now, and I love that you are a strong, intelligent, kick-ass woman who is being recognized for her talents. Don't worry about your mother, what does she know anyway."

"Thank you, Ed," she replied, the tears coming again. "You're amazing, and I couldn't ask for a better, more loving husband."

"And don't you forget it. Good night, beautiful lady, sleep well," he said, rolling over to switch out the light.

Emily lay in the moonlight, processing the events of the day. She thought the empty house, and the precious memories that had encircled her as she stood alone in her home for the very last time. She thought of Liz, and how happy and content she had sounded, now that she had Lauren and Naomi in her life. She thought of her mother, and a sadness fell over her as she realized they would never truly see eye to eye. Finally she thought of Ed, her dear, sweet Ed. He had always watched her with pride and admiration. He was her knight in shining armor, and she was his princess.

She reached out in the darkness, slipping her hand under Ed's pajama shirt, stroking his stomach. His muscles tightened, and he put his hand on top of hers. He whispered,

"I'm sorry, darling, I'm not really in the mood. I'm just tired from all the craziness today. I love you so much, though."

"Of course, I understand," came Emily's standard response. Why would tonight be any different, after all?

She turned over, and with a sigh, she allowed her thoughts to drift far away. Soon she was sitting on the sand beneath the swaying palm trees, smelling the saline of the deep, blue ocean. She shaded her eyes as she watched the surf and the glimmering sun as dawn broke on the horizon. She felt a draw and a deep longing as she drifted off into delicious, faraway dreams.

41

Diagnosis
Monday, July 15th - Pasadena

Chrissy nodded a greeting at the receptionist as she checked in at the front desk of the breast clinic. She tried to smile, but it wouldn't come.

"Are all your details still the same Mrs. Miller?" The receptionist said with a bright, professional air.

"Sorry, what did you say?"

"Are all your details still the same? Address, insurance, etc?"

"Oh, yes. Yes, they are."

"Ok, thank you. Please take a seat and the nurse will call you in a moment."

Chrissy sat, holding her purse against her. She was alone in the waiting room. She hadn't wanted to worry Scott, so she hadn't told him about the doctors' call that morning. After all, why raise alarm bells before it was necessary?

The waiting room had a clean, polished ambiance that reminded her more of a spa that a medical facility. Purple orchids placed on chic modern side tables, complimented the crisp white walls and stylish chairs. The prints on the walls were minimalist, depicting various birds in flight, and there was a hint of lavender in the air.

Chrissy jumped as the door opened. A friendly nurse called her name and ushered her down a hallway.

They sat together on a mauve couch. Chrissy could feel the rough weave of the cushion as she gripped it.

The nurse offered a soft, reassuring smile. "I understand you're here for a follow up, Mrs. Miller?"

"Yes," replied Chrissy in a faltering voice. "The doctor called me this morning to say there were some 'anomalies' on my mammogram, and that he wanted me to come in straight away to have them checked."

The nurse spoke gently. "Yes. So, we are going to redo the mammogram, and then do an ultrasound. Once the doctor has taken a look at the results, he will come and speak to you about next steps."

Chrissy nodded.

"Do you have any questions at this time?" the nurse asked in a warm tone.

Chrissy shook her head. After all, what could she ask? Do I have breast cancer? Am I going to die? This well-meaning nurse didn't have the answers to these questions, or any of the others that swirled about in Chrissy's head. How could she?

The nurse led her to a changing room where she exchanged her t-shirt and bra for a blue paper gown that opened in front. She placed her belongings into a locker and slid the rubber band with the dangling key around her wrist.

She waited in yet another white chair.

Glancing up at the TV, she could make out the low dulcet tones of a man's voice explaining metastatic breast cancer. A simple diagram of a woman's breast appeared, the breast, shoulder and arm outlined in a bold red color, while the cancer was depicted as a neat little bundle of yellow cells, shown just above the nipple. As the narrator continued, the imaged animated, showing small blue arrows appearing from the yellow cell bundle and heading in all directions.

"They make it look so orderly," thought Chrissy, *"like something from a high school textbook. Like the water cycle, or a diagram detailing how flowers pollinate. They're presenting it as something so day-to-day. As if it's a natural part of life, instead of the end of it."*

Her chest tightened as the fear welled up inside her.

She thought of her family, those three individuals who made up her entire world.

"How will they cope if I'm seriously ill? Will they be brave and tell me that everything will be OK? Will they cry at night when no one can hear? Will it change who they are, or how happy they will be in the future? Poor Scott, what a burden to have to care for me and raise two kids at the same time. And my babies, I can't leave my babies."

Tears fell as she imagined the 'coping' that would need to be done. The sacrifices that would be made. Terror and hopelessness loomed like shadows and she shut her eyes, knowing she could do nothing to stop it.

A nurse called her name, and Chrissy took a sharp breath. They were ready to perform her mammogram.

The technician was efficient but distant. She seemed far more interested in getting a clear image than in consoling Chrissy. But Chrissy wasn't in the mood for small talk anyway, so that suited her just fine.

Shortly, Chrissy found herself back in her white chair.

"It can't be cancer," she thought to herself. *"I've had no symptoms. I've had no pain and I've not been losing weight or anything. It has to be cysts or something like that. Something benign. People don't just get cancer out of the blue, there would be signs, surely?"*

But why would the doctor have been so concerned if it was just cysts? Why would he have asked her to come in for a same-day appointment? Chrissy wasn't so naïve that she didn't know what that might mean.

"Mrs Miller?" asked yet another nurse.

"Yes?"

"Can you follow me, please? I'm going to take you for your ultrasound."

"Of course." Chrissy followed along behind.

She entered a dimly lit room and was greeted by the ultrasound technician.

"Hi Mrs. Miller. Please lie down on the bed and open your gown. This will take about twenty to thirty minutes. I'm going to apply some gel, it may be a little cold."

Chrissy nodded and opened the rustling paper gown.

She lay in the semi-darkness, her mind drifting as she gazed about her, taking in the various carts and apparatus that lined the walls.

On the opposite wall there was a canvas print, a beautiful image of butterflies in flight, their wings almost iridescent in the half-light.

As she stared, they seemed to lift off the canvas, and she felt their fluttering wings as they darted about her. She slowed her breathing for fear of blowing them away.

Now she was lost in the darkness with those beautiful butterflies. They were painfully delicate, yet gloriously vibrant.

She watched as their wings slowed down, as if an old movie projector was running to a stop. She heard a click, and the whir of a camera capturing a single image. A moment of perfection, preserved forever.

She could see Rachel's eyes behind the lens, shining with wonder and adoration.

And she finally understood.

In that moment, she saw the world as Rachel had.

Rachel had seen butterflies.

She had seen them everywhere, in everything, and in everyone.

While others saw fragility, she saw strength. Where they had seen only pain and suffering, she had seen vibrance and splendor. She understood that beauty was not perfection, far from it. She recognized that the struggle was part of the beauty; it was the source. One could not exist without the other. She saw what others could not, that it was the struggle that forms us, it gives us our wings; it makes us who we are meant to be.

Rachel knew that life was brief, and it broke her heart that most of us never fully embrace it. That was her sorrow. That was what she was trying to show us, but we couldn't see it. In a world of vibrant color, we saw only black and white. Always waiting for the next day, and the next, until there would be no more days, and we would be gone.

The tears ran down Chrissy's face, and the nurse placed a hand on her arm.

Chrissy jolted, shocked to be pulled back into the dark room.

"Oh, I'm sorry. I didn't mean to startle you. You seemed so sad, that's all. I'm sure everything will be just fine," she said, smiling and nodding encouragement.

Chrissy whispered a thank you. She couldn't explain that her tears had not been for herself, but for Rachel. The deep sorrow she felt was for the loss of her old friend.

Until that moment, she had never understood what Rachel was trying to convey. But now she did. Now she recognized Rachel's precious gift.

Fully dressed, Chrissy sat once more on the mauve couch, waiting for the doctor.

"Mrs Miller?" asked a tall, elderly gentleman. Chrissy

looked up and nodded.

He sat beside her and smiled.

"I've looked at your mammogram and your ultrasound, and I don't think we have anything to worry about. You have dense breast tissue, which makes it somewhat harder to detect breast cancer early on. That was why I wanted to take another look, just to be on the safe side. You have a couple of darker spots of tissue, but I'm pretty certain those are just benign fibroids. We'll have you come back in three months to check they haven't grown in size, but I think you're in the clear."

He smiled as Chrissy exhaled a deep, shaky breath. She wanted to hug him and cry, but she was drained.

As she walked through the parking lot, she felt an unusual sense of calm.

She sat in her car and watched a bird flit from palm tree to palm tree against the azure blue sky.

She thought of her two closest friends, their strength, their bravery, their vulnerability, their own iridescent glow. She could see their beautiful wings. And now, for the first time, she could see her own. She could finally see her own, and she felt at peace.

"Thank you," she whispered to Rachel.

42

"Can we get two glasses of Prosecco and a dozen oysters? Thanks so much."

"Of course, sir. I'll put the order in right away," replied the server.

"Do you want to get the peach salad as well?" suggested Chrissy.

"Ooh, good call," replied Scott, winking at his beloved wife.

As the server moved away, Chrissy grinned at Scott and raised an eyebrow.

"Prosecco and oysters, eh? Are we celebrating?"

Scott looked at her with so much love in his eyes it made her heart ache.

"We've got a lot to celebrate, no? It makes me go cold to think about what might have been."

Chrissy's smile faded as she nodded.

"Yes, it was so scary. I never want to feel that way again."

Scott reached across the table and took her hand in his. He

looked deep into her eyes and said,

"Please promise me you will never face anything like that alone again. I am here for you, and you don't need to protect me."

Chrissy felt the tears welling up.

The Prosecco arrived, and they toasted to health and happiness.

As Chrissy sipped the delicious sparkling drink, she said, "Do you think we made the right call on the house?"

"Yes, I do." Scott replied with a decisive nod. "I have to admit it surprised me when you hit the brakes on everything. Part of me was already in that old house, my sleeves rolled up as I stripped layers of wallpaper off the dining room walls."

Chrissy chuckled.

"You would have gone, wouldn't you? You would've scraped wallpaper and wiped kids' noses at the family practice?"

"Totally. If it would make you happy, I'd become a pirate and be known as the terror of the high seas!" he said, laughing. "But seriously, Chrissy, I'd do anything for you."

"I know, and it makes me love you even more, if that's at all possible."

They smiled at each other, and the years seemed to roll away. Beneath the flecks of grey and the faint wrinkles, she saw the young man she had fallen in love with.

The oysters were delicious, and they ordered a bottle of Pino Noir to accompany their lamb and steak entrees.

"Remember the night we met? What was that bar called?" Chrissy asked.

"Oh, jeez, I can't remember the name anymore. I just remember it was in USC Village. You were so standoffish that night, such an attitude," he said with a chortle.

"How dare you, I was not," replied Chrissy, feigning

offense. "You were awful, laughing and joking with your friends, all preppy and arrogant like you owned the place."

Scott raised an eyebrow. "Oh really? I think the real problem was that you hated how gorgeous I was, and how hopelessly in love you'd fallen."

Chrissy laughed and swatted him. "You give yourself far too much credit. OK, I admit it, you did look kinda cute, and I guess I just assumed you would be a self-absorbed asshole because of it."

"Well, you certainly made me work hard for your affections that first night. You were so sullen and aloof, but when you finally smiled, the whole room lit up. I knew at that moment I wouldn't ever look at another girl again. It was simple, you were the one for me."

Chrissy blushed and smiled at the memory. How young they had been, and how simple everything had seemed.

"Although, you almost lost me forever over that fight at Stacie's house, remember?" she said.

Scott raised his eyes to heaven and groaned, "This? *Again*?" and he chuckled with amused resignation.

"Well, you were so rude to me."

"No, you were drunk and being sassy, and you took the first verbal swipe at me, remember? You should have known not to tease me about politics. I take my civic duty very seriously."

"Well, maybe now I can see I was being a little unfair, but you called me out in front of all our friends. I was so embarrassed."

"Yeah, and I would do it again in a heartbeat. You were mad about it for ages, though. The next time we met up at the coffee shop on campus, you were acting all prickly and formal, remember? I couldn't work out what was up with you, so I just started telling you all about my professor, who'd been caught sleeping with one of his students. I thought the gossip might get a reaction from you, but it didn't. So then I told you how the Dean of the School of Medicine had asked me to be a speaker at one of the student conferences, and how nervous I felt. And then I asked you if you would help me buy a suit for the occasion."

Chrissy laughed.

"I know, you were chatting away, and all the time I'm thinking 'when is he going to apologize? Doesn't he realize how terribly offended I am? I am mortally wounded by the humiliation of it all, and I refuse to concede without a formal apology.' I was sitting there seething, and you'd forgotten all about it."

Scott grinned and shrugged.

"Water under the bridge. I've never held grudges. Just say what needs to be said and move on. That's how I was raised, and I've never changed."

Chrissy's heart overflowed with love for this man.

"I know. It was at that moment I knew I wanted to marry you. I was still livid, of course, but I couldn't help myself. You are a good, honorable man who is straight as an arrow, and I wouldn't change that for anything."

Scott chuckled. "In other news, Mom told me they still haven't had an offer on the Rectory."

Chrissy wrinkled her nose in concern. "I hope they sell it soon. I'd love to see a family move in there and care for it the way it deserves."

"Yeah," Scott agreed. "Someone is going to be very happy in that house, I'm sure of it."

They smiled at each other.

Scott continued, "Have you spoken to Ryan since we took the house off the market?"

Chrissy made a face. "No. Needless to say, I am not his favorite person right now. I reckon he'd already spent that fat commission check, only to have it snatched away from under his nose."

Scott grinned.

"So am I to assume your realtor days are over? Or will you move to another agency?"

"Oh, God, no! I am done with real estate. I don't have the balls for it."

"Well, I'm very glad to hear it!" Scott chuckled.

Over dessert they talked about the kids, and their hopes and concerns for the coming school year.

"Don't worry, they are more resilient than we give them credit for."

Chrissy smiled and thought of Rachel, and said quietly, "Yes, you're right, they are."

Once the plates were cleared and the check paid, Scott smiled and said, "Well, that was delicious. I'm so full. Full and happy. Talking of the future, if real estate is off the table, have you thought about what you might to do instead?"

Chrissy looked conspiratorial and said with the flicker of a smile, "Actually, I do have an Idea."

43

New Horizons
Saturday, August 3rd - Pasadena

Emily put the key in the front door of the luxurious penthouse apartment.

"Ed, are you here? I think I found our house!"

Ed came round the corner from the kitchen where he'd been making dinner, delicious smells of roasting vegetables wafting after him.

"Really?" he said, his eyes shining. "Was it the one you had the good feeling about?"

"Yes!" squealed Emily, "and it was everything I was hoping it would be." She kicked off her shoes and added them to the pile by the door.

"OK, let me pour you a glass of wine, and you can tell me all about it," said Ed, beckoning her into the kitchen.

Glass of wine in hand, Emily talked through every step, every room, and every design aspect of the house as Ed listened, enthralled.

"It's a modern one story home with four bedrooms and two bathrooms. It feels enormous because of the open floor plan. The outside is neat and well maintained, with orange trees in the front garden. It's shady and set back from the road, so it's quiet. The front door leads directly into the living room, which has soaring ceilings with skylights that flood the room with natural light. The walls are cream and there's beautiful hardwood flooring throughout."

She took a sip of wine and continued.

"The living room leads into the kitchen, which is *huge*. It has a central island with a breakfast bar, and all new appliances. Oh Ed, you've never seen a fridge as big as this one, you're going to love it. Best of all, there are sliding doors that lead out to a pool and an outdoor kitchen area. It's on a hill near the golf course, so the view is spectacular."

"Hey, Mum. Sorry, I didn't hear you come in," said Philip wandering into the kitchen, his eyes on his phone.

"Hi baby, I was just telling Dad, I think I've found us a house."

"Nice! Is it big? Will I get my own bedroom?"

"Yes, and yes. Plus, there's a swimming pool," said Emily, her eyes gleaming with excitement.

"No way! Hey guys, Mum found us a house with a swimming pool!" and he dashed off to tell the other kids the good news.

"Ooh, it sounds perfect!" Ed said, "I can't wait to see it."

"The realtor said you should go at look at it tomorrow morning first thing. He said that it won't be on the market for long, and that we should 'strike while the iron is hot' if we want to make an offer before someone else does."

"Oh, Emily," said Ed, "it's all falling into place, isn't it? It's so exciting!"

"I know. I can't believe it. I feel like that we're going to be really happy here," she replied, sighing.

She wandered into the living room to find her two youngest children lounging on the deep leather sofas. They were engrossed in some inane kids' TV show, so she kissed each of them on the top of their heads, and they grunted their hellos. She smiled and walked out onto the balcony.

She stood, sipping her wine and drinking in the views of Pasadena in the soft evening light. From this vantage point she could gaze out across the city, and although they had only lived in the apartment for a few weeks, she knew she would miss this view. She watched the groups of pedestrians on Colorado, most of them weighed down with shopping bags from fashionable clothing stores. She chuckled at the sight of a lady walking her tiny dog, their outfits perfectly coordinated. As she breathed in, enticing wafts of garlic and cinnamon filled the warm air, signaling that the multitude of Pasadena restaurants were preparing to greet their evening patrons. Soon, lights began to flicker on in windows, and she could hear the faintest lilt of jazz music coming from one of the apartments below.

She sighed with blissful contentment as the last rays of the sun caught the dome of city hall, casting a shimmering golden glow across the tops of the palm trees. Leaning against the railing, she sighed deeply, knowing she would never tire of this beauty.

Her phone rang, and she pulled it from her back pocket. Her heart leapt as she saw the caller ID.

"Hi, Brody," she answered.

"Hey there. I just wanted to check in and see how things are going. How's the apartment?" he said in his smooth, drawling accent.

"It's amazing. It's far more than we needed. Thank you so much, we're very spoiled."

"Nothing is too good for you, girl," he said with a warm, bubbling laugh.

Emily's cheeks burned.

"Actually, I might have found a house to rent," she blurted

out. "It's a good size and I love the style. Ed's going to check it out tomorrow, and if he likes it as much as I do, then we're going to put in an offer."

"Hey, that's fantastic news. You don't hang around, do you?" Another warm laugh. "I was wondering if you wanted to come sailing tomorrow? I just bought a new catamaran, and I wanted to try her out. I've called her 'New Horizons' and I thought, who better to take her out with but you, appropriate, no?"

Emily chewed her lip.

"I've only sailed once before, and that was when I was very young. I'm worried that I'd be more of a liability than a help, to be honest."

"Don't worry, I'm an experienced sailor and I'll teach you the ropes, if you'll pardon the pun. I won't let anything happen to you, I promise," he said earnestly.

Emily's heart was thumping.

"Um, well I should probably go and look at this house with Ed. Although, that's in the morning, and he'd planned to take the kids to a museum in the afternoon. Let me just check that he'd be OK taking them on his own."

She muted the phone and shouted through to Ed, who was pulling the roast chicken out of the oven.

"Ed? It's Brody on the phone. He's asking if I'd be free to go sailing with him tomorrow afternoon. What do you think?"

"Sure! Sounds like fun. You should go."

"Will you be OK managing the kids on your own, though? Maybe I should stay."

"No, no, go and enjoy yourself, we're going to have a fun day out together."

Emily took a deep breath and unmuted the phone.

"Sure, I'd love to come. Thank you so much for the offer, I'm really excited."

"Great! I can't wait to see you. I'll message you the address," said Brody. "Bye for now, and I'll see you tomorrow," he said with a smile in his voice.

44

Downsizing
Saturday, August 3rd - London

Liz heard the doorbell ring, and she steeled herself. As she pulled open the door, she affixed a sunny smile.

"Hi Mum, it's so nice to see you. Please, come in,"

"Oh darling! You look amazing!" her mother beamed, air-kissing both her cheeks before walking through the front door and into the hallway.

"I brought you a little housewarming gift," she said, handing Liz a potted plant and a bottle of champagne.

"Thank you, it's lovely," said Liz, smelling the tiny flowers. "Please, come through to the kitchen."

Cynthia followed her daughter into the kitchen and, at Liz's invitation, sat gingerly on a chair beside the breakfast table.

Liz put the champagne in the fridge and turned to her mother. They both smiled, trying to ignore the awkward silence that hung between them.

"Tea?" asked Liz.

"Do you have decaffeinated?"

"No. Sorry."

"I better not, then. If I drink caffeine after 4pm I have terrible insomnia," she said and looked around the room.

"Um, wine then? I have a white open, or I could open a bottle of red? Or we could have the champagne if you'd prefer?"

"I shouldn't if I'm driving. Thank you, though. Just come and sit and tell me how everything's going," Cynthia said, beckoning Liz.

Liz sat opposite her mother and cleared her throat.

"Well, it's been great. We've been here for a week now, as you know, and we've done most of the unpacking. It was chaos for the first couple of days. We just ate takeout and rummaged around in boxes, trying to find forks and loo paper."

She grinned at the memory of it.

"Naomi loved it. She was like a little hamster diving in and out of all the empty boxes and making forts. It's completely screwed up her bedtime routine, that's why Lauren is trying to put her to bed now. If she starts at 6pm, there's a chance she might be asleep by 8, but you never know. She's such a little rascal," Liz said, and smiled the wide, beaming smile reserved for her little angel.

Cynthia said in a soft tone, "I love watching you talk about her. You love that little girl so much, don't you?"

Liz looked at her mother, surprised to see such tenderness in her eyes.

"Yes, I really do. I'd do anything for her. I'd die for her in a heartbeat," she whispered.

Cynthia looked fragile for a moment, as if she might cry. With a quick breath, she stood and said in a bright, almost brusque manner.

"Well, are you going to give me the tour?"

"Um, sure. Although we can't go upstairs just now, Lauren

will kill me if we wake up Naomi."

Liz walked her mother around the small but cozy home and the tiny walled garden. She pointed and chatted with enthusiasm, explaining all their plans to make the place their own, her eyes shining with joyful anticipation.

"So, do you think you'll be here for a while?" Cynthia asked.

"Well, it was only ever meant to be temporary, but I'm hoping it becomes permanent. I can't imagine being without them now. Naomi will start school next year and the local school has a great reputation, although I have to admit I've already started looking into private school options. Lauren says it's ridiculous to spend so much money on a school when she's still so little, but I want her to have the best start, you know?"

Cynthia gave a rueful smile. "Shall we go for a walk? There's a beautiful park just around the corner and I'd love to get some air," she asked.

"Um, sure," said Liz, somewhat taken aback. "Let me grab my keys."

They walked in silence along the path that intersected the grassy areas of St Martins Gardens. It wasn't what Liz would call beautiful, but it was neat and well kept, and it had a pleasant, safe atmosphere.

"I wanted to talk to you, Liz, if that's OK?" Cynthia said. "Can we sit?" she signaled to a nearby wooden bench.

Liz's hackles rose. "*Of course, this had all been too good to be true. The housewarming gifts and the pleasantries. She's such a bitch, she's here to talk me out of it, isn't she? I should have seen this coming.*" Liz braced, ready for a fight.

"Mum, if you think..."

But Cynthia cut in,

"Elizabeth, I owe you an apology."

Liz stopped in her tracks, thrown by both her mother's

words, and the genuine remorse in her eyes.

There was silence as Cynthia searched Liz's face, looking for permission to continue.

"Go on," Liz said.

Cynthia took a long, shuddering breath and said, "A lot has happened over the past couple of weeks, and I've had to face some rather uncomfortable truths. One of which was my reaction to your relationship with Lauren and Naomi, and how..." she swallowed, "inappropriate my behavior has been."

She stopped, looking down at her manicured nails, and Liz saw the shadow of age pass across her mother's face.

Cynthia looked up, her pale eyes meeting Liz's sharp, inquisitive gaze, and she sighed again.

"That afternoon I called you. I could hear Naomi in the background. I heard her bubbling laugh, and her little voice with the East London accent, and I instantly began to make assumptions about who she was, and what her family would be like. It was terribly wrong of me, I can see that now. I was judging her without knowing her. I saw little Naomi and Lauren as a threat to you. I know it sounds ridiculous, but deep down I believed I was protecting you. I didn't see how bigoted I was being until Xander called me to tell me about his plan to take Naomi away from Lauren. It horrified me how heartless he was being, but then I realized that, at some level, I was as guilty as he was."

Cynthia looked at the ground, twisting the straps of her purse as she spoke.

"It's no excuse, but I believe my suspicions were due in part to my upbringing. As a child my entire life was structured and molded to represent the epitome of sophistication and breeding. How I dressed, how I spoke, even how I laughed, were constantly criticized and controlled. We were taught that our position in society defined not only who we were but also our value in the world. My parents were so distant and they showed us such little affection. I can see now the pressure they were under, but at the time I just wanted them to hold us, and tell us they loved us. That wasn't their way, though. Growing up in that environment I felt so stifled, and yet, so lonely. I hated the garden parties and the formal functions. All I wanted to do was run away and hide. I think I married your father as a rebellion against my parents' expectations. And look how that turned out."

Cynthia snorted derisively.

"When you and your brother were born, I swore things would be different. I wanted to be a loving parent; to play and have fun with you, but I couldn't find it in myself. I was still so preoccupied with our reputation that I could never show you how much I truly loved you."

She sighed, her shoulders sagging uncharacteristically.

"And now I watch you talk about Lauren and Naomi, and I see how energized and vibrant you've become. You obviously love them very much, and I am grateful you were able to find the connection you never had at home. I've realized that instead of protecting you and your brother, my prejudice and fear has driven both of you away. Elizabeth, I can see it now. I'm a snob and a bigot, and I've done so much damage because of it. I'm here to ask for your forgiveness. I'm going to try my hardest to make a change."

Cynthia shot Liz a pleading, shameful look before her gaze shifted back to the ground beneath her.

They sat in silence for a time. It was the silence of a truth long known, but never admitted. A silence that didn't need to be filled with reproaches or forgiveness, but only with stillness.

As the streetlights blinked on, Liz placed a hand on her mother's knee and said, "It's OK, Mum. Everything is OK."

Cynthia looked up with tears in her eyes and said,

"I'm so sorry, munchkin. I'm sorry for a lot of things."

Liz flinched at the pet name she hadn't heard since she was young. But then it was as if a door unlocked inside her. She felt the tears rising, but before they could take hold of her, she stood up.

"We'd better get back. Lauren will wonder where we've gone."

As they walked, Liz was quiet. She was deciding whether or not to open her heart to the woman walking next to her. She stopped, and turning to her mother, she said,

"Thank you, Mum. I know how hard that must have been for you. And you're right, I was ashamed of how you reacted to Lauren and Naomi. But if you honestly mean what you say about making amends, then maybe we can try to make things right."

Cynthia's lip trembled, and she held out her arms.

Liz hesitated for a moment, then walked into the embrace.

As her mother's arms closed around her she felt, for the first time in as long as she could remember, the genuine love as they held each other tightly.

They cried right there in the park, laughing and wiping their faces.

Cynthia reached into her purse for a handkerchief. "God, I must look a fright," she said, beaming a relaxed, comfortable smile that was so unfamiliar but so welcome.

"Yup, I'm pretty sure we both do," Liz said, smiling back at her, her eyes glistening.

As they walked home, Cynthia cleared her throat and said,

"Liz, I have something else to tell you. Your father and I have parted ways, and I'm afraid I'm going to have to sell the house. I don't believe you and your brother were ever very comfortable there anyway, so it will probably won't be too much of a hardship for you."

"Why are you selling the house?" Liz asked, bewildered.

Cynthia took a deep, shaky breath. "It seems your father isn't the man I thought he was. As you know, I'd never put much stock in his business acumen, and for the last eight years his art and antiquities business had been running at a loss. We'd been selling assets and funneling money from savings accounts into the business in order to keep it afloat. Several years ago I told him that enough was enough. That we couldn't afford to keep doing this, and he'd have to close the business. That's when he confessed to having a gambling problem. He told me he owed a large sum of money to some unsavory characters, and that the lenders had threatened him. I didn't know what to do. I didn't want to tell anyone because I was too ashamed of what they might think. So we sold almost everything we had to cover the debt. Family heirlooms, the cottage in the Cotswolds, everything."

Cynthia stopped and turned to look at Liz.

"Then last week he told me he needed to visit a sick relative. Three days after he left, I received a letter from the bank. It stated that the loan we'd taken out against the house was in arrears. I called the bank to inform them we had no such loan. It seems your father had forged my signature in order to take out the loan, and he'd transferred the money into an unconnected account."

Cynthia was struggling now, the tears welling up in her eyes.

"I hired a divorce lawyer, and their forensic team has been going through our financial records. Apparently there was no gambling problem, and your father knew exactly what he was doing all along. For the last few months he has been systematically emptying our long-term savings accounts. For years he'd been moving money into various accounts across the country, but now it's all vanished. His last known location was at the family chateau of a wealthy French artist, with whom he'd been having an affair. The solicitor informs me he has been swindling the artist as well, and the French police are looking for him. He's emptied all the bank accounts and vanished into the ether. Oh Liz, I always thought he was a bumbling idiot with no business sense. I took him for a fool, but it seems I was the fool all along."

Cynthia's eyes filled with tears and she hung her head, defeated.

Liz's heart went out to her mother as she tried to process what she'd just heard.

"I always suspected he was up to no good, but I would never have imagined he could've pulled off something like this. How bad is it? Do you know yet?"

"The solicitor thinks I'll have enough to live on. Just. But I'm going to have to make some significant changes to my lifestyle. Let's call it 'downsizing' shall we?" Cynthia said with a look of bitter irony.

Liz squeezed her mother's hand. "It'll be OK. We'll work something out. Let's let the lawyers sort out what they can, and then we'll pick up the pieces and move on, yes?"

Cynthia looked beaten.

"Maybe it's a fitting punishment for my behavior all these years?"

"Nonsense," said Liz, in a matronly tone. "Now, let's get you home and give you a nice cup of tea, shall we?"

Liz quietly unlocked the front door, and the two of them walked into the kitchen. Lauren was there, and she turned to greet them with a wide smile, which changed to concern when she saw Cynthia's white, drawn face.

"You OK, Mrs Cavendish? You look like you saw a ghost." she asked.

"Lauren, this is my mother. Mum, this is Lauren."

Cynthia blinked hard and said, "It's a pleasure to meet you, Lauren. You have a lovely home."

"Thanks. Now what's up with the two of you?"

Liz sighed heavily. "Mum's broke. My dad took all her money and ran off with an artist. Now he's screwed over the artist as well and he's disappeared. I told you he was an asshole."

"Elizabeth!" said Cynthia, looking aghast.

Lauren tutted and smiled supportively at Cynthia. "Oh, don't worry, Mrs. Cavendish, we're all family here. In fact, the very same thing happened to my nan. Her husband took all her money and did a runner, never to be seen or heard from again. That's why she came down here to London. It's pretty rough, but you'll get through it."

Cynthia smiled at Lauren with a mixture of admiration and relief.

Lauren continued. "Why don't you come for Sunday lunch tomorrow? You can meet Naomi, and we can help you make some plans for getting back on your feet?" Lauren asked with an enquiring glance at first Cynthia and then Liz.

"Oh yes, I'd love to! Thank you, Lauren, that's very generous of you," replied Cynthia, her eyes shining through the tears.

"Great," said Lauren decidedly. "We got to get to know each other a bit better, don't we? After all, we're family, and we've got a lot of time to make up for," she added, smiling at Cynthia.

45

Home
Saturday, August 3rd - Pasadena

"Morning Judith," Chrissy said as she waved to her neighbor, "Your roses are looking beautiful."

"Thank you, my dear. It's the pruning that does it, 'treat them mean, keep them keen' that's what they say." Judith laughed as she snapped her clippers in the air. "Your little scamp is looking a lot more confident now, isn't he?" she said, as she came to fuss over Doogie. She ruffled his scruffy ears, and he panted, staring up at her with adoration.

Chrissy beamed with pride. "Yeah, he's settling in really well, although there's been some howling, hence the name." She grinned, but Judith missed the joke. It appeared that 1980s sitcoms were not her strong suit.

As Chrissy and Doogie continued down the street, she thought back to the day they had picked him out at the pound. They had struggled to come up with a name, but after several sleepless nights of scratching and howling, a sleep deprived Scott had hit upon it. He'd stood up from the breakfast table, raised a finger to heaven and said, "I've got it!

Doogie Howler, MD. The MD stands for My Dog!"

Chrissy and Scott had fallen about laughing as the kids stared at each other blankly. The adults had explained with the help of YouTube, and the kids had groaned and begged for something better. But Doogie it was. It fit him perfectly.

Doogie and Chrissy took early walks every morning, watching the neighborhood stretch and rub its eyes in the cool morning air. She had come to know the early birds like Judith and the mailman, both of whom greeted her warmly and always took the time to ruffle Doogie's ears. He would make a terrible guard dog as, despite his tough start in life, he was the most affectionate dog you could ever meet, always willing to make new friends.

Chrissy loved their walks, listening to the birds and dodging the yard sprinklers that swayed back and forth, making the vibrant grass glisten in the morning sunlight. She always felt refreshed by the time she got home, ready to wake the kids and start the day.

Today she paused at the end of the road to watch the light play on the mountains as the world woke up from its slumber. She breathed in, smelling the freshly cut grass from the golf course below, while the tiny figures of the greens keepers went about their duties. She looked to her right at the beautiful Rose Bowl stadium shining white against the green grass, and she felt a warm contentment at the familiar sight.

Doogie whined and tipped his head on one side in an inquiring manner.

"OK, you," Chrissy said, smiling down at him. "Let's go home."

The kitchen was bustling as they walked through the front door. Josh had summer training for his new track and field team, so he was making himself a sausage omelette while drinking an enormous glass of fresh orange juice. Jackie was nowhere to be seen, still in bed and making the most of the last weeks of summer freedom.

"Hi gorgeous, and my little champ," Scott said as he rushed past Chrissy, coffee mug in hand, giving her a quick peck on the cheek and ruffling Doogie's ears. "We're only going to play nine holes because it's going to be crazy hot today," he said. "Do you want me to grab lunch on the way back, or should we go out somewhere?"

"I got some steak from Taylor's yesterday, so I thought we could have steak salad? Nothing too heavy," Chrissy replied.

"Ooh, sounds yummy," replied Scott, smiling and leaning in for a kiss.

Josh groaned. "Oh God, stop it, you two. You're disgusting."

Chrissy and Scott grinned at each other and giggled.

"OK, bye guys. Good luck Josh, knock 'em dead. You can tell me all about it when we both get home," said Scott as he pulled the door shut behind him.

"*Home*," echoed Chrissy to herself, and smiled.

She set about tidying the kitchen as Josh scoffed his breakfast and stared at his phone. Doogie danced in between Chrissy's legs before trying to clamber into the dishwasher, much to her amusement.

"You're the worst," she scolded him gently, bending to pat him on the top of his head.

Not long after Josh had left for practice, Chrissy heard the mail truck pull up. Doogie barked, but his wagging tail betrayed his enthusiasm.

"Thank you," called Chrissy through the window, and the mailman acknowledged with a wave and a smile.

She opened the door to find a package addressed to her. She sat at the kitchen table and opened it. There was a note, and a beautifully wrapped parcel, which was strange because it wasn't her birthday, or any special occasion she could think of.

She opened the note and saw her mother's handwriting. It read:

My Chrissy,

It was so lovely to talk with you yesterday. You sounded so happy and content, and it filled my heart with joy. Thank you so much for calling. I know we haven't spoken as much as we should have over the years, but I'm hoping we can change that in the future.

I've included a little gift for you, I hope that's OK? My friend is a crystal healer and she makes crystal charms you can hang in your home. This one has hematite and smoky quartz for grounding, and red jasper for stability and security.

I know you're skeptical of these kinds of things, so if I've overstepped the mark, then please go ahead and re-gift it to someone else.

I was always a restless spirit, and I worried that I'd passed the same nature on to you. When you moved to L.A. I hoped you'd found where you belonged, but you still seemed so unsettled. When we spoke yesterday, though, you seemed at peace. You sounded content, and I cried a little afterward, hoping it was true. My little girl, all I could ever wish for you is that you find your place in the world, and I'm hoping with all my heart and soul that you have finally done that.

Trish

Chrissy smiled and unwrapped the gift. She gasped in amazement as she held it up to the light, watching the sun reflect off the crystals, shooting tiny rainbows across the kitchen.

She walked to the kitchen drawer, took out some thread and tied it to the loop at the top of the charm. Standing on a chair, she hung it above the kitchen window where the light could catch it.

Standing back, she admired its beauty as she shook her head and laughed, not quite believing her eyes.

"What's that, Mom?" asked Jackie, bouncing down the stairs and into the kitchen.

"It's a crystal charm. It's from Trish. It helps with grounding and stability."

Jackie nodded and said, "It's pretty. It looks just like a butterfly. Can you pass me the cereal?"

Chrissy smiled to herself and reached for the cereal box.

46

"Hey you guys! It's so great to see your faces!" Liz beamed as the FaceTime connected and her two best friends appeared on the screen.

"Hi!" replied Chrissy and Emily in unison.

"Are you guys in swimsuits? God, I'm so jealous," Liz said with a huge smile.

"Yes, we've just been chilling by the pool this morning," Chrissy said. "These guys moved into their rental yesterday, so we thought we'd celebrate. The kids have been in and out of the pool for hours, but they're playing computer games inside now."

"Wow, that was fast, Emily. Wasn't it only last week you found the place?"

"Yes, but there was a lot of interest and we didn't want to lose it, so we signed the lease right there on the spot. Moving wasn't too much of a chore because we only had a couple of suitcases. Everything else is still in a shipping container on its way from England. It should be arriving in Long Beach sometime next week. Talking of new houses, how's your place? Does it feel like home yet?"

Liz beamed and nodded. "Yes. It's amazing and we all love it. I'm now totally domesticated. You wouldn't even recognize me. I get excited about trips to IKEA for God's sake!"

They all laughed.

"Oh, and you'll never guess," Liz continued. "My Mum is babysitting next week so Lauren and I can go out for dinner to celebrate."

"What?" was the chorus of disbelief from the others. "What happened?"

"Well, it's a long story. Let's just say that she saw the error of her ways. She and Naomi are best pals now. You should see them playing tea parties together, they're adorable. It's all very new for Mum, but she's learning how to open herself up to people, and she's blossoming because of it."

"Any sign of the awful Xander?" asked Chrissy hesitantly.

"Ha," Liz snorted. "He texted me last week. I let Lauren write the response. I won't tell you what she said, but I haven't heard from him since, and I don't expect I will ever again."

They all laughed.

"Serves him right," said Chrissy.

"So, Emily, how is everyone settling in to L.A. life?" asked Liz.

"They're loving it. We went to the beach last week and Philip bought a boogie board. He was in an out of the surf for hours, while Sophie and Harry played in the sand."

"What the hell is a boogie board?" asked Liz.

The other two laughed as Emily explained, "Its kinda like a short surfboard, it's for smaller waves that are closer to the shore."

"Wow, you've only been there for three weeks and already

you're a native," Liz said, smiling with pleasure. "I'm so glad it's all working out for you. When do you start work, Emily?"

"Next week. I'm so excited, but nervous too."

"Have you spoken to Brody recently?" Liz asked with a weighted look.

"Yes, he's been very supportive since we arrived. Actually, he invited me to go sailing on his new yacht last weekend. I said yes at first, but then I called him back and politely declined. I think it would be better if we didn't see each other outside of work," Emily's cheeks colored, and, keen to change the subject she added, "The kids start school next week as well, so that will be a big step in settling in."

Liz took the hint. "That's much earlier than the kids in England. Our kids don't go back until next month. How are they feeling about starting at a new school?"

"Actually, they're really excited. Sophie and Harry will be at the same school, so they're comfortable because they'll have each other. And Philip will be in the same class as Chrissy's daughter, Jackie. Isn't that crazy? It didn't even cross my mind when I found our rental house, but it turns out we're in the same school district as Chrissy, so they will be classmates!"

Liz laughed. "That *is* crazy! How fantastic that it worked out that way."

Chrissy smiled her agreement. "I know, right? And they've been getting on so well. Jackie is normally a little standoffish with new people, but she seems to have really taken to Philip. It's as if they've known each other for years."

"Do I hear wedding bells in the future?" Liz said with a devilish grin.

"Oh, stop," Chrissy said, tutting and smiling. "It's purely platonic, but it'll be lovely for them to have an ally as they both start a new school."

Everyone sighed for a moment, a contented, happy sigh.

"Wow," said Emily. "What a roller coaster of a year. I could never have imagined all the things that would happen to us, and how our lives would be changed forever."

"It's true. That reminds me. I got your parcel in the mail, Chrissy. The note said not to open it until we spoke today. Why the mystery? It isn't my birthday for ages."

"I'm so glad you got it, and now this is totally perfect." Chrissy said, her eyes shining. "Wait one second. I have one for Emily as well. It's a housewarming gift."

She dashed off into the house as the other two stared at each other, bemused.

"Here we go. This is for you," Chrissy said, returning and handing Emily a simple white gift box with a ribbon around it. It matched the box that Liz was holding.

The friends opened their gifts at the same time.

"Oh, it's beautiful," Emily exclaimed. "Oh Chrissy, thank you," and she held up a crystal charm to watch it sparkle in the sunlight.

"Chrissy, it's gorgeous. Thank you so much," Liz said in a choked voice as she examined her own charm.

Chrissy glowed with happiness. "I'm so glad you like them. My mom's friend makes them. They are custom pieces. Emily, yours has moonstone for luck in a new job, and tiger's eye and citrine for focus and prosperity. Liz, yours has rose quartz for unconditional love, jade for compassion and protection, and garnet for self-empowerment, strength and safety."

"Look how it catches the light," marveled Emily. "It's so delicate. The shape looks like the wings of a butterfly," she said in awe.

Chrissy's heart overflowed with joy as she said quietly, "Well, we are all Rachel's butterflies, after all."

Emily looked quizzical. "How do you mean?"

Chrissy gave her a tight squeeze and replied, "I'll explain

later, I promise. In fact, I need to ask you both something. As you know, I quit my realtor job, and I've been doing some soul searching to work out what I want to do next. I've been thinking about this for a long time, and I've finally mustered up the courage to do it. I need your permission though."

Liz broke in.

"What are you talking about? What do you want to do?"

Chrissy took a deep breath.

"I want to start writing again, and I was thinking of writing a novel. I want to write about the four of us, and dedicate the book to Rachel and everything she has given us. I'll change the names, of course, but I wanted your permission first before I start."

Emily laughed and hugged her old friend.

"Of course! It makes complete sense. You have always been a storyteller. Why did I only just see it? You have the soul of an artist, Chrissy, and you *have* to do it!"

Chrissy looked at the laptop screen as she bit her lip.

"Liz? What do you think?"

Liz chuckled, "I think it's a fantastic idea, with one condition."

"What's the condition?"

"Don't dumb down my language. Use all the swear words you can come up with! I can't swear at home anymore and I worry I'm turning into a big softy. At least in your book let me keep some of my old fire and brimstone."

Laughter rocked the three friends, and Emily reached for her glass.

"Let me propose a toast," she said, "To Rachel, who gave us more than she could ever have known, may she always be with us."

The friends raised their glasses, and with tears in their eyes, they said in unison.

"To Rachel."

Vicki Childs Online

Thank you for reading my debut novel 'Rachel's Butterflies', I hope you enjoyed it!

Reviews are the lifeblood of a novel, especially for independently published authors, so I would be incredibly grateful if you would take a moment to leave a review on Amazon for 'Rachel's Butterflies'.

Want access to a **SECRET, BONUS, DIRECTORS-CUT CHAPTER** of 'Rachel's Butterflies'?

Just go to **www.vickichilds.com/rachels-butterflies-bonus-chapter**

Finally, let's get to know each other better! Come hang out with me online at:

www.vickichilds.com
Facebook.com/vickichildsauthor
https://www.instagram.com/vickichildsauthor

Acknowledgements

Writing my first novel has proven to be an incredible adventure, one I could not have achieved without the help and support of some amazing individuals.

I would like to thank Brady Brady, the published author of a series of funny, poignant, and heartwarming novels, for his advice, insight and patience in helping me through this process.

Thank you to my long-suffering husband, Richard, you are my soulmate and the inspiration for Scott.

To my wonderful, inquisitive children Nicholas and Eleanor, for believing in me and bringing joy and light to my life.

Thank you to my mother, Alex, who shared her love of reading and stories with me from a very young age. You opened my eyes and my heart to the wonder of books, and changed the course of my life because of it.

Thank you to my two closest friends Pippa and Joe who inspired this story. Your love and support over the years has taught me the true power of friendship, and allowed me to see my own butterfly wings.

And finally to my beta readers and advocates, Lynne, Aine, Judith and Rebecca. Thank you for your considered feedback and insight, without which 'Rachel's Butterflies' would not be the book it is today.

About the Author

Vicki grew up in England, not far from Windsor Castle. She studied Psychology at the University of Surrey and spent most of her career working in talent acquisition and training.

She relocated to California with her husband in 2008, just before the birth of their first child.

She now lives in Pasadena with her husband, two children, two dogs and a cat.
'Rachel's Butterflies' is Vicki's first novel, but she is already hard at work on her second.

Made in the USA
Monee, IL
15 August 2021